THE BEST THING ABOUT BENNETT

ALSO BY ...

All That Lingers

Short Tales and Ruminations

An Amusing Alphabet

The Clay Canvas

The Clay Canvas, revised edition

Creative Painting on Everyday Ceramics

THE BEST THING ABOUT BENNETT

IRENE WITTIG

©2021 Irene Wittig

This work is a work of fiction, Any resemblance to actual persons, living or dead, is purely coincidental

ISBN 9798746367600

Cover art by Emily Cotton ©2021

For Wayne

1

Bennett Hall's sudden departure one Friday went unnoticed. This did not surprise her. She had become more and more invisible as the years went by. To be honest, she was relieved that it was lunchtime and her cubicle neighbors weren't at their desks, sparing her the humiliation of whispered comments as she was escorted out by a security guard.

There had been a time, earlier in her twenty-seven years with Bancroft, Chandler and Co., when the future had looked bright. In recognition of her Superior Performance Review, she was moved to a windowed cubicle. Her confidence surged. Seeing people outside walking briskly, often arm in arm with a companion, inspired her to find ways to reach out to her colleagues. She filled a bowl on her desk with candy, but only the young receptionist stopped to take one when she delivered office mail. So Bennett brought a dozen donuts and placed them next to the coffee machine. They were gone in an hour with no-one the wiser as to who had left them. After that, Bennett waited until she saw people going in for coffee.

"How nice of you," they said, though the women often smiled and added "I really shouldn't."

Bennett was pleased, though she wasn't sure how to expand on these bits of conversation. Then one day her store-bought offerings were upstaged by homemade pastries brought in by the young receptionist, who placed them temptingly on her desk and seemed to have a lot to say.

Despite her social setback, Bennett felt professionally encouraged when she was asked to participate in an important new effort—the only woman so chosen. In the end, her conclusions were set aside as not being in the interest of the Company. The injustice of this assessment, combined with recognition that she might never have personal adventures to share or jokes to tell, almost defeated her, but for the sake of the Company and its goals, she pulled herself together. She continued to do what was asked of her until the very day she was deemed "redundant."

With little expectation of happiness, Bennett was saved from desperation by the very restraints she put upon herself, somewhat like cattle soothed into acceptance of their path to slaughter by the narrowing of their confines.

Bennett looked up at the security guard tasked with accompanying her downstairs, and straightened the last, unfinished report on her desk. To make sure the guard understood she wasn't stealing it, she showed him a leather folder beautifully embossed in gold, with the words: *Bennett Hall, Bancroft, Chandler and Co.* before placing it in the oversized handbag she always carried.

"Sounds like a grand place," the guard said.

She nodded, not bothering to tell him that Bennett Hall was her name, not a place. She'd had enough of that.

As she passed through the marble-floored lobby a voice called out.

"See you Monday, Miss Hall!"

"Not this time, Frank," Bennett replied, wondering whether she should explain. She'd bought her morning newspaper from Frank all these years. Although they'd grown old together without knowing a thing about each other, Bennett would miss him. Frank had been the only one who'd always greeted her when she arrived and wished her well when she left. So perhaps she should explain after all. But if she did, Frank would have to say he was sorry even if he wasn't, and their relationship would end in awkwardness. It was best to let things be.

2

Bennett stepped off the bus and walked the half-block to the large mansard-roofed house with a columned porch to one side in what used to be the better side of Wilmington.

Stumbling over a broken step, she reached inside the mailbox hanging crookedly on the wall and retrieved her key. Inside, the house was dark and smelled of life long gone stale.

Bennett had no memories of life before this house. She and her parents had moved in with Aunt Mary when she was a baby. When her father died, she and her mother had stayed on. One evening, when Walter Cronkite announced on the news that it was the ninetieth day of the Iran Hostage Crisis, Bennett had whispered, *Mommy, are we Aunt Mary's hostages?*

Her mother had grabbed Bennett's hand and shuffled her upstairs. *That was a terrible thing to say! Aunt Mary can be difficult but she took us in when we had nothing. Never forget that!*

It was only a few years later that her mother died as well, leaving Bennett with a woman willing yet ill-equipped to fill a mother's shoes.

Without turning on the light, Bennett passed the library where Aunt Mary's bed still filled the space a sofa and chairs should have occupied, and walked upstairs to her narrow room, where nothing but the clothes in her closet and the sheets on her bed had changed in years.

When Aunt Mary's will was read, Bennett learned that Aunt Mary was not a relative at all, but as Mary had no family, the house was left to her. Bennett roamed the massive house she liked to call *The Old Beast*, wondering what she should do with it. It was filled with her aunt's belongings: dark, ornately carved chests and armoires, worn brocade-covered sofas and chairs; chipped porcelain figurines, crowded together like people on a New York subway train, and even a tarnished silver menorah whose provenance Bennett had always wondered about, as Aunt Mary had been raised Catholic. Dusty gold tassels hung from cupboard keys and fraying twists of silk tied back the aging drapes. Leather-bound classics were stuffed unread into dark mahogany bookcases. There'd always been a perverseness in the pride Aunt Mary took in the house's pomposity and arrogant pretense, since that pride had never led to repairing or preventing its decay.

Bennett, as heir, had been free to change the house, but having never practiced change, it did not come easily to her. What if she made a rash decision that could not be undone? She could have started with little things—straightening the crooked mailbox, fixing the broken front step—but even that seemed daring. And now that she'd lost her income, what difference would it make to change the little things if she couldn't change the big ones?

There had been a time, long ago, when she'd looked forward to change, when life seemed to shine with possibilities—a time filled by Stephen. With Stephen.

She'd fallen in love with him the first time she saw him struggling to get his father's wheel chair through the door of the neighborhood library. She'd stopped to help him and thought he was the most handsome young man she'd ever seen, with his soft blue eyes and dark brown hair curling slightly at the nape of his neck. And when he thanked her, his voice had been warm and his smile even warmer.

"My dad can't see very well," he said, "so I take him to the library every Friday afternoon and we choose books I can read to him."

Bennett had brazenly passed by the library every week after that, so it didn't take long before he invited her to walk with them and have some lemonade on the front porch.

When he read a passage he thought she would like, he'd write it down for her. *For Bennie*, it would say in handwriting that was like no other.

He was the only one who called her Bennie, and she probably loved him more for that than for anything else. She'd never had a name before that was hers alone. Bennett had been her mother's maiden name, Hall had been her father's. Together the name sounded like an orphanage in a Victorian novel. Even her middle name, Mary, was borrowed, rightfully belonging to the woman who wasn't even her aunt.

In school, the boys had teased her by calling her Benedict or Traitor, or Eggs, all of which had made her feel discarded like the empty cans the boys kicked down the street. She thought of using her initials as A.A. Milne, C.S. Lewis and H.G. Welles had done, but when she told her classmates to call her BM, they had laughed. When she asked why, they'd made crude noises and laughed even harder. So she stuck to Bennett. No one thought to give her a nickname again until Stephen. And never again after.

Stephen encouraged her to go to college even when Aunt Mary said she didn't have money for that, and the stupid boy should mind his own business. So Bennett began evening classes and paid for them herself, with money she earned working part-time at the library.

It wasn't long before Stephen and she were making plans to marry. Then, after he earned his degree and found a good job they would look for a house. His father would move in with them because he couldn't live alone. Bennett didn't mind. She admired Stephen's loyalty, and Mr. Bannister was a very kind man. She wondered for a moment if Aunt Mary would have to come too, but as Stephen didn't mention it, neither did she.

When she told her aunt that her professor had recommended her to the Financial Reports Division of Bancroft, Chandler and Co. because she was so good with numbers, her aunt warned her not to count her chickens before they hatch. When the personnel office called to offer her a job, Aunt Mary worried about being left alone all day.

Bennett and Stephen's marriage plans were put on hold when Mr. Bannister's health suddenly deteriorated. His final wish was to spend his last days near his sister, so he and Stephen moved to Baltimore.

Bennett put down a deposit on a furnished apartment so that Stephen could stay with her when he came to visit.

She'd been in her room packing when Aunt Mary flung open her bedroom door. She was wearing her ugliest orange and purple muumuu, and her eyes were red from crying.

"You can't leave me... I can't breathe," she said, barely audible as she leaned her body against the doorframe. She clasped a hand to her heaving chest and waited for a response. Bennett put her arm around Aunt Mary's shoulders and explained that she was grown up now and it was time to move out.

Aunt Mary pulled away and wheezed "I don't want to die alone."

Then, with a choked gasp and a resounding thump, she fell to the floor and Bennett called for an ambulance.

The next morning, Aunt Mary had recovered enough for Bennett to fetch her. A few blocks from home, Bennett slowed the car to look at a gaggle of preschoolers on the other side of the street. The last two had tangled themselves in the rope meant to keep them together.

"Aren't they sweet, Aunt Mary, like two puppies sharing a leash. One day, Stephen and I will have little ones like that."

In that instant of inattention they were hit from the rear, lurching the car forward and causing Aunt Mary's head to hit the windshield.

Within minutes she was back in the hospital with a concussion. A mild one, they said, yet even after her release she continued to be troubled by dizziness and unexplained weakness in her legs. The downstairs library room was changed into a bedroom for her. After days of careful thought, Bennett asked if she could take her aunt's large upstairs bedroom for herself so that Stephen could stay when he came.

"How can you be so selfish when it's your fault I can't walk?" had been Mary's answer.

It *was* her fault, but Bennett wondered if her aunt pretended not to walk just to punish her; then hated herself for suspecting her of such malicious deceit. Aunt Mary had taken her and her mother in when they were in need. Bennett owed her as much. She had no choice but to cancel the furnished apartment and take care of her. Stephen would understand.

Loyalty no matter how difficult was what she and Stephen had admired in each other. Even loved—although perhaps not enough, as it turned out. She thought she'd put his abandonment behind her long ago, but memories of hurts and disappointments had a habit of rising up when least expected.

Only Bancroft, Chandler and Co. had been solid ground beneath her feet, so Bennett had remained steadfast and constant even when her rise in the company had not been what she'd hoped. Yet in the end, they'd abandoned her too.

No longer bound to anyone or anything, Bennett felt unmoored, destabilized. She would have to start anew—though the thrill of the unknown no longer held a candle to the comfort of familiarity.

Still, might a new place not become familiar with time?

With that hope in mind, she decided to sell the Old Beast and find a smaller, more manageable house where she wouldn't have the burden of costly and intrusive renovations.

It took Bennett some weeks to come to this decision.

Despite her trepidation—and with the efficient assistance of a friendly real estate agent who'd slipped a flyer under her door—she sold the Old Beast fully furnished, and bought the new, empty house in less than three months, leaving her with a tidy nest egg in the bank.

Bennett's new home was a modest, three-bedroom, brick semidetached on a tree-lined street in a neighborhood she knew little about except that the agent said it was quiet and relatively crime-free. She might not have chosen it had she not been enchanted by the sunlight streaming through its uncurtained windows, illuminating the house's creamy white walls. The clean simplicity of it was a relief after living so many years with heavy velvet drapes and faded olive-brown wallpaper.

She asked her realtor where she might buy some modern furniture for the new house. Something that wouldn't cost her an arm and a leg.

"I like traditional myself, but my kids seem to love Ikea," the realtor said. "They find them reasonably priced and you can check their catalog online."

The next day, Bennett purchased everything she needed for her new life in less than two hours: furniture, linens, lamps, a mirror, file boxes, and a newlyweds' set of dining essentials for four—just the right number for her not to have to wash dishes after every meal—

and a plain glass pitcher that could be used for any number of things. Thrilled by such efficiency, she ordered everything to be delivered and assembled on the day she took possession of her new home.

The day before closing, she packed her few reference books in a cardboard box, added her Waterman pen and pencil set—a gift from Stephen she still kept in its original case. In the back of her dresser drawer, she found a piece of paper with a list of names—boys on the left, girls on the right—written in that singular hand so delicate it looked as if the names had been written with a needle dipped in ink. The letters were balanced neatly on an invisible line, with only the ends of lower case h, k, and n swooping down like flycatchers' tails.

Stephen had written the list one day as they sat on his porch and planned the children they would have. Four at least, she'd said, so they'd never feel lonely. And a girl first—hopefully—as she'd be more likely to help with the littler ones.

He'd made lists of everything—books he'd read, movies he'd seen, museums he wanted to visit—and kept most of them in neat little notebooks. Bennett wondered if he still had them, and if he'd had children and used any of the names on their list.

It was a melancholy memory now, but one she couldn't bear to lose, so she folded the paper and slipped it into the notebook of lists she kept herself and carried in her handbag. Back then, his habits had quickly become hers, although she no longer added to the list of places to visit, as she had never traveled anywhere, except once on business. Why keep dreaming the improbable?

The next morning, Bennett piled her belongings into her car and drove to the realtor's office to complete the final paperwork and take official possession of her new home.

She arrived at 123 Spring Street moments before the arrival of the Ikea truck.

By evening, everything had been assembled and put into place.

For the living room she had ordered an easy chair with a foot stool, a sofa, a floor lamp, a simple television console, and a coffee table big enough to hold feet and a newspaper; for the kitchen, a plain table and four chairs. Tomorrow she'd go out and buy a flat screen TV. Maybe even a big one. Meanwhile, she had a radio.

Upstairs, she'd chosen the largest of the three bedrooms for her office and the middle-sized one for her bedroom. Unable to think of any purpose for the smallest yet, she'd simply closed the door.

She admired the smooth, sleek surfaces of her new furniture, confident that she would never tire of their clean simplicity.

In the office, she'd had the deliverymen place the long part of the L-shaped desk under the window so she could look out into the garden. The short part would be perfect for the new large-screen iMac she was going to buy, along with a scanner-printer-copier, and a small three-drawer organizer where she would keep ink cartridges and paper.

If her sensible investments remained reliable, she would not have to look for other employment. Some of her coworkers who'd retired had moved to Florida or to where their children lived. Bennett wondered how those who stayed filled their time once their routine was gone.When the early evening news on the radio interviewed a genealogist, she thought doing research might be just the thing for her, so she placed a row of Ikea file boxes on the horizontal bookcase behind her chair in anticipation of the reports she'd write.

She would start work every morning at nine o'clock to give her day structure. It would feel like going to the office again—only there'd be no boss or co-workers to ignore or be ignored by.

She unpacked her reference books, lined them up alphabetically by category in the bookcase next to the window—Almanacs, Biographical dictionary, Dictionaries, Statistics, Thesaurus. The Atlas had to be placed out of order at one end because of its size.

She withdrew all her documents from her handbag and placed them in the fireproof box she'd bought for their safekeeping. She'd reorganize the rest of its contents tomorrow.

Then she moved on to the bedroom to unpack her clothes. She flicked a piece of lint off her dark blue suit, and smoothed the jacket with her hands. She loved the suit, the way it made her feel professional and respected. It was her favorite of the three suits she owned. She had few other clothes, other than the jeans and two dresses that had belonged to her mother.

When she attached a full-length mirror to the back of her bedroom door, she was surprised to see a face no longer defined by deep creases between her brows and dark circles under her eyes. Was it happiness or merely a trick of the light?

Pleased with the arrangement of the upstairs rooms, Bennett went downstairs and walked out onto the front stoop to gaze with satisfaction at her new, quiet street. As she glanced to the left, she noticed her neighbor's curtain move. Before she could go back in, the door opened and an old woman came out and leaned against the railing separating their front door landings.

"Hi there, welcome to the neighborhood," the woman said. "My name is Carmen-Aida McElroy. My mother wanted me to be an opera singer but I didn't have any talent."

Bennett thought it an odd comment but smiled politely. "Mine is Bennett Hall."

"Sounds like a place Jane Austen would go to," she chuckled.

"Yes. I've been told."

"I mean, because of Elizabeth Be—"

"I really must finish unpacking," Bennett said, and turned to go back in.

"Oh, well, good night, then," the woman said. "If you want to know anything about the neighborhood, let me know. I've been here fifty-six years, ever since my husband and I got married. He died three years ago of a heart attack. It was a terrible shock to—"

Before she had a chance to continue, Bennett closed the door. She couldn't bear to have to deal with another lonely old woman.

3

When Bennett opened her front door again the next morning, Mrs. McElroy was sweeping her front stoop.

"Good morning, Miss Hall. It's almost Christmas. You must be off to do last minute shopping."

Bennett froze, not sure she wanted to be pulled into conversation, but then nodded and held up the list she was holding.

"My, you must have a lot of people to buy for," Mrs. McElroy replied, leaning with both hands on her broom as if she were settling in for a long chat. "Aren't you lucky? I don't have anyone now that my husband's gone."

At a loss as to what to answer, Bennett mumbled sympathetically before rushing down the steps. When she turned to look back Mrs. McElroy was smiling and waving to her. To Bennett's surprise, she felt a rush of unfamiliar warmth toward the old woman and raised her hand, if not quite in a wave at least in response. Alarmed that she'd taken a risk she shouldn't have, her fingers moved down the narrow scar along her temple. The result of a childhood accident, it was barely visible, though Aunt Mary had always made a point of saying what a shame it was for a young girl's beauty to be scarred like that—ignoring the fact that it had been her fault.

Bennett got in her car and drove down to the Apple Store where she found a parking space in a lot around the corner. The brightly lit store was packed with customers. Young men and women in blue Apple T-shirts and jeans wove in and out of aisles answering questions as customers sat at counters trying out the newest devices, while others, like Bennett, stood patiently waiting their turn.

"Good morning, may I help you?" a young man finally asked over the din.

Bennett handed him her list of requirements.

"All this?"

Bennett nodded and watched the young man key the information into his hand-held device. How wonderful to have a list and not have to explain. She knew what she wanted, there was no need to discuss it.

"Very good, and may I see your credit card?"

"Don't I have to go to a cashier?"

"No, I can do it right here. And your email address, please, so I can email your receipt. And do you have a car? If you drive to our back door, we can load you right up."

"Yes, and yes," Bennett said, delighted at this unexpected efficiency. Minutes later, another Apple-shirted employee met her at the loading dock with a cart neatly laden with an assortment of white boxes.

Bennett found herself humming as she drove off. When she stopped at a red light a girl appeared at the window, smiling and holding up bouquets of roses.

"Why not? In fact, make it two," she said, feeling quite reckless. Without bothering to ask the price, she rolled down her window and exchanged a crisp twenty dollar bill for the two bouquets.

A good day all around, Bennett thought, when she arrived home and found the parking spot directly in front of her house still vacant. She unloaded her purchases and carried them carefully into the house. One bouquet of roses she unwrapped and placed in the plain glass pitcher she'd bought at Ikea. The other she placed still wrapped in a glass of water by the sink.

In her office, she unpacked the new iMac and admired how sleek and clean it looked on the blond desk. She stacked the other packages neatly at the other end to be opened and dealt with later and returned to the kitchen. Wavering for a moment, she dried off the bottom of the still wrapped bouquet, opened her front door, and ran down her steps and up Mrs. McElroy's.

"Merry Christmas!" she said, as the door opened, her hands trembling as she handed her the roses.

"Why Miss Hall, how very kind of you. They'll look lovely on my table. Won't you come in for a cup of coffee."

"No, no, thank you." Bennett responded, "I have to get back to work."

Running down her steps and back up hers, she looked over their shared railing and thought she saw a tear slipping down Mrs McElroy's cheek. She hurried to shut the door, embarrassed at having viewed something so private.

Private moments were not something she'd shared or even witnessed with Aunt Mary.

Bennett wondered if Mrs. McElroy had children, then remembered that she said she had no one since her husband died. She had no one either, of course, but at this point it seemed better. No one to hurt, no one to be hurt by.

She lay awake in her new bed that night, enjoying the crisp freshness of new sheets, and listened to the silence. No brakes squeaking as nighttime buses rumbled over potholes. No one shouting for her over the intercom.

Bennett awoke at 7:15 the next morning, well-rested and looking forward to the day. She showered, and was about to put on a suit as she had done every day for twenty-seven years, but realized there was no need. Jeans and a top would be good enough.

It was only when she walked down to the kitchen to make breakfast that she realized she'd forgotten to eat dinner the night before and hadn't thought to buy food. She'd hoped to start working on her project early, but with all the shops closing for Christmas the next day she couldn't put off going to the market. Unexpected complications distressed her, but when one was starting over one had to expect them.

She'd never had to shop for food before. Aunt Mary had done all the shopping in the early years, and later farmed the responsibility out to whichever cleaning lady was then in her employ. There must have been dozens over the years. Only Juanita had stayed more than a few months—years, in fact, tolerating Aunt Mary's moods and managing to create a sense of home in a house that had never felt like one. Bennett had been sorry to let Juanita go, but there'd been no point in her staying on once Bennett lost her job.

Bennett might have gotten a higher price for the Old Beast, had it been in better condition, but the young couple who'd bought it viewed themselves as being on the forefront of a great revitalization and didn't seem to mind how it looked. Here in her new, smaller house she could manage without help—though she'd have to learn how to cook. Aunt Mary had decreed the kitchen off limits to her *and* her mother, afraid perhaps that they would end up thinking the house was theirs, so Bennett had never tried her hand at cooking anything except tea. When she was young, she was too afraid to question Aunt Mary's pronouncements. Later, it was easier not to oppose her.

She took a small pad of paper out of the kitchen drawer. Eggs, bread, she wrote, cheese, tomatoes. What else? She couldn't think. Never mind, she'd manage without a list. How hard could shopping be? All she had to do was walk down every aisle and pick out what she needed.

When she opened the front door, she found Mrs. McElroy struggling to pull a rickety shopping cart down her steps.

"Well, hello, Miss Hall! Are you off to work?"

"No, I've retired."

"Oh. I thought …" Mrs. McElroy seemed to be waiting for her to explain.

"I'm going grocery shopping. I realized I have no food."

"You're in luck, Miss Hall. The farmer's market is today and they have wonderful things if you get there early. Good prices, too. That's where I'm going. I'll show you the way, if you'd like."

"How far is it?"

"Not far. About seven blocks. It's not so bad," she said, seeing Bennett eyeing her cart with its tottery wheels and dented frame. "It's all down hill on the way back. I do it every week."

Bennett hesitated, rubbed the scar on her temple, and said, "We'll go by car."

"Oh, that would be a treat! My husband always took me by car. We had an old Ford. Almost 300,000 miles on it."

"You must have traveled a lot," Bennett said.

Mrs. McElroy didn't answer at first, perhaps lost in a memory, but then she straightened her back as if to shake it off and replied, "Not too much, mostly we drove around here, and we went to my brother's every now and again—before he and his wife died—and we did almost go to the Grand Canyon once. We had that car for years. He was very handy, my Jimmy. I was sorry to let it go, but I never did learn to drive."

Mrs. McElroy slipped her cart back under the front steps and accompanied Bennett to her car.

"I've never been to a farmer's market," Bennett confessed.

"Really? Well, I'll show you who the honest farmers are—the ones you can trust. Some of them don't grow their own vegetables. Sometimes I think they just buy old ones from the supermarkets and pass them off as fresh."

Bennett began to regret her offer. What if this was the beginning of a long litany of complaints? But no, Mrs. McElroy was smiling, her hands lying peacefully in her lap. She needn't worry, Mrs. McElroy was nothing like Aunt Mary.

"This is a very nice car, Miss Hall. Elegant. My Jimmy loved a good car."

Bennett and Mrs. McElroy spent an hour walking through the market stands, yet between the two of them, they filled only half the trunk with their purchases.

"As there's still room," Bennett said. "would you mind if we stopped at the supermarket after this?"

Mrs. McElroy was more than pleased to have the chance to buy things too heavy for her rickety cart, and Bennett appreciated her advice on household products. It was a well-spent morning, but she was eager to get to work, so when Mrs. McElroy invited her to come in for a little lunch when they returned, she declined.

After unpacking and putting all the purchases in their proper places, Bennett went upstairs and turned on her new computer, happy to have a project. She uploaded a genealogy program, but before entering any names, she googled how to do genealogy research online. It was exciting to think that the further back she researched, the broader the reach of the family's roots would be. One person meant two parents. Two parents meant four grandparents, and so on. She'd read that common Anglo-Saxon names like her family's were the easiest to trace. She could already picture what a neat, carefully drawn family tree might look like. After that, she would research the details of their lives for the family history she planned to write. If she worked hard, that task might see her through much of her unexpectedly extended retirement years.

She began by entering the information she already had on the two birth certificates she'd found in a rusty strong box inexplicably hidden in the linen closet. First hers: Bennett Mary Hall, daughter of Ernestine May Houseman and William Bernard Hall. Then her mother's: daughter of Gladys Pearl Wheeler and George Henry Houseman—names she'd never even heard spoken.

Bennett entered the information, toggled over to another window and googled her own name. Nothing came up, of course. She googled Aunt Mary, thinking how funny it would be if she found clues to a long ago scandal that explained her aunt's loneliness, but there was nothing.

She imagined herself spending weeks in the city archives reading through old newspaper files and census records, looking for stories to accompany the names and dates she found. Although as far as she knew, neither her father nor mother had ever accomplished anything important, Bennett hoped she'd find more compelling stories among her earlier ancestors. There were so many people named Hall, it would take her months to check them all, but how satisfying it would be if, in the end, her roots traced back to someone of consequence.

Bennett looked up from her computer. Time had passed so quickly she was surprised to see that it had grown dark. Seven o'clock. Time to shut it down, and a good time to take an undisturbed stroll around the neighborhood. Most people would be indoors eating dinner or watching the news.

She noticed an odd flashing of tiny lights in Mrs. McElroy's window: red then green, yellow then white. It took her a few moments to understand they were Christmas tree bulbs flickering on and off. Aunt Mary had disliked decorating for the holidays. A waste of time and money, she'd said. Who's going to see it anyway? She was right, no one ever came, but a little sparkle just for themselves would have been nice.

Bennett ambled around for an hour, glancing into people's windows as she passed, listening to the soft sounds of Christmas carols floating out of neighborhood churches: Catholic, Methodist, Episcopalian, Lutheran, all in close proximity. She hadn't been in a church since her mother died. Aunt Mary wouldn't go. Saw no point in religion anymore, she said. Nor in anything else, Bennett thought.

Bennett wasn't sure how she felt about religion. Long ago, she would have talked to Stephen about things like that. She would have liked to have girlfriends, but it had never happened. And at Bancroft and Co., she'd worked with middle-aged married men who—despite her finely chiseled face and tall, slender figure—found little reason to look beyond the self-imposed wall she hid behind. She'd thought of taking a drawing class, or learning French so she could meet people, but that would have meant leaving Aunt Mary alone evenings or weekends too, which would have been ungrateful. Mary had taken them in when things were really difficult. *Never forget that,* her mother had said. And so she hadn't. Loyalty and kindness were more important than learning French or how to draw—or being happy, it seemed.

Bennett quickened her pace to clear her head. She didn't like thinking about not being happy.

When she returned home, she made herself a simple supper and belatedly read the morning paper. She heard children running by and wondered what they were doing up so late, forgetting once more that it was Christmas Eve.

The next morning she rose at her self-appointed hour of 7:15, eager to resume her research. Breakfast could wait. By the time she felt the rumblings of hunger it was already eleven.

She was about to break an egg into a frying pan when she heard a knock at the door.

She opened it a crack. She really should get a peephole.

"Oh, Mrs. McElroy, good morning. Is something wrong?"

"No, Miss Hall. It's Christmas Day and since you seem to be all alone ... Are you? ... all alone, I mean."

"Yes, I am. I'm working."

"But it's Christmas. I baked Jimmy's favorite cake and thought you might like to share it with me, being we're both alone, I mean. Just for a bit. I won't keep you long."

"I don't know...I suppose I could. Yes, I will. Thank you, Mrs. McElroy. That's very kind. I'll just finish up and then come over. Just for a bit, if that's all right."

"Oh, I'm glad, dear. For as long as you like," she said, a smile lighting up her face, making her look almost young. Bennett couldn't help but smile back.

Mrs. McElroy's floral wallpaper was the first thing that caught Bennett's eye. It covered every wall, while the sofa and easy chair were covered with a chintz of pink roses. On her table lay a white cloth embroidered with delicate sweet pea vines. Rows of African violets were in full bloom on the windowsills, and even the lace curtains had a daisy pattern.

"It's like being in a flower shop," Bennett blurted out.

"Well, thank you, Miss Hall. Do sit down. I've made a pot of tea. I hope you like Earl Grey. In the morning I prefer Irish Breakfast. It's a bit stronger, don't you think? A nice pick-me-up when the body is not quite ready for the day."

The heavy teapot—a porcelain one with hand painted flowers, of course—wobbled a bit in her hands, so Bennett held her cup as close to the spout as possible.

"Thank you, dear. My Jimmy preferred coffee, but I don't drink it any more. I find it upsets my stomach. My doctor says it's the acid. Do you find that, too? That it upsets your stomach, I mean?"

"No."

"Oh. That's good then. Won't you have some cake? It has apples in it, and a shot of bourbon to give it a little punch."

Bennett took a bite. "It's delicious, Mrs. McElroy. You must have been a big hit at family parties," she said, immediately regretting it. Hadn't she said she had no one?

"I'm afraid, we didn't have much family. It was just us most of the time. We didn't seem to need anyone else...." Her voice faded for a moment. "Sometimes we visited my brother and his family—though not too often. They were rather quiet themselves even though his wife was Italian. She wasn't the happy-go-lucky kind you see in the movies. I think she must have been homesick for her people. I could understand that. I don't think I would have liked living in a foreign country, having to speak another language with people who didn't know anything about my country. She never got to go back, not even for a visit."

Bennett had often felt like a stranger in a strange land, except that she had no place to return to.

Mrs. McElroy poured her another cup of tea.

"She was still young when she passed away, Miss Hall. Cancer it was. Such a sad thing. She was afraid to go to the hospital, so her son took care of her. Never left her side all summer. The poor boy was only fourteen. We offered to take him to live with us afterwards, but he wouldn't leave his father—even did the cooking and cleaning for him and never let his school work go. He went to college and paid for it himself. He had real spirit, that boy. Sure wasn't going to let life get him down."

For a moment Bennett had the irrational thought that she was talking about Stephen.

"Does he live here?" she asked.

"No, never did. They lived in Philadelphia. But he's not there anymore. He had dreams of being a doctor, wanted to see the world. My brother never liked the idea, but when he died in an accident at work, there was no one to stop him. I haven't seen in him in a long time. He used to write, but you know how young men are."

"I knew a boy once who took care of his father too…we were going to get married but his father grew very ill and wanted to be near his sister so they moved to Baltimore. He promised to write but he didn't either."

Bennett's face turned red. She'd never revealed that much of herself to anyone before.

"Oh, how sad," Mrs. McElroy said, who must have been used to such confessions for she didn't seem shocked at all. "There must have been a reason, don't you think? Did you try to find him? Baltimore isn't so far."

"I couldn't. I had my job… and my aunt to take care of…but I did check the crime reports and call the hospitals, just in case … you know?"

"I'm sure you did the best you could," Mrs. McElroy said, smiling kindly.

"I suppose," Bennett answered, though she knew the real reason she hadn't looked for Stephen was that she'd assumed he'd found somebody better. Aunt Mary had warned her he would. *Out of sight out of mind,* she'd said. Well acquainted with disappointment, Bennett had believed her. What other explanation could there have been?

"You have a lot of books, Mrs. McElroy," she said, hoping to change the subject.

"Yes, I love to read. It's another way of seeing the world, don't you think? What kind of books do you like?"

"I like reference books and almanacs best, I suppose, though I do read history and biographies, even science occasionally. I liked adventure stories as a child but I don't have the personality to live that sort of life—so I don't read them any more. Nor any novels actually."

"Really? I always liked a good novel best," Mrs. McElroy said. "You learn about people from them, and that's the most important thing, isn't it? Understanding people."

Without waiting for an answer, she went on to talk about her favorite books, chatting so cheerfully that Bennett barely noticed her slipping into the kitchen for fresh plates—also floral—and silverware.

"I made a roast, dear. Just in case. You'll stay, won't you? Everyone deserves a special dinner on Christmas."

After they'd finished, Mrs. McElroy brought out the last of Jimmy's brandy and they drank a toast to their new friendship.

"You're very easy to talk to, Miss Hall, so I hope you don't mind if I ask you a personal question. Are you really retired? You seem too young. My Jimmy worked to the day he died." She paused. "He was tall and slender, like you, but he sure liked his food."

"I don't blame him. You're a wonderful cook."

"I'm so glad you think so. I hardly ever do it now and was afraid I might have forgotten how."

"Not at all... though I think I'd better be going." Bennett folded her napkin and placed it neatly next to her empty plate.

"Oh dear, I've kept you too long, haven't I? But before you leave, dear, may I give you something?"

Mrs. McElroy walked down the hall to her bedroom and brought back a lumpy package wrapped in tissue paper and tied up with a red ribbon.

"I made this for my Jimmy for his birthday but he didn't live to see it. I gave away all his clothes after he died—there are always people who need them—except that I couldn't bear to give this away without knowing who was going to wear it. I put so much love into it, you see ..."

Bennett's fingers fumbled nervously with the ribbon. She unfolded the tissue paper and revealed a hand-knit sweater the silvery gray of an early morning sky, its slight mothball odor a sign that it had been cared for and protected. She held it up to her chest.

"Oh, Miss Hall, it is a little big, but the color really suits you. You will accept it, won't you?"

4

Bennett found herself humming as she left Mrs. McElroy's house and caught a last glimpse of the light in her window. It had been a surprisingly pleasant day, as sweet and soothing as the honey in tea. She'd hang the sweater over the curtain rod in the bathroom. By morning the odor of mothballs would be gone and she could wear it as a reminder of this, her first happy Christmas.

Bennett climbed into bed and pulled the comforter up and over her shoulders. Within minutes she was asleep. She dreamed of eating lunch on Mrs. McElroy's patio on a warm summer day, pots of geraniums all around. On a table, a bowl overflowing with fresh fruit sat next to a platter piled high with freshly baked and fragrant blueberry scones. With the rumble of nearing thunder, the sky grew dark and Bennett felt a sudden chill. Black-green vines sprouted from the ground along the fence between their gardens, twisting and turning until they'd grown high enough to latch themselves firmly onto the back wall of their shared house, then over and through the back of Bennett's chair and around her ankles. As she struggled to untangle herself she heard Mrs. McElroy's friendly laughter turn cold and her face darken.

You are pathetic, Miss Hall, blathering on about Stephen like an idiot. Don't think we're friends now because I said you were easy to talk to. I'm old. I have no one else.

Bennett woke with a start to find herself curled up and shivering, her comforter twisted around her feet.

She thought of the sweater and the intricate pattern of stitches Mrs. McElroy must have worked so hard on. It was a man's sweater and too big. Aunt Mary would have scowled and asked what she meant by giving it to her? Best to put it away and not wear it.

Bennett pulled the sweater off the shower curtain rod, folded it gently into a pillow case, and placed it in the very back of the top shelf of her closet.

From the window above the desk in her office, Bennett saw Mrs. McElroy take the trash down to the curb, and then look up at her window as she walked back. She thought she heard her knock but ignored it. When the old woman pulled her rickety shopping cart down the street and turned left at the corner, Bennett wondered where she was going. She couldn't possibly need groceries again. She could catch up to her and take her by car, but she knew she wouldn't. Christmas had been a happy day, but it couldn't last. Mrs. McElroy was lonely. She would expect things Bennett didn't have the capacity —nor the courage— to give her. She would disappoint her and Mrs. McElroy would be even lonelier than before. That's why she'd had the dream—as a warning not to get involved.

That night she hung a sheet across the office window.

There were no more knocks on her door after that, although Bennett did hear a loud thump against the wall one afternoon. When she snuck out for a walk that evening, she noticed there was no light in

Mrs. McElroy's window, no flickers of Christmas cheer. She turned away and didn't let herself wonder why.

A few days later, when the mailman couldn't fit any more mail into Mrs. McElroy's mailbox, he knocked on Bennett's door.

"Mrs. Hall, do you know if Mrs. McElroy is away?"

"No, I don't think so. I mean, I don't really know."

"Then we'd better call the police. She never goes away. There must be something wrong."

Bennett hesitated but receiving an impatient admonition from the mailman, she agreed to call and then joined him at Mrs. McElroy's door.

When the police arrived they found her on the floor, next to several open boxes of letters and a stepladder that had fallen over. There was dried blood on the floor and on the back of her head where she must have hit it when she fell.

"Looks like she was trying to reach something and the step ladder toppled over," the police officer explained to Bennett who was still standing motionless in the doorway. "It's a shame. She was a nice lady. I remember her husband, too. He used to give me a hand with my car when I had trouble. Good, decent people...guess you didn't think to check in on her, did you?"

"I just moved in," Bennett said.

The police officer nodded.

"Didn't know her well then?" he asked, his eyes narrowing to a squint.

"No."

"Funny, then, that she should write you this letter," he said, looking hard at Bennett as he handed it to her.

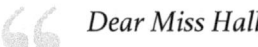
Dear Miss Hall,

I had such a lovely time with you on Christmas Day that I'm afraid that my giving you the sweater may have embarrassed you. And in my chattiness I may have said something to upset you without knowing it, for we have not spoken since then. I hope that is not the case and that you have just been busy with your project. If I offended you in any way do please accept my apologies.

I hope you have had a happy beginning to the New Year.

Sincerely,

your friend and neighbor,

Carmen-Aida McElroy

"May I keep it?" Bennett asked.

"I guess there's no point in our holding it, seeing that her death was an accident."

Bennett remained seated on her front step long after the police had removed Mrs. McElroy's body and locked her door, with one hand still holding the letter with its neat Palmer script, the other tracing the scar on her temple. Mrs. McElroy had shown her only kindness. If she'd answered the knock on the door, Mrs. McElroy might not have climbed the ladder alone. Absent or present, she was responsible for a terrible accident once again.

Late that night, Bennett pulled out the sweater that had been knitted out of love, even if not for her, and placed it in her dresser drawer. Then she ripped the sheet from the office window, as if so doing she could undo her indifference to the thump against the wall.

When morning came, Bennett raked the leaves that still lingered in the corners of Mrs. McElroy's garden. When snow fell a few days later she carefully swept a path to the stairs and pulled the rickety old cart from under the front steps so she could repair its wobbly wheel.

As the days and weeks went on, she cleaned both their gutters, repaired the latch on Mrs. McElroy's fence, and ordered a book on Mid-Atlantic gardening.

"You might try aerating the soil before you plant," the mailman suggested when he delivered it. "Mr. McElroy used to do it every year."

Two months passed before Bennett turned her attention back to genealogy. When she did, she found her mother's roots deeply planted in the region and easy to trace. She'd hoped to find relatives she might like to meet, but discovered her mother had been an only child of only children. She felt a moment of sympathy for her as she imagined her living a childhood as lonely as hers. Census records revealed that all her mother's ancestors had been laborers, factory workers, street cleaners, housewives, domestics or laundresses, living in the poorest sections of the city, generation after generation. How surprised they'd have been to learn her mother had ended up living in a mansion, and not as a maid.

Bennett set out to answer questions she never thought to ask before. As if she'd suddenly discovered curiosity, she pored through newspapers files online and at the central library seeking a simple explanation for Aunt Mary's wealth—a lottery win or lawsuit settlement perhaps—but found nothing, not even an undeserved inheritance. In fact, she found no trace of a Mary O'Reilly at all.

When it finally occurred to Bennett to check the county records on the Old Beast, she was shocked to discover that it had been bought by an Alfred and Thelma Morgan. Upon their deaths the property was transferred to Mary Margaret O'Reilly Morgan.

Bennett didn't understand. Had Mary been married? How could she not have mentioned that? What should have been an exciting discovery was a mystery Bennett was afraid to tackle. It might change all her assumptions, when all she'd wanted was an orderly way to pass the time.

She shut down the computer. Someday she'd research her father's family but for now she'd had enough. Her father's ancestors would have to wait.

As if fulfilling an unpaid debt, Bennett restarted her Tuesday and Friday visits to the farmer's market and bought only from the stands Mrs. McElroy had shown her. She began to speak to the vendors, asking advice on vegetables or how the weather affected their crops. It was a slow and sometimes painful process but she felt she owed it, and it gave her peace of mind.

Mrs. McElroy's house remained empty.

"There's no one to sell it, I suppose," the mailman said. "Probably belongs to the state now."

"Then I'll consider it my civic duty to take care of it," Bennett said, and when she felt the first warm breezes of spring, she ordered the soil aerated, bought a new rake, a hoe, several bags of potting soil and mulch, several pots of pansies that she was told would survive a late frost. After all danger of one had passed, she would plant new flower beds in both their gardens.

It was comforting to have a plan that didn't involve a lot of questions.

5

Once she'd completed her garden preparations, Bennett embarked on a plan to explore different parts of the city on foot. Although she'd lived in Wilmington all her life, she hardly knew it. She began with the oldest part of town and was intrigued by its mixture of turn-of-the-century factories (now shuttered or turned into artists' studios), old family businesses, and modest places to eat. She ended most walks by stopping at her neighborhood library. There she'd rummage through the stacks, seeking out accounts of the city's history in the hope she might stumble across mention of a Hall or a Houseman.

After a while she thought the histories too dry and, remembering Mrs. McElroy's love of novels, resolved to set herself a more literary goal. Perhaps reading all the Pulitzer Prize winners in chronological order, or a book by every Nobel Prize winner in alphabetical order. Unable to decide which was better, she randomly plucked a book from the library's new-fiction shelf. When she started reading it later that evening, she found it was a badly written and violence-filled police procedural. She returned it early the next day, mostly unread.

Feeling unsettled, she left the dim lights of the old library and walked aimlessly along the river, finally wandering into an unfamiliar area lined with kitchen suppliers, furniture refinishers, and fabric wholesalers. She caught sight of a sign that read *Schimmerling's Rare and Used Books* and decided to go in.

A small brass bell tinkled overhead as Bennett opened the door. The shop was dusty and cramped, but the rows of bookcases appeared to be well-organized and clearly marked.

"May I help you?" asked the old man sitting behind the cash register.

"I can't decide whether to read the Pulitzer Prize winners or the Nobel Prize winners."

The man pulled at his scraggly goatee and gave the statement careful thought.

"You may find some of the early Pulitzers a bit dated. On the other hand, some of the Nobels can be challenging, even esoteric at times, yet just the thing if you are looking for insightful introductions to a variety of cultures."

Bennett waited for the man to make the final decision for her, as the man pushed his glasses down his nose and gave her a long look.

"Yet sometimes," the man said, "one can find exactly what one needs in little-known books that haven't won any prizes at all. I've also found pleasure in reading a series, where one has the chance to live in someone else's world for an extended period of time. I like to compare it to traveling by ship rather than plane."

"I haven't done much of either so I wouldn't know, but I'll take a look around."

"It'll be worth the effort. Stay as long as you like. We're open until six, every day but Sunday."

Bennett worked her way through the shelves, choosing books at random merely because their titles or covers intrigued her. By the time the shop was ready to close she had accumulated more than two dozen books. The old man looked approvingly at most of her choices, quizzically at a few.

"Wisdom, knowledge, love, and humor," he concluded, as he piled the books into two grocery bags. "All the necessities of life. And because you have chosen well, but do not have any Nobel Prize winners, I would like you to consider adding this." He turned and pulled out a boxed set of ten leather-bound books from the shelf behind him: Galsworthy's complete *Forsyte Chronicles*, all three trilogies plus interludes.

"I'm afraid I've used up all my money."

"No charge then. You only have to promise to read them. You won't regret it."

"That's very kind of you," Bennett said. "I'll try, and if I finish, I'll come back and tell you what I've learned." Adding the set to her already bulging bags, she thanked the old man and walked out the door, leaving the sound of a tinkling bell in her wake.

As she stood on the sidewalk, a bag in each hand, her oversized handbag over one shoulder, she felt inexplicably happy. Looking right and left, trying to remember which way she needed to go to get back home, she noticed a slender young woman in slacks opening her car door and paused for a moment, struck by how beautiful she was.

"Señora Bennett, is that you?" the young woman said as she turned and saw her. "It's me, Maria Morales, Juanita's daughter."

"Oh, my goodness. I almost didn't recognize you. You were just a girl …"

"Yes, it has been a while."

"How is your mother?" Bennett asked, with a pang of guilt. "Did she find work? I was sorry I had to let her go but I--"

"It's all right, we're managing. Now that I work full time she helps me by taking care of my daughter."

"You have a daughter? I didn't know."

"What are you doing here, Señora Bennett, and why are you covered with dust?"

"I've been buying up the book store. It's a dusty place."

"Poor Señor Schimmerling, I really need to help him clean again."

"You know him?"

"I work next door," she said, pointing to the sign that read Vecchietti's Antiques. "You're not planning to walk home with those heavy bags, are you? I'd be glad to give you a lift."

"If you're sure it's not out of your way ... but wait, I've moved. I live on Spring Street now."

"Really? That's not far from us at all." She reached for one of the bags. "Come on in the shop for a moment—"

"I don't care for antiques."

"Just to get you another bag. This one is tearing."

"Oh, I see. Thank you."

The door creaked as Maria opened it, and a bell rang as they stepped on the mat. Pottery shards lay strewn on the floor under a shelf, one side of which no longer hung on the wall adjacent to the door.

"Señor Vecchietti?" Maria shouted. When he didn't answer, she ran to the back of the shop and pulled aside the curtain.

"Señor Vecchietti, are you all right?"

"Yes, yes. I was just fixing that shelf when I got a little dizzy and leaned on it."

"You shouldn't be climbing on things."

"I'm fine. It was the nails. They're no good. I should have used screws. What are you doing back anyway? I thought you were going home."

"I am, but I needed a bag for an old friend I just ran into. Come and meet her."

She held his arm as they walked to the door, where Bennett was still standing in the same spot.

"Señor Vecchietti, this is Señora Bennett. My mother worked for her aunt for many years."

"Any friend of Maria's is a friend of mine," he said, holding out a small, wrinkled hand. He barely reached Maria's shoulder, and looked to be in his nineties, despite a full head of thick white hair.

Maria reached out to catch his arm again when she saw him wobble. He steadied himself on the back of a chair, and gave Bennett a probing look.

"You look familiar, have you been here before?"

"No, this is my first time." She found the old man's look disconcerting.

"Are you sure?"

"I'm afraid we have to be going, Señor Vecchietti," Maria interrupted. "Leave the shelf, please. I'll fix it in the morning. And please go home. You've worked enough for today."

"I'm worried about him," she said to Bennett, once they were outside. "He's not well, and shouldn't be working at all but he won't listen. He says he wants me to manage the shop but he won't let me make any changes. He wants me to organize his records but won't let me get a computer, or even do a proper inventory. He says if he wanted to be modern he'd sell cell phones not antiques. He's the most stubborn man I know but I love him dearly. He's funny and kind and incredibly knowledgeable. I'm always learning something."

"When did you start working here?"

"When I was in high school." She turned to look at Bennett. "You know, it's funny that he thought you looked familiar. He usually has a really good memory for faces."

6

April rains started a few days later and were forecast not to let up for two weeks. Unable to take her now customary walks, Bennett arranged her new books alphabetically by author, then googled each author and printed up anything interesting she found, slipping the relevant printout into each book. That only took a day, and it was still raining, so she reorganized her underwear, folding each pair of briefs in half and putting them into two side by side piles at the front of her dresser drawer, placing her camisoles folded in half and then in half again behind them. Finding the results pleasing, she pondered whether it was better to hang or fold her blouses. She probably didn't need so many now that she didn't wear a suit every day. In fact, she hadn't worn one in quite a while. Maybe she should buy herself another pair of jeans, or a skirt or two, and a few tops. And another pair of walking shoes. Hers were almost worn out now.

After three days, Bennett needed a new project—a bigger one—and decided it was the perfect time to tackle the complete *Forsyte Chronicles* Mr. Schimmerling had given her. She filled a large thermos with hot coffee, made herself comfortable in the easy chair, and was soon so engrossed in *The Man of Property*, she almost didn't hear the phone ring.

"Señora Bennett, this is Juanita. Do you remember me?"

"Of course. Did your daughter tell you that I ran into her?"

"Yes, that is why I am calling you. She said you bought many books."

"I did. And she showed me where she works. She seems happy there."

"She was. That is why the news is so terrible."

"Did she lose her job?"

"No, it's not that exactly."

"Well, that's good then," Bennett said. "I'd better get back to—"

"No, please, Señora Bennett, I don't mean to bother you—you did not really know them—but Señor Vecchietti was driving Señor Schimmerling home after work as he always did, when they had a terrible accident. The police think he had a heart attack, poor man. They were both killed. We knew Señor Vecchietti was not in the best of health, but we never expected this."

"I'm very sorry to hear it... but I don't understand. Why are you telling me? I only met them once."

"It's because Maria has inherited both shops."

"Both? ... well, that's not a bad thing, is it?"

"No, and she is grateful, but it may be more than she can handle."

"There are advisors she can hire for that sort of thing."

"We have no money for that." When Bennett didn't respond, Juanita added, "I was hoping that since you are retired now and have time... you could help her."

"Me? I don't have—"

"Not with money, Señora Bennett! I wouldn't ask you that. No, I meant with advice. Just to get her started."

"I don't know anything about running a shop."

"Oh, but you know business, and you are an intelligent woman, and honest. I thought if you could take a look at the books... give her a little advice until she's on her feet."

"I'm not an accountant... it's a big responsibility. I might do it all wrong and she would lose the business. I couldn't live with that ... Besides, I have a project of my own now, and a house. I even take care of the house next door..."

"Please, Señora Bennett, I have no one else to ask."

Juanita had always been so kind.

"Let me think about it."

"Thank you. If—"

"I'll let you know."

Juanita had never taken advantage of her. Why would she now?

She was kind to you. Never forget that, her mother had said. She meant Aunt Mary, but it would apply to anyone who was kind, wouldn't it?

She called Juanita back and told her she'd see Maria in the morning and to please not call her Señora anymore. Just Bennett would be fine.

∽

A new large, hand-lettered sign hung on the wall between the shop doors: *Shops Temporarily Closed in Memory of Mr. Vecchietti and Mr. Schimmerling.*

Maria opened the antique shop door as soon as she saw Bennett getting out of her car.

"I can't thank you enough for coming," she said, smiling and shaking Bennett's hand with both of hers. "And I'm sorry I look such a mess. I've been cleaning."

"I don't know how much help I can be..."

"Don't worry, I won't make you clean," she laughed. "I'm trying to make some order so I can keep the shops open if at all possible. They would want that. I just don't know where to start with the paperwork."

"As I told your mother, I'm not an accountant..."

"I know, but Mama says I can trust you. I'd hire someone, but I don't want some guy telling me that it would be more efficient to close the shops and invest in the stock market instead. Besides, I can't afford to hire anyone—which means I can't pay you either—not right away—but I don't want to take advantage of you, so if you can help me keep the shops going I thought maybe I could give you a percentage—that wouldn't be unusual, would it?"

"No, but we don't have to talk about that now. I'll look at the files and bank records, and see if I can figure out your financial situation—but please remember, I'm not an accountant."

"I understand. The two of them shared the storage room and used it as their office as well—as you can see, it opens to both shops—but they kept their financial records separate. We can start with Mr. Vecchietti's records—I'm at least familiar with them—but not in your good suit. It's dusty back there. Let me get you a smock."

Whereas Bennett's old office in the insurance division had been an anonymous cubicle lined with neat filing cabinets on the eighth floor of a nondescript office building, the storage room was cluttered and looked out on a courtyard. On Mr. Vecchietti's side, crammed between three floor lamps and two treadle sewing machines, stood an old rolltop desk of the sort the curmudgeonly editor of a city newspaper might have used. On Mr. Schimmerling's, surrounded by tall stacks of books threatening to topple over, sat a 1950's red and white dinette table, on the right side of which lay a large ink blotter covered with notes and telephone numbers, and on the left two desk lamps, an early 1900's photograph of a family, and six small metal boxes filled with index cards.

"I'm afraid this is not what you're used to," Maria said.

"No, but that's not necessarily a bad thing. I've been used to many things I didn't like."

"Before we start, can I show you a list I made of what I'd like to accomplish?"

Bennett's list would have been typed, with bullet points and indentations and placed in a folder. Maria's was handwritten on yellow legal pad paper, with little doodles and asterisks pointing to things she'd thought of later.

First item was to have a new sign that said Vecchietti-Schimmerling Antiques and Books. Maria said she had a friend who could do that.

Second was to open the wall between the shops so that customers would see that they were now one business. For that they'd need a carpenter.

Third, and obviously most important, since it was written in red and underlined, was to get a computer so they could computerize earnings and expenses, and keep track of inventory.

Fourth, create a website.

"I don't think we're ready to sell online since we'd have to ship things," Maria said, "but wouldn't it be fun to send our customers periodic emails in which we told them what item or items we were featuring on our website. The website would have photos and the item's history. I found a drawer full of notes on most of the things in the shop—all handwritten, and most of them in pencil, but together we should be able to decipher them."

"It's a good plan, Maria," Bennett said, "but before we do anything, we have to see where you stand financially."

"Oh, I agree. I know we won't be able to do everything at once. You'll find I'm actually a very practical person and don't like wasting money."

"That's good," Bennett said, looking around, "One of the first things we have to do is an inventory. It's a big job, everything has to be written down. Mr. Vecchietti seems to have accumulated quite a collection."

"It won't be so bad." Maria didn't sound in the least discouraged. "We can do one section at a time. The books will be much easier. Only a matter of counting."

"Don't we have to know what everything is worth?"

"It's all marked. I thought we could work on it an hour or two before we open every day."

Bennett felt suddenly energized by the idea of organizing a whole business, not just insurance records.

"I'll start on Mr. Vecchietti's papers—if you can show me where he kept them. Did he have a safe? There might be something in there I should see as well."

Maria revealed a small safe hidden behind a painting on the wall.

"I hope you know the combination."

"I do, because Mr. Vecchietti called it his American safe."

She pushed the buttons 07041776 and the safe clicked upon. Inside they found no papers but a small box with enough cash to buy a computer.

"Terrific! It wasn't the first item on my list, but it's the one that will help us the most, so let's go get one now."

"Can you manage by yourself, Maria? I have something I'd like to do at home."

"Sure. Will you come back tomorrow?"

"I think I can help for another day or two."

That evening, Bennett read up on small business needs and found the right software for inventory management for a small shop like theirs.

The next morning, she downloaded the software onto Maria's new computer, and then started on the financial records.

The finances of both shops were in surprisingly good order despite their haphazard filing systems. Eager to have the papers put into a manageable order, the one or two days Bennett said she could come stretched to two weeks. Then three. At the end, all the files were in order and the herculean task of inventorying was also behind them. From then on, all receipts and expenditures would be entered in the computer on a regular basis. The shops were ready to reopen.

"Would you consider staying on, Bennett, to keep all these things running and up to date? You would be an enormous help."

Bennett took a deep breath. It was a commitment. She could always quit, though that would be a terrible thing to do to Maria. But why not try it, if she really needed the help. She had nothing she had to do at home. The genealogy had already been put on hold.

"Yes, I think I would like that, as long as you feel I'm contributing."

"That's great! How about coming for dinner on Sunday to celebrate and discuss what your percentage will be. Mama will be there and I'd like you to meet my daughter. Is seven o'clock all right?"

"I don't know ..." Bennett said, tracing the scar on her temple with her finger. What if accepting would spoil everything, just when it all seemed to be going so well? "Maybe I ..." she stammered, but then thought of Mrs. McElroy, and how much she had lost by not accepting her friendship. "Maybe I can bring the wine?"

Bennett arrived precisely at seven, opened Maria's apartment building door, from which two panes of glass were missing, and took the elevator up to the eighth floor. The hallway was long and narrow and lit by harsh fluorescent lights. The building was part of a large complex that had seen better days. Affordable housing had been its aim, but now all the buildings were marred by graffiti, and the hall carpeting was stained. Bad tenants or bad management, she wondered. She worried that Maria wasn't safe there and was glad she had her little house on Spring Street to go back to.

Before she had a chance to knock, the door to apartment 803 opened, revealing a dark-haired little girl in sparkly pajamas.

"Hi."

"Who are you?"

"Isabella. I'm four."

"I'm Bennett and I'm more than four."

"I know. You're big. Mama's in the kitchen. She told me I can open the door because it's seven o'clock and that's when you are supposed to come and you wouldn't be late."

"Come in, Bennett, and make yourself at home," Maria called from the kitchen. "We'll be there in a second. Isabella was very excited about your coming."

Bennett sat down on the nearest chair and smiled at the child, who was now standing on her head on the sofa, revealing pink underpants with three rows of ruffles. She couldn't remember the last time she'd spoken to a child.

"You look funny upside-down," Isabella said and watched as Bennett cast a glance around the room. It was bright, and tastefully decorated, and Bennett found it touching that Maria had created such an inviting home in the confines of such a run down building.

"What's that?" Isabella asked, now right side up and pointing to the brown paper bag in her lap.

"Wine."

"Mama will drink it 'cause I only drink milk. And juice, sometimes, but not too much because Mama says it has too much sugar."

"Your daughter and I were having an interesting conversation about drinks," Bennett said, standing up as Maria and Juanita came out of the kitchen.

"She'll have to tell me all about it, but now she needs to go to bed. Say good night, Isabella."

Isabella kissed her grandmother and then reached up to her mother and whispered something in her ear.

"If you want to," Maria said.

Isabella walked over to Bennett and kissed her on the cheek, then took her mother's hand and skipped down the hall to her room, leaving Bennett with a happy grin on her face and the brown paper bag still in her lap.

Bennett and Maria developed what they agreed was a fair division of labor and profit, and Bennett's days took on a new and pleasant rhythm. On the days that she worked—anywhere from two to four times a week—she rose early, read the morning paper over breakfast, walked down to the shop—when the weather allowed—and entered earnings and expenditures while Maria cleaned and polished and rearranged the window displays when new items arrived.

Soon Bennett found herself helping customers search for books, often picking up one or two for herself. Maria said she should be careful, soon she would be spending more than she earned. She told Maria she wouldn't mind. It helped their earnings and the books gave her something to do in the evening.

Maria knew far more than she about antiques, but with the help of Mr. Vecchietti's notes and Mr. Schimmerling's books on the subject, Bennett was learning. She avoided the big, ornate pieces that reminded her of Aunt Mary, preferring to learn about things that she wouldn't have thought would interest her—such as pottery and porcelain markings. Her discovery that British makers had kept precise registry files for shapes and designs manufactured between 1839 and 1883, made it easy—and enjoyable—to tell customers the exact ages of their selections. Thanks to an old book on faience, she determined that a plate with a Chinese motif Maria had found at a flea market was actually French, from a pottery near Strasbourg, dating back to 1780, and worth much more than she paid. Bennett was tempted to buy it herself but thought it would look pretentious hanging over her Ikea table.

Her next goal was to learn silver markings, especially British ones which again were the most precise and informative.

Customers came looking for a vast variety of things, from bed frames to teapots, and grandfather clocks to postcards. Bennett couldn't understand the appeal of old postcards until she started reading the backs of them. Intrigued by the messages, the beautiful handwriting, as well as the exotic places of origin, she began collecting them also, keeping them in an archival album she bought in an art supply store. She suggested to Maria that they might offer such albums to postcard collectors, along with good furniture polish and jewelry cleaner for their other customers.

Once they'd settled into a steady routine, Maria began to leave the shop periodically to check out estate sales for pieces to refresh their stock, leaving Bennett in charge. That was how Bennett first met Lola Wiskowski.

7

A woman unknown to Bennett threw open the shop door and wiped her feet on the mat, making the bell ring frantically as she made her entrance. In her fifties, bleached blonde, overweight in what used to be called a pleasantly plump way, she wore a shimmery print blouse over a tight-fitting black pencil skirt, a three-strand necklace of large, multicolored glass beads, three cocktail rings, and leopard print high-heeled shoes. She was hard to overlook.

"Hi, honey. Sure looks different in here," she said loudly. "I was sorry to hear about the old guys but I'm glad to see the place is still open."

She looked at Bennett intently.

"Are you a Vecchietti or a Schimmerling?"

"Neither," Bennett answered, startled. "I just work here."

"So who owns the place now?"

"Maria."

"Oh, yeah, the pretty girl. She looks Italian. She must be a Vecchietti."

"I'm afraid she's not here," Bennett evaded. What business was it of hers? "Can I help you with something?"

"Sure, honey. I'm always on the lookout for good jewelry. Costume jewelry, that is —I can't afford the real stuff. I like pieces from the thirties and forties. Old Vecchietti always saved the best ones for me. You know, Miriam Haskell, Schiaparelli, Weiss. And Bakelite, I have a thing for Bakelite."

She held up a wrist for Bennett to see her butterscotch and green bracelet.

"I'm afraid I'm not very familiar with jewelry yet. I'm rather new to this business."

Lola's eyes took a quick tour of Bennett's wrist, neck, and ears.

"That's all right, honey. I see you don't wear jewelry, but I know my way around. I'll take a look at what you've got in now. Just no clip-ons. No one wears them anymore and they're too much trouble to convert."

Bennett nodded, remembering the box of Aunt Mary's gaudy earrings she'd thrown out. As she watched Lola bend her head over the glass case by the cash register, she was fascinated by the unusual intricacy of her hairdo. Her hair was pulled back into a braided bun, which was topped with a pink satin bow. A small pony tail hung from the bottom of the bun, partially obscured by the enormous ruffle at the neck of her blouse, which continued around and down both sides of the front. The whole image made Bennett think of ice cream sundaes topped with curls of whipped cream.

"Nothing today, honey, but don't worry, I'll be back," Lola said with a wink, leaving Bennett to think about her own hair. It had been a long time since she'd thought about hairdos. When she was a child she'd wanted long, flowing hair, and had loved her mother to brush it. But when her mother died, Aunt Mary had it cut short. *Much more practi-*

cal, she'd said. Bennett kept it that way until she met Stephen. The growing-out stage looked awkward for a while, and by the time it was an attractive length he'd left for Baltimore. When she didn't hear from him, she had it cut again. *Much more practical*, Aunt Mary said again, though her own hair was long and worn curled into a tiny bun. The older and heavier Mary grew, the further up her head the bun went, as if the back of her head had run out of space. Her only concession to beauty was bright red lipstick. *You'll never keep a man if you don't wear it*, she said, though wearing it hadn't helped her. Yet, it did make Bennett wonder if Stephen would have written had she worn it.

When Maria returned, Bennett told her about the brash woman who'd come in looking for jewelry.

"Oh, that's Lola. Lola Wiskowski. She's a character, but she's all right. She often bought pieces from Señor Vecchietti. A few times she even sold him some."

"How much jewelry does one person need?"

Maria laughed.

"It's never a question of needing, Bennett, just wanting, but Lola resells most of her pieces at trade shows. She has a good eye and she's a good negotiator, so she usually makes a profit. The whole antiques business is just buying and selling the same things over and over again. I like to think of it as the art of recycling."

Lola returned before the week was up, buying a rhinestone cat brooch she pinned on the lowest point of her neckline. Bennett couldn't help notice the tiny tattoo on her breast.

"It's a forget-me-not," Lola said. "Men always comment on it."

"I can imagine."

The next week Lola came in twice, and the one after that three times, always in a different outfit, and always finding a way to engage

Bennett in conversation, even if she was not the one at the register, and whether she was making a purchase or not.

"She likes you, Bennett," Maria teased, when they sat down to go through the days' receipts.

"Oh my God, I hope not," Bennett stammered.

Maria laughed. "Don't worry, not like that. Lola definitely prefers men, but she's always looking for company—I think because she travels so much—and flirting is the only way she knows to get it. You should join her and her friends sometime. You might have fun. You shouldn't be alone all the time."

"How about you, Maria?" Bennett deflected, bending down to pick up an imaginary piece of paper so she wouldn't see the blush she knew was rising to her cheeks. "Your mother said it's been two years since you were widowed?"

"Widowed? Is that how Mama put it? That's not quite how it was."

Bennett had no idea how to continue this line of conversation, but Maria must have taken her silence as an invitation to talk for she put down the receipts and said, "I was sixteen when I met Carlos. He was eighteen and already in trouble and I guess that's what made him attractive. I was going through my rebellious phase."

"Why were you rebelling? Juanita seems like a good mother."

"She was. She is, but I guess I was one of those kids that needed to rebel just for the sake of it. Weren't you ever like that?"

"No." Bennett shook her head. "Is that why you married Carlos?"

"Not exactly. We dated for a while, but then I slept with him and got pregnant, which scared him off. Two years later he got shot during a robbery. Mama thinks it would be best for Isabella if we just say I was widowed ... but why am I telling you all this?"

"I'm sorry, I didn't mean to be so ... personal."

"No, it's all right. I don't mind your knowing. In fact, I'm glad."

"And now? Is there someone else?"

"No, but I haven't been looking. I have time. I'm only twenty four and I want to focus on Isabella and make sure I can make a go of this business. Then I can think about looking."

"What would you look for?"

Maria laughed. "You mean, what kind of man would I choose this time? A better one, I hope. Someone kind, adventurous, intelligent, willing to work; someone who likes kids and has a good sense of humor. Not that I would be put off by good looks and a little money. I might as well aim high. How about you, what's your ideal person?"

Bennett shrugged, embarrassed. "I don't know. It's been a long time since I've thought about it. Right now having my own house and a job I enjoy is enough. I don't want to risk spoiling everything by being greedy. Why dream the impossible?"

"Come on, Bennett, don't give up. You never know. You might meet just the right guy."

"I doubt it. My choices are limited."

"Lola might open your horizons," Maria said, smiling.

Bennett was still trying to decide whether she could be friends with someone like Lola, when Lola returned to the shop a few days later. Bennett showed her an especially fine piece of jewelry Maria had bought at an estate sale over the weekend.

"Wow, honey, wasn't Hitler fantastic for costume jewelry!"

"What a terrible thing to say."

There was no way they could be friends.

"All I meant was that if it wasn't for Hitler all those European jewelers wouldn't have come here. They had skills, honey, and they knew how to design. They didn't have the money to buy platinum and diamonds, so they made stuff they could afford to make, and people like me could afford to buy. Sometimes changing your expectations can open new doors, you know."

"What kind of skills?" Bennett asked, still wondering whether she could overlook Lola's heartlessneess.

Leaning over the glass case, Lola explained the intricacies of cutting and setting gems.

"I had no idea," Bennett said, turning the piece over in her hand.

Encouraged by her interest, Lola patted her hand and suggested she join her at The Green Parrot Piano Bar after work on Friday so they could talk some more.

Remembering what Maria had said about getting out, Bennett agreed.

"I'll meet you here at closing time, and we can go together. They've got a great happy hour," Lola told her. "Half-price drinks and all you can eat oysters—and you know what they say about oysters."

Bennett nodded uncomfortably, wondering if there was any truth to it.

On most evenings, The Green Parrot Bar—up a steep flight of steps over a French restaurant—was a quiet place to have a drink and listen to old standards, but on Fridays local wannabe stars gathered for their weekly sing-along. Intimate seating arrangements were undone and chairs pushed against the wall, so that drinkers could listen to the singers gathered around the piano. Stacks of sheet music sat on the piano unopened as Pat, who had been rehearsal pianist on Broadway for years, played every song by heart.

Feeling out of place in the boisterous crowd, Bennett picked up a book of lyrics from a shelf near the bar and pretended to follow along. When Lola looked over, she smiled and mouthed the words, her silence unnoticed.

"This is a blast, isn't it honey?" Lola slipped her arm in hers. "After this we usually go on to Sal's on the boulevard for pizza."

"I can't. I'm sorry... maybe another time?"

"Sure, honey, I understand. I'll be at the gift market next week, but how about a week from Saturday? We'll go dancing. I know a great little place where they do line dances and the Texas two-step. It's a group thing. No dates required, but it still seems a little pathetic to arrive alone. Much better with a friend." She pulled a business card out of her purse and handed it to her. "Here's my address."

"I've never .. I mean, I'm not a good dancer."

"Don't worry about that. There'll be lots of people to show you. Why don't you come to my place around seven, and we can have a drink before we go. Loosen us up a bit." Then she turned toward her friends, who were already halfway out the door. "Hey, guys, wait up."

Bennett looked down at the card Lola had given her. Between two angled photographs, one of a rhinestone brooch, the other of a porcelain doll, was her name in a ridiculously curly font:

Lola Wiskowski

Glorious Jewels and Gorgeous Dolls

lola@jewelsanddollsforever.com

On the back, in big, loopy handwriting she'd put her address, telephone number and a smiley face.

Bennett drove home, relieved to have gotten away, and wondering if she could cancel Saturday by email, tell her something had come up, though nothing would. When she wasn't at work or taking a walk she stayed home.

She glanced over at Mrs. McElroy's empty house as she unlocked her front door and felt an unexpected pang of loneliness. She'd missed her chance for friendship then. There was no point in making the same mistake again. She'd go to Lola's on Saturday.

Bennett arrived precisely at seven, wearing her best blue suit and matching pumps.

"Well, look at you," Lola said, though it was unclear from her tone what she meant. "Come on in and make yourself a drink."

She pointed to a small mirrored bar where she had set out two glasses, an ice bucket, a bottle of bourbon, and a bottle of Coca Cola. Next to it, a life-sized painting of a gaudily lipsticked woman sitting on a bar stool, her carrot red hair falling over one eye, hung incongruously over a floral love seat on which a half-dozen, elaborately dressed, porcelain-faced dolls perched against lace-trimmed, heart-shaped pillows. Bennett had the uncomfortable feeling they were staring at her.

Gold lace curtains covered the windows. A tall mahogany jewelry cabinet stood in the corner, its drawers open and overflowing with necklaces, bracelets and brooches. Stenciled roses and vines crept along the ceiling, and framed the doorway to the hall. Not knowing where to sit down, Bennett stood awkwardly in the middle of the room, holding her oversized handbag in front of her as she watched Lola in the kitchen prepare a plate of cheese and crackers.

"Don't you just love my place?" Lola said, turning to look at her.

"It ... looks like you."

"Thanks," she said, clearly pleased. "I think a home should reflect its owner, don't you?"

"I ... I do, I mean it does," Bennett said, glad Lola didn't notice her stammer.

"Put down your bag and pour us a drink, won't you, honey? Not too much ice, and just a splash of Coke for me."

Bennett walked over to the bar.

"How was the gift show, Lola?" she said, as Lola brought over the cheese and crackers.

"Pretty good."

Lola sat down on the love seat in front of the dolls and motioned for Bennett to join her. Bennett hesitated, seeing there would be little space between them, but not wanting to be rude, she perched on the edge of the cushion and handed Lola her drink, then listened as Lola told her about the miles she'd walked, going from vendor to vendor, making contacts, giving out cards.

"I have a bunch of regulars who buy from me," she explained, "but you've got to keep making new contacts. You never know who's going to die or go out of business. My first husband didn't understand that. He got jealous when I talked to people. It broke us up. My second husband, on the other hand, was a real charmer, could sweet talk anyone into buying anything. He's the one that got me into selling dolls. He was great for my business but then he died."

"Oh, I'm sorry," Bennett said, trying to absorb the idea of two husbands.

"C'est la vie." Lola shrugged and put down her glass. "Come on, honey, time to go dancing. What do you have in that big sack of yours?"

"It's my handbag. I always carry it. It was my mother's."

"Oh. I thought maybe you brought a dress or something. You look a little proper in your suit. Next time you should wear something with a skirt. Looks good when you're dancing, especially with your figure. I could lend you some lipstick, if you want."

Bennett shook her head. "I never wear it."

Lola laughed. "Really? I feel naked without it. But to each his own. Do you mind driving? We could walk from here, but I hate doing it in my dancing slippers."

Bennett looked down at Lola's feet, surprisingly dainty in their gold sandals, and then at hers, in her boat-shaped, size 10, low-heeled pumps.

"Perhaps we should go somewhere else?" Bennett suggested. What was she thinking, going dancing with strangers?

"Oh, no, honey, we gotta go. It's my favorite place."

It was only a two minute drive. Bennett let Lola out at the front door and then had to drive almost all the way back to find a parking space. Worried she would be upset at having to wait, Bennett ran back, but found that Lola was too busy talking to the ticket-taker to have noticed.

"My treat this time. You can spring for it next time," she said.

DANCELAND filled the ground floor of an erstwhile fabric warehouse. A slight formaldehyde odor still lingered in the air. Styrofoam-backed posters lined the cinderblock walls in a futile attempt to absorb the sounds that reverberated through the immense space. The old pine flooring, newly refinished, reflected the lights hanging from pipes in the ceiling. People stood in scattered groups chatting as they awaited instructions for the first dance. Lola entered with a wave of her hand, and shouts of greeting surrounded them.

"Do you know everyone?" Bennett asked, feeling both impressed and irritated.

"I try to." Lola took her hand and pulled her along from one group to another without ever introducing her. Bennett wondered why Lola had bothered to bring her.

Within minutes the music began and despite unintelligible instructions from the man holding a microphone the crowds fell into lines and began to dance. Having long ago become adept at following rules, Bennett soon caught the hang of it. By the end of the evening, she could almost say she'd had a good time.

Maybe sitting home every evening as she'd done until then, thinking about what might have been or should have been was no way to live. Hanging out with a husband collector was probably not what she would have chosen, but it was better than all those years of not making friends at Bancroft, Chandler and Co. So when Lola asked her to join her again a week later, Bennett could find no reason not to accept. Lola was fearless, open to meeting people, and happiest in a crowd where everyone knew her. She was willing to try anything new, not caring what people thought. As different from Aunt Mary as anyone could be. Bennett admired that. Even more, she envied it. Lola was who she was and that was good enough for her.

Lola let little time slip by between invitations and pulled Bennett into her many social activities. When Bennett felt like a fish out of water and suggested outings that were more to her liking, Lola said *sure, as long as it isn't too quiet*. This meant they did not go to concerts, plays, lectures, or basically anything she had to listen to without talking.

8

*D*riving home from her weekly trip to the farmer's market, Bennett rolled open her car window. It was the first August day that wouldn't steam the pleats out of a skirt. A perfect time to have taken the day off. She had almost reached her house when she was slowed down by a moving van creeping along in front of her. She pressed her foot hard on the accelerator to pass it, only to see the van follow her onto Spring Street and park directly behind her.

She carried her groceries up to her door and, once inside, pulled the living room curtains closed, leaving an opening just wide enough to be able to watch the movers unload.

"Watch that trunk, please, it's very old!" a man shouted unexpectedly from the upstairs window. When had he arrived? A few moments later he walked out the front door: a tall, slender man in his mid- or late-forties, with short brown hair, graying at the temples, and wearing khaki shorts and a black T-shirt. Attractive, Bennett thought, but no clue as to whether he sat at a desk all day or shingled a roof or fixed the plumbing.

Two small children ran laughing and screaming out of the house, then in again. And out again. And in again. They, unlike the man, were a dark mahogany brown, with curly black hair cropped so short that only their clothes indicated which was the girl and which the boy.

"Papa, I can't find my bicycle!" the boy shouted.

"It's in the backyard," the man called back. "Both of you, please stay where I can see you, and don't get in the way. You might get hurt."

So he was the father. And the mother? Where was she? No one had told Bennett people were moving in. She liked her nice, quiet neighborhood the way it was, and now everything might change.

"I guess, you've lost half your garden, Miss Hall," the mailman said the next day, when he delivered the mail later than usual, and arrived at the same time as Bennett. "But it'll be nice to have neighbors again."

"I suppose," Bennett said, hoping she wouldn't have to deal with them at all— though there was no reason to assume the worst about people she didn't know, as Aunt Mary had always done,

Bennett nodded farewell to the mailman, unlocked her door and went inside, her feelings still unresolved.

The next morning the man, dressed in light blue cotton pants and scrubs, drove off at 7:45 with his children, and did not return until after six. This schedule was repeated every day for the next three weeks. Evenings they stayed home, but there was little to be heard, save for the muffled sound of running up and down the stairs, which was no more disturbing than the sound of squirrels scampering over the roof. Bennett could almost forget that the family lived there at all if it weren't for the weekends when the children spent most of their time playing in the backyard. To her surprise, Bennett found herself enjoying the shouts and squeals of laughter that seemed to be a part of every game. She envied the ease and affection they all showed each other: child to child, father to children, children to father. How different things would have been if her father had lived. And her mother. If things had been different, she might have been a mother herself.

Still no sign of a mother next door. Divorced? Or maybe she was dead. Or in the military. Women did that now. Or prison. Though probably not. The father and children seemed happy. Bennett would have liked to know more about them, but it wasn't in her to ask. Besides, it might not matter. Who knew how long they'd be there?

The beginning of the school year brought a change to her new neighbors' routine. Father and children left the house just when Bennett was eating breakfast, with the boy carrying a backpack and the girl a lunch box. Mid-afternoon the children were brought back by a woman who stayed with them until their father returned at six. On the afternoons Bennett was not at work, she looked forward to hearing the children playing ball or hide and go seek, or swinging in their new hammock. When she heard crying she'd run to the window to make sure they were all right. When she saw scraped knees tended and bumped elbows kissed, her heart ached for the lonely, neglected child she'd once been. One day, the children noticed her watching and waved, but the moment quickly passed as they returned to their games, and Bennett returned to the stillness of her books.

She was reading a book on Chinese porcelain she'd brought home from the shop when she was startled by a sudden frantic ringing of the doorbell accompanied by urgent knocking. She leaned out the window and saw it was the children's minder.

"I'm coming!" she shouted , then ran down the stairs.

"My son!" the woman cried, tears streaming down her face. "He's had a terrible accident ... I have to leave. Can you watch the children?"

"I couldn't ..." she stammered.

"Please! I have to leave now. Right now. He's in the hospital, I can't take them with me. Dr. Muir will be home in less than an hour."

Bennett nodded. What else could she do? She grabbed her keys, locked up and followed.

"I will call when I can," the minder shouted as she ran to her car, leaving Bennett standing speechless with the children as she drove away.

She felt a tug on her pants leg.

"Can you play Uno with us?" the boy asked, a deck of multicolored cards in his hand.

"I can try," Bennett said. "But shouldn't I know your names first?"

"You have to tell us yours first," the boy said, putting his arm protectively around his sister's shoulder. "We're not supposed to talk to strangers."

"You're right. My name is Bennett Hall and I live next door."

"We know that already!" the girl laughed. "We've seen you lots of times."

"I'm Medi but sometimes I'm called Simon," the boy said and then added: "And her name is Hope. She doesn't have another name."

"Why are you sometimes called Simon?"

"I think it's my school name, but Papa calls me Medi for short. What are you called for short?"

"Just Bennett."

"That's not very short. Do you want to know how old I am?"

"Yes, I do. Will you tell me?"

"I'm six."

"And I'm four!" Hope added, clearly quite proud of the fact.

There was a moment of silence as each tried to figure out what to say next.

"Come on, let's play Uno," Medi said, pulling on Bennett's sleeve.

"I don't know how to play."

"How come?"

Bennett shrugged. "Guess I never had the chance to learn."

"That's okay. We can show you," Hope said, taking Bennett's hand and pulling her down to the floor, which was cluttered with paper and crayons, and a variety of plastic knights and dragons.

Medi dealt seven cards to each person.

"It's easy," he explained. "Everyone gets seven cards."

"I can count to seven," Hope said to Bennett. "Can you?"

"Of course she can," Medi answered. "She's a grown-up."

Bennett smiled. "What do we do once we have the seven cards?"

"If you get a red two you can put down a two or a red."

"How about if you get a three, Medi?" Hope asked.

"Same thing, silly. Don't you remember?"

Bennett soon saw that she needn't worry about secret strategies. Hope and Medi had laid their cards out on the floor in full view because the cards were too big for their little hands to hold.

"Now let's play baby," Hope suggested after a few minutes.

"I have to confess. I don't know anything about babies."

"That's all right," she said. "You can be the big sister. I'll be the Mommy and Medi is the pirate."

"That's an interesting combination. Are you a good pirate or a bad pirate?" "Arrgh!" Medi answered, pulling a cardboard sword from the toy box.

"Don't hurt me!" Bennett cringed and held her hands to her face like Munch's screamer.

"Don't worry, Bennett, it's only paper. See?"

"What a relief! You looked terribly fierce."

"Sometimes I practice in the mirror," Medi explained.

"Medi says I have a big sister, too," Hope interrupted.

"Is she a pirate also?"

"No, silly, she's a person like me."

"I thought you were a baby."

"I am, so you have to give me a bottle."

"I'm glad you reminded me."

Bennett got down on her knees and was bending over Hope when the front door opened.

"What's going on here?"

Bennett jumped up, her face red.

"I can explain. We were just playing baby ..."

"But why are you here? Where's Mrs. Jackson?"

"She had to leave. Her son was in an accident ... she asked me to stay with your children until you returned. I haven't been here long ... I'm sorry if I startled you."

"Oh God, he's her only child ... sorry I didn't mean to be rude ... I have to call her."

Bennett got up off the floor and turned toward the door.

"I understand completely. I should leave ..." What must he think, finding a strange woman bending over his child?

"No, please, can you stay a moment longer while I call her?"

Bennett felt a tug on her sleeve as she watched him pace back and forth, switching the phone from one hand to the other. She looked down to see Hope looking up at her.

"Can we still play baby?"

"I think I'll have to go in a minute," Bennett said.

"I don't know what to do," the man said as he got off the phone. "Mrs. Jackson won't be coming tomorrow. Probably not for a while ... I'm in the middle of an important project. I can't just take off ... how in the world can I find someone by tomorrow?"

He sat down, then suddenly realizing he was ignoring Bennett, he stood up again.

"I'm so sorry, I'm talking to myself. It's Miss Hall, isn't it? You've been so kind and I haven't thanked you or even introduced myself. I'm Joe Muir," he said, holding out his hand. His eyes were the darkest brown, his handshake firm and warm.

"Joe? Short for Joseph?" Bennett blushed. What an inane question.

"Funny you should ask. It's actually short for Giordano. My mother was Italian. It was supposed to be Gio with a G but people kept saying Gee-o so I spell it like Joe instead. Sorry, that was much too long an explanation. Listen, Miss Hall.. I'm sure you don't— there's no reason you should—but you don't by any chance know anyone trustworthy who takes care of children?"

"Actually, there is one person ... someone I've known a long time and trust completely. She takes care of her granddaughter. She might—"

"— be just perfect. Do you by any chance know her number?"

"Yes. I think I have it with me."

Bennett took out her wallet and removed a small, folded piece of paper on which she'd long ago typed the few telephone numbers she might have reason to call: her office, her doctor, her dentist, the nearest pharmacy, and Juanita Morales. To those she'd added Maria, the shop, and in pencil, Lola.

"I'll talk to her first and explain the situation, if you'd like, and then I'll leave you to negotiate the details."

9

The morning after her unexpected childcare adventure, Bennett found a handwritten note slipped under her door.

Dear Ms Hall -

It was too early to bother you this morning but I wanted to thank you again for yesterday. I don't know what would have happened if you hadn't been there. Thanks also for directing me to Juanita. If all goes as expected, I will give her the house key and she will pick up the children this afternoon and stay with them until I return. I said she could bring her grandchild along. It makes me feel more confident that the children will be in good hands.

You certainly saved the day and I can't thank you enough.

Medi and Hope said they hope you can come and play again.

Gratefully,

Joe Muir

Bennett folded the note and after a moment's thought, added it to her file of important documents.

Forgetting all about breakfast, she set out for a long walk. The air was cool but the bright sun felt warm on her face, and she felt something she could almost call happiness. Her new address could not have been more appropriate: 123 Spring Street. When she said it aloud she could almost feel the lift in her step. One two three ... spring! Out of the old life and into the new. Out of darkness and into the light. Was it really possible that her life had turned around so completely?

After two hours, she returned energized and ready, even eager, to get back to her genealogy research and deal with whatever Hall family secrets she unearthed.

William Bernard Hall, born July 2,1930 in New York City, to Bernard Maurice Hall and Luigina Maria Bruni. The Italian name was a surprise, as was her father's place of birth. Had he grown up there? No one had ever mentioned New York, but then no one had ever told her things she would actually have wanted to know.

She logged onto the census records website and searched for William Bernard Hall in 1930, and found endless William Halls but none with a middle name. It would have helped to know where in New York her father had lived. Perhaps Bernard or Luigina would be easier to find, but even if she found them, the census wouldn't tell her the important things, like what they looked like, how they met, who their friends were, or even who their parents were.

You're wasting your time, Bennett. Nobody cares.

Bennett shook her head. It's what Aunt Mary would have said, but she'd been dead for months and it was time to stop hearing her voice. Why didn't she ever hear her mother's kinder voice? Or was hers just too long ago?

Bennett entered the data on her computer and resolved to keep searching the census records the next day. But it was five o'clock and she wanted to know how things had gone with Juanita.

Bennett knocked at their door and saw Hope standing on tiptoes, knocking on the window pane in reply. As soon Juanita opened the door, Hope ran up and grabbed Bennett's hand.

"You've made a friend, Bennett," Juanita said. "She's been talking about you all afternoon."

"Hello, Hope. And how are you, Juanita? Thank you so much for coming to their rescue."

"It is I who must thank you—once again. First Maria, and now this. If Dr. Muir and the children are happy with me, I am very happy. With Isabella to take care of, I have not been able to work since your aunt passed away. To have a job where I can bring Isabella is a gift. I am very grateful."

Bennett looked fondly at Juanita, as she stood at the counter with her apron tied around her ample waist, her gray hair loosely pinned back. She remembered how often Juanita had brought them salteñas and baked plantains from her own kitchen because she knew Aunt Mary rarely cooked, preferring to let fresh meat and vegetables rot rather than let Bennett cook. Fried chicken and biscuits, or hamburgers and fries, delivered by neighborhood fast-food restaurants had become their usual fare, supplemented with an occasional piece of fruit Bennet brought home from the office cafeteria. Aunt Mary rarely left the house after Bennett's mother died, and never at all the last few years. She'd grown slower and fatter until all she did was sit on her bed and watch television, snacking on potato chips and fast food leftovers until Bennett came home.

"You'll be surprised to hear that I have taught myself how to cook, Juanita. Only simple things, of course."

"Then I guess you won't want any of my salteñas," Juanita said, her eyes twinkling.

"Oh, I do. I was just remembering how much I liked them."

"Come in and have one then. And you, Hope? Would you like another one?"

Hope shook her head.

"I'm full."

"Then go on and do some more coloring with Isabella. I need to talk to Señora Bennett for a moment."

Hope waved to Bennett and ran off into the dining room where Medi and Isabella were busy coloring at a table covered with construction paper and crayons.

"Do you think Dr. Muir will be happy with me?"

"I have no doubt."

"He's a very special man, you know, taking in those children when they had no one else."

"They are not his?"

"Now they are. He and his wife adopted them."

"So there is a wife? I've never seen her."

Juanita shook her head and leaned forward so only Bennett could hear.

"She was killed. In Uganda."

"Killed?"

"In an accident. Such a tragedy. That's why Dr. Muir came back."

"I don't understand... the children are from Uganda? How do you know all this?"

"I asked. I had to know what family I was bringing my Isabella to," she said, looking at Bennett sharply as if to say it would have been quite irresponsible not to.

"Yes, of course, but ..."

"You can ask him yourself. He will tell you."

Bennett nodded, though she knew she wouldn't. But she would listen if he brought it up. She was good at that.

"Bennett! Come look at my picture," Hope called from the other room.

With exaggerated concentration Bennett examined the drawing of a large head and two long, spindly stick legs.

"Hmmm... Yes, that's very good. Clearly a portrait of .... um ...?"

"It's Isabella, can't you tell?" Hope said.

"The green hair threw me off for a second, but I recognize her smile. She looks very happy."

"Yes, Isabella's always happy because Juanita brings us cookies."

Bennett laughed. "I guess it's not just Isabella that's happy."

She looked at her watch. She'd better go. Dr. Muir would be home soon and she didn't want him to think she was taking liberties.

"Don't leave," Medi said when Bennett walked toward the door. "We haven't played Uno yet."

"Next time," Bennett said. "I promise."

She put her hand out to touch Medi's head. His wiry hair felt scratchy yet soft under her fingers. She was overcome by a rush of tenderness toward these little beings who had so quickly and inexplicably captured her heart. She mustn't spoil it.

10

Lola announced that she would be away for at least six weeks. Every fall she showed her jewelry at trade shows up and down the East Coast, and this year she was adding Chicago and Atlanta to her schedule as well.

"But don't you worry, honey. I'll be back."

Bennett wasn't worried at all. In fact, she was relieved she wouldn't have to cut short her now frequent five o'clock visits to Juanita and the children. While Bennett taught Medi how to play Monopoly and chess, Hope and Isabella would sit on the floor "drawing" and "writing," eager to present Bennett with countless pages of their free-form scribbles and indecipherable words.

"You are very good with children," Juanita remarked one afternoon, while cutting meat and vegetables for a Salvadoran soup she called *Sopa de Rez con Verduras.*

"Only because they make it easy," Bennett said. "Your soup smells heavenly."

"I'll give you some to take with you," Juanita said, ladling some into a plastic container.

"Oh no you don't," a man's voice said, startling Bennett. "If you're going to eat our soup I'm afraid you'll have to eat it with us."

"I didn't mean—"

"Don't be silly," Joe said, throwing off his shoes and giving each child a hug. "You want Bennett to stay, don't you?"

"You can sit next to me, Bennett," Hope said, making it impossible to refuse.

With Juanita's continued gastronomic encouragement, Bennett was asked to dinner again. And again.

Used to her own tidy rooms, so purposely devoid of memories, and despite her fear of becoming an unwelcome obligation, Bennett felt more and more comfortable in Joe's house with its jumble of belongings reflecting the many facets of his life. He'd replaced Mrs. McElroy's floral wallpaper but had kept her well-worn furniture. Bookshelves overflowed with books and photographs. African carvings and Italian ceramic plates hung together in the living room alongside a framed poster of Albert Schweitzer. On a table-sized bulletin board in the kitchen, school announcements and appointment reminders vied for space with Hope and Isabella's drawings. And none of it made Bennett feel claustrophobic the way Aunt Mary's decaying clutter had.

So it didn't take long for Bennett's visits to extend to the children's bedtime. Hope dozed off as soon as her head touched the pillow, but Medi struggled to stay awake so he wouldn't miss Bennett reading to him about dinosaurs and pirates.

"You've been really good for them," Joe said, making Bennett blush.

As winter approached and the cold evenings called for hot tea and fireside conversation, Joe began inviting Bennett to stay on after the children were in bed. He'd sit in the easy chair while Bennett sat on the sofa, and they'd talk—about the children at first; then an interesting patient Joe had had, or a movie Bennett had watched when she couldn't sleep. They discovered they shared a love of black and white movies from the 40's.

"But recently I've been watching Italian movies," he said. "They seem to have compassion for human flaws in a way we don't... I would have liked to have gone to Italy with my mother, so she could show me where she grew up, but she died before we had the chance. Someday I'll go with the kids."

Bennett heard a sadness in his voice she hadn't heard before. It would be childish—as if she were competing with him—if she told him that her mother had died when she was young, and her grandmother was from Italy, too, but she didn't know her and didn't know where. So she didn't say anything at all.

That night she made a list of the Italian movies he said he'd liked.

One evening, about a week later, Joe asked Bennett to stay on after the children went to bed. He brought out a bottle of wine and poured them each a glass.

"Are you all right? You don't seem yourself," Bennett said.

"I saw a young man in the ER today—I'd gone down because they were short-staffed—he was so skinny and weak. I think he was Sudanese, but he reminded me of all the young men with AIDS that Laurie and I used to treat in Uganda." He paused. "You can't imagine what it means to have AIDS in Africa."

"It must be so ... sad," Bennett said, inadequately, distracted by Joe's fidgeting with his wedding band.

"It's worse than sad. When these young men die it's not only families losing loved ones. It means no workers in the villages, no incomes for their families. There is no safety net. No welfare or unemployment insurance..."

He poured them each a second glass of wine.

"I thought I'd read that things had gotten better ..." Bennett said.

"They have. But a million and a half are living with AIDS and a quarter of them are still not getting treatment. So thousands die every year...Sometimes I wonder if I should have left. We were making a difference, Laurie and I."

Bennett wanted to say something meaningful, something comforting, but could only stammer, "Did she... get sick? Is that why—"

Joe shook his head.

"No. But one night, a doctor from a small clinic a long way from ours called, desperate for help. All his nurses had fallen sick. I begged Laurie to get some rest before she left—she had been working all day and it had just rained and the roads were a mess—but she wouldn't. I had patients and the children to take care of, or I would have gone with her. The next day they found her body and the Jeep in a ravine. She'd broken her neck."

"Oh my God."

Bennett could feel his eyes on her, asking for her understanding.

"She was such a good person, Bennett. We had so many plans for the clinic."

Bennett yearned to reach out and hold him, wipe away the tears that made his eyes glisten, but all she could manage was to reach into her pocket and hand him her crumpled handkerchief. She was no good to anyone. What a fool she was to imagine he could ever be interested in her.

Joe blew his nose, straightened his back and took a deep breath.

"Thank you for being such a good listener, Bennett," he said, "but now's your turn. Tell me how your genealogy research is progressing."

Bennett shook her head.

"It's not that interesting."

"No scandals?" Joe teased.

"No, just some unexpected things—but then I didn't know what to expect since no one ever told me anything."

She sounded like an idiot, complaining about something so trivial when he'd just talked about losing his wife and people dying of AIDS.

But Joe smiled and said, "I wasn't told much either. Not by my parents anyway. The few things I know I found out when some distant cousins of my mother's came for a long weekend and reminisced about when they were young in Naples. A few long-kept secrets were revealed that weekend. You'd better take your Italian records with a grain of salt."

"What do you mean?" she asked, unsettled, her voice sharper than she meant it to be.

"Well, a married man, for instance, couldn't recognize a child out of wedlock. Since there was no divorce until 1970, and most annulments weren't approved, many children were born outside official marriage. To avoid having their children being labeled illegitimate, wives and husbands who were long separated recognized each other's children by their new partners. Or sometimes a bachelor brother recognized a child so that the child would have his father's name. But in that case the mother was marked as unknown, which was equally misleading

—and usually ridiculous. Italians were good at making adjustments to the truth, so you'd better be careful."

Bennett bristled. She wasn't a child. There was no need to be condescending.

"Then what's the point of doing genealogy in the first place?"

"None, probably, with all the real problems in the world," Joe said, patting her hand, "but it can still be fun, even if it doesn't matter. "

Bennett felt her face redden.

"Maybe it matters to me," she said, standing up abruptly and almost knocking over the table lamp. "We can't all be as noble as you and Laurie..."

Before Joe could respond, she'd stumbled out the door and rushed home. As soon as she closed her door she knew she'd ruined everything.

11

Bennett blamed the motor scooter racing down Spring Street for awakening her at two in the morning. Then the screeching of a cat fight at three. Or was it the wind rattling her window? Even the ticking of her clock, which she normally didn't hear at all, echoed through the room. Of course, it wasn't noise that niggled at her. It was Joe smiling as he mocked her. That was what he was doing, she was sure of it.

She'd been embarrassed and her reaction had been childish. He'd probably rolled his eyes when she left in a huff, glad to be rid of her.

She should have spent more time with Lola. She might have learned how to deal with people. Lola would have brushed Joe's comments off. She wouldn't have interpreted an off-hand comment as a judgment on her whole life—even if he was right that her life was inconsequential.

Lola had talked about the men in her life—sometimes in embarrassing detail—without drama, accepting them for what they were. Yet she was divorced, so maybe she hadn't really? She'd never shown interest in the men in Bennett's life, but as there weren't any, it was a good thing she hadn't. Bennett would have had to admit how ridiculously, unforgivably, long it had been since sex had been a part of her life. It had been once with Stephen—after all, they'd planned to get married—but then he'd left. There'd been a few other times, when she was in her late twenties and thought time was running out. She barely remembered them, as they hadn't led to anything.

Only once was there someone from the office. She liked him, but he soon moved on to someone else. Aunt Mary said there was no point moping. Men were unreliable. And they didn't like tall women. It made them feel small. But Bennett knew it was because the other woman was better. And more fun. No one in the division would have ever described Bennett as fun. No one mentioned it, but they must all have known about her humiliation, so she didn't dare risk it again. The last time she had sex at all was with a man she met in the bar of her hotel when she was in New Orleans on business. Lonely and a little drunk, she'd gone up to his room. Years later all she remembered was the shame she'd felt, and the grayness of the sky when she left the next morning. Not his name.

It was a pathetic tale that Lola would never understand. Just thinking what Joe would think made her stomach knot.

Standing in the shower, with hot water washing away the last remnant of a morning headache, Bennett remembered that she'd put Lola off when she called to say she was back from her trip. But only two days had passed. She wouldn't think it odd if Bennet said her plans had changed.

It had to be better than staying home knowing she could never go next door again.

"Oh good," Lola said. "How 'bout going for a big juicy steak? I have lots to tell you."

Bennett thought she'd hear about the trade shows, but Lola preferred to talk about the people she'd met. More specifically, the men.

"One guy was a real charmer, so I invited him up for a night cap. He was happy to accept, but afterwards, he was so out of breath I thought he'd die of a heart attack. How would I have explained a naked dead man sprawled across my bed?"

"Oh my God, Lola. What did you do?"

"Nothing. He didn't die, but I did have a moment of panic, though it wouldn't have been the first time such a thing happened in a hotel."

"No, but…"

"I think I would have gotten dressed, covered him up, and called the front desk—you know, as if I wasn't involved."

"But you were. You would have felt terrible."

"Of course," Lola said. She seemed annoyed.

"I didn't mean—"

"Steak's getting cold," Lola said.

They ate quietly for a few minutes.

"Have you gone back to DANCELAND?" Lola asked, having moved on.

Bennett shook her head, and drank a sip of her wine.

"Oh no, not without you. I could never do that."

"Well, then, it's good I'm back."

So Bennett went on seeing Lola, accepting invitations to social activities she would never have considered otherwise. They helped push aside the painful memory of her last visit with Joe. Her whiny petulance had ruined any chances might have had with him.

She might have apologized, but Juanita came to tell her that Joe had started an evening course and she would be minding the children at her house for a while.

∽

Bennett had spent most of her life facing one day at a time, meeting obligations, keeping anger and unsatisfied desires at bay. She'd stopped expecting more. Then everything changed. She was pushed out by Bancroft and Co., sold her house and bought a new one. Found a new job, though, to be honest, it had found her. And met Joe and Medi and Hope. She hadn't earned any of those good changes. Why then did she find herself wanting more?

As October slipped into November, seeing Lola became a habit that softened the pain of knowing that what she desired she couldn't have —and worse, what she desired *to be* she wasn't.

Sometimes Lola let them substitute a movie for the weekly singalong, or a musical at the civic center instead of Sal's for pizza. They never talked about anything more consequential than whether Lola should get a booth at the winter market or wait for the spring one, until one night as they were eating take-out at Lola's, Lola asked if Bennet had ever had cybersex?

"I don't know what that is," she had to admit.

Lola laughed.

"You're behind the times, honey. You have cybersex with people you meet online. It's pretty exciting. People are real honest when they think no one knows who they are."

"Or totally dishonest."

"Maybe, sometimes," she said, "but who cares? I've had some real thrills online. You wouldn't think cybersex would be arousing, but it is."

Bennett didn't know what to answer.

"See, I met this guy online once and we ... well, you know, and then he invited me to join him and a few of his buddies at his hunting lodge in Louisiana."

Bennett's eyes widened. Was Lola crazy? Didn't she see *Deliverance*? Or worry about AIDS?

"You didn't go, did you?"

"Sure I did. He sent me pictures first, so I knew what the guys looked like and they seemed fine. Real fine, actually. So I went and we had a ball, even if the lodge turned out to be nothing more than a cabin in the woods. In fact, that's where I met my third husband. Lane Bashford. Don't you just love that name? He was one of the buddies. The best looking one of the bunch, if you really want to know. He had the cutest pony tail."

Lola leaned back in her chair and smiled, remembering.

"One of your date's friends, Lola? Didn't you feel ... disloyal?"

"Nah, he didn't care. Besides, the marriage didn't last. Looks weren't enough, it turned out."

Third husband? Cybersex, hunting cabins with a bunch of men ...

"My God," Bennett muttered. "Why would you think I'd want to hear about that?"

12

*B*ennett hadn't meant to leave Lola's so abruptly but she couldn't think of anything more to say except that she should be careful and that she had to go because she had an early morning appointment. When she got home she rinsed her mouth twice with Listerine, as if it could wash away the bad taste in her mouth. How could she be friends with someone whose view of life and relationships and propriety were so far removed from hers?

But Bennett knew that Lola wasn't the problem. A few disparaging words by Joe about her genealogy findings had totally discombobulated her. He had awakened desires in her she had long forgotten she could have. Was it simply greed to want more than she had, or was it the realization that without desire there was no joy, no passion, no sense of purpose or accomplishment. After all, what interest would one have in food without hunger?

The next day, Bennett called Maria and said she wasn't well and wouldn't be in. She made herself a cup of coffee and then sat at the kitchen table watching it get cold. She might have wallowed in confused self-pity all day if the phone hadn't rung again and again until she could no longer ignore it.

"Ms. Hall? I'm so glad you answered," an unfamiliar woman's voice bubbled through the line. "I tried several times before but you didn't answer and I couldn't leave a message—guess you don't have an answering machine."

"No, I don't. Who is this, please?"

"Oh, I'm sorry. This is Shannon Butler. You may not remember my name since we didn't get a chance to meet, but my husband and I bought your house."

When Bennett didn't respond, she went on. "Your realtor gave us your number. See, I was up in the attic and found a box I thought you might want."

Why was this woman bothering her? Bennett had purposely left everything behind.

"There was nothing in the house I wanted to keep."

"I know, but I think this might be different. Someone must have hidden the box on purpose because it was all wrapped up in an old quilt and stuck way in a corner where you wouldn't normally see it. You probably wouldn't want the quilt anymore, though. It looks pretty ratty though it—"

"What kind of box?" Bennett interrupted, feeling assaulted by the woman's relentlessly cheerful chattering.

"Well, I told my husband I didn't feel right looking through it, but I did happen to notice that there were some documents, and a bunch of newspaper articles about a young pianist named William Hall. He must be a relative, don't you think?"

"Pianist?"

"Yeah, like a child prodigy or something. Don't you want to come get the box? I'll be home for another couple of hours but then we're going away for three weeks and I'm sure you wouldn't want to wait that long to see it."

"All right, I suppose I can come. It'll take me about an hour."

"Great!" Then the woman laughed. "I was just about to give you directions. Isn't that silly?"

Bennett smiled weakly into the phone and hung up without saying good-bye. She took off her nightgown, threw it in the hamper, took a shower, and got dressed. She could get there in less than thirty minutes, get the box, and be back in an hour.

When she first saw the Old Beast again she could almost feel it reaching out to capture her and hold her prisoner again. Her heart hammered so hard against her chest she could barely breathe. But then she noticed that the overgrown evergreens that had darkened the living room had been removed and replaced by young azalea bushes. She stepped gingerly onto the porch and realized that the floor had been repaired and painted a light gray. A new brass door handle had taken the place of the old black knob, and the gargoyle-like knocker was gone, replaced by a shiny new doorbell. When Bennett rang it, she heard the melodic tinkle of bells.

A young woman in black jeans and a pink T-shirt that said *I ♥ Paris* opened the door and greeted her with a broad smile and an outstretched hand.

"Ms. Hall? I'm so glad you could come. It gives me a chance to tell you how much we love it here. We've changed it a bit. I hope you don't mind. But you know how it is, you want to make a house your own. You understand, don't you?"

Yes, oh yes, Bennett thought though she just nodded.

The house was so altered Bennett could hardly take it all in. How had they done it so quickly? All the wallpaper had been stripped and the rooms were painted the kind of colors Maria liked, with silly names like mango cream biscuit or lazy caterpillar green. The old rugs were gone, the floors refinished. No more heavy drapes. Some windows fearlessly had no coverings at all. The sun seemed to stream in from all directions at once. How was that even possible?

"Mrs. Butler, could I possibly see the kitchen?" she asked, remembering the few happy hours she'd spent there with her mother when Aunt Mary was not about.

"Of course. That's my favorite room. We've kept it a little retro. We didn't want to make changes that didn't go with its age, but were up-to-date at the same time. Does that make sense?"

"Very much. I can't get over it. You've expelled all the ghosts."

"Ghosts?"

"Sorry. That was more a comment to myself. You've done a wonderful job. I wouldn't have known how to begin. I can't thank you enough for showing it to me. It has given me enormous hope."

"Are you renovating a house too?"

"No, just myself."

The young woman looked puzzled.

"Don't mind me." Bennett turned to go. "I won't bother you any longer. I know you are leaving."

"You can't go yet, Ms. Hall. I haven't given you the box." She paused for a moment. "And there's one other thing. I hope you aren't too disappointed that we didn't keep all the furniture and things. We did sell some of it, but a lot of it wasn't in good enough condition to sell, so we gave it away. It wasn't our ... our style, if you know what I mean."

"I understand. It wasn't mine either."

"We didn't sell the silver menorah, though. It's probably the most beautiful thing we have and looks great in the dining room, even though we aren't Jewish. But then it occurred to us that you might be, and maybe you didn't mean to leave it behind. It must have a sentimental value, and be worth a lot of money, as it's silver. So if you want it back, we'd understand."

Bennett smiled. "I wouldn't think of it. I'm not Jewish, or anything really, and don't know why we had it. I'm delighted that it brings you pleasure. You must keep it."

"Oh, you are the best. Thank you so much!" The young woman reached over and kissed Bennett's cheek, and handed her the box.

"It is I who should thank you," Bennett said. "You couldn't have picked a better day to call me."

13

*B*ennett was still smiling when she walked up her front path and saw Medi and Hope sitting on their front stoop.

"Is that a treasure box?" Medi asked when he saw what Bennett was holding.

"I hope so but I haven't looked in it yet."

"We'd better go, kids," Joe said, as he came out, carrying a cooler and a pair of cleats. "Oh, Bennett! Haven't seen you in ages. Today is Medi's last soccer game of the season so we have to run, but how about joining us for dinner?"

His smile was warm. He seemed pleased to see her. Was it possible that she hadn't ruined everything after all?

"I'd like that. About 6:30?"

"Could you make it six? They have school tomorrow and need to get to bed early."

Bennett watched as they ran down the stairs to their car. Every few steps the children turned around and waved. She waved back until she saw their car pull around the corner. Only then did she go into her house.

Eager to remove the remnants of the gloom that had overwhelmed her earlier, she removed the rumpled linens from her bed and washed the dirty dishes in the kitchen sink. Then she called Lola to offer an explanation for leaving her so abruptly. She owed her that, at least. But what could she say? That Lola's life wasn't what she wanted?

"Lola? It's me. I should have called earlier, and I don't know how to say this as kindly as I want to—because you've been so nice to me—but I'm afraid we're just too different to be friends."

"I thought we were having fun."

"We were, but—" Lola would never understand that fun wasn't enough.

"Well, never mind," Lola said cheerfully. "I won't hold it against you—and hey, we'll still see each other at the shop. Don't forget to save me the good stuff. You've developed quite a good eye, you know."

Bennett was relieved, albeit a bit disappointed that Lola didn't care. But why would she? She was only one of many people in Lola's life. She was right about one thing. Bennett did have a better eye now, and not only for jewelry.

Grateful the situation was so easily behind her, she put up water for tea, then changed her mind and poured herself a glass of wine instead. Pulling up a chair, she sat down at the kitchen table and let her finger trace the delicately inlaid lines of silver that curled around the top and sides of the mysterious box. Whose was it and why had it been hidden away?

Inside she found three envelopes. The first contained documents. She'd look at them later. It was the second envelope, filled with yellowed newspaper clippings, that intrigued her. Why had they been kept? Afraid the brittle paper would crumble in her fingers, she gently unfolded and smoothed out the clippings one by one. Most of them were reviews cut carefully from newspapers, praising the performances at concert halls and university auditoriums around the country of an accomplished, even masterful, young pianist from New York named William Hall. Slipped in amongst the reviews were fan letters, most of which were from starstruck young girls who dotted their i's with little circles.

Stuck to the back of yet another review, was a clipping from the New York Times:

Gifted Young Pianist Gravely Injured in Accident.

William Hall and the driver of his car were injured in an accident downtown early Thursday morning. Mr. Hall, a gifted pianist recently returned from a national tour, and winner of the prestigious Otto Grünbaum Young Pianists Award when he was only thirteen, was gravely injured as the No. 4 Bus was struck in the rear by a truck, forcing it into Mr. Hall's vehicle. The driver of the bus and six passengers were taken to Lenox Hill Hospital where they were examined and then released with only minor injuries. Mr. Hall remains in critical condition. His driver is expected to be released tomorrow.

Bennett gasped. This was her father. How could she have lived with a grand piano in the middle of the living room and not known that it was his? No one ever played it or even talked about music, so to her it had been another one of Aunt Mary's pretenses. She had so few memories of her father. No one had ever spoken of his success or his injury. So why did she feel guilty for not knowing?

She glanced up and saw the minute hand move on the kitchen clock. Ten to six. Almost time to meet Joe and the children. With so much to think about, she was glad to take a break. She opened the door and found Joe and the children already outside waiting for her.

"Hello, everyone. How was your soccer game, Medi?"

"They lost," Hope said.

"The coach said we did our best. Papa says that's what counts."

"What kind of pizza do you want, Bennett?" Hope chimed in. "Papa says we're walking there."

"That's a good idea," Bennett said, taking each child by the hand. "I need some exercise. Do you know any marching songs?"

"What's a marching song?"

"Something we can sing to make us walk in rhythm. I heard one in a movie once. I'll teach it to you. When I say left you have start walking with your left foot. Ready?"

Medi and Hope looked down at their feet and then at Bennett's and stuck out their left feet.

"Now let's say it together: Left, left, left a wife and seventeen children in starving condition with nothing but gingerbread left. Again! Left left left..."

It was an odd phrase to march to so cheerfully, but no one questioned it or even noticed. Hope soon forgot to keep up with the rhythm and started skipping, laughing and holding Bennett's hand, but Medi kept his eyes focused on Bennett's left foot and soon got the hang of it. Joe laughed and kept up with them. "Never thought of you as a military type, Bennett."

"I'm full of surprises."

After pizza and another march home, the children were ready for bed. Joe invited Bennett to stay but she declined, saying there were still some papers in the box to look through. "But thanks for letting me join you and the kids for dinner. I needed it."

"Why? Is something wrong? Maybe I can help."

"Thank you, Joe. That means a lot to me, but there are some things I should figure out for myself."

Once home, Bennett returned to the kitchen table and began to read through the remaining newspaper clippings. *Child prodigy, talented, sensitive pianist, acclaimed, gifted, gifted, gifted. A success.* The words whirled around in her head. Could they really have once described a man who'd left so little impression on her?

She lifted her shoulders and straightened her back, trying to relieve the tightness. Her head ached. She reached for the open bottle of wine, brought it closer to her and poured herself a glass.

She reached for the documents she'd set aside before. The first two were the birth certificates of her maternal grandparents. She'd enter their data later, whether it mattered or not.

The next document was different and unexpected: a Certificate of Citizenship issued by the Department of Justice declaring that Bernard Maurice Hall—her grandfather—born in France on March 26, 1896, and now residing at 279 Riverside Drive, New York City, became a citizen of the United States of America on the one hundred and fifty-first year of its independence—four years before Bennett's father was born. Interesting. Curious. Though not as curious as the fact that at the time of his birth—according to the French birth certificate that followed—his name was Bernard Halévy, son of Avrom Halévy and Milka Bialik.

French Jews, not Anglo-Saxon Halls? Why had that never been mentioned? Stupid question. Wasn't it clear by now? Nothing had ever been mentioned. Joe said it didn't matter—but it did. No one seemed to be who she thought they were. Did that change who she was, or was Joe right that it didn't matter?

As she pushed her hand to the bottom of the envelope to make sure she hadn't missed anything, she remembered the menorah. It must have been her grandparents', a treasure brought from the old country. Perhaps their only one? And she had given it away without a thought.

She'd call Shannon Butler and get it back.

Bennett picked up the phone then remembered that Shannon had said they were going away. She'd loved the menorah for its beauty when it meant nothing to Bennett. Was it right to ask her to give it back?

Bennett replaced the receiver and returned to the envelope. Nothing more, she thought, until her finger nail caught the corner of a sheet of paper flattened against the back of the envelope. Gently, she peeled it off, pulled it out, and found it was her father's death certificate. Cause of death: *cardiopulmonary arrest due to multi-organ failure as a consequence of an overdose of alcohol and sleeping pills.*

Her father had left them on purpose.

She had few memories of her father—except of the night before he died. She remembered that well. They had all been in Aunt Mary's kitchen and she'd spilled grape juice on her dress.

Bennett!

Startled, she'd let the glass slip out of her fingers and it shattered into a million tiny pieces on the floor.

My best glass, you clumsy oaf!

Aunt Mary had lunged at her and swiped her face with the back of her hand. The sharp edge of her diamond ring sliced a thin line down her temple so that Bennett's blood added crimson to the stain on her dress.

Mary, how could you?

William, help for God's sake!

Bennett remembered how pretty it looked, the red curling through the purple, voices swirling around her, competing for attention, her father running out of the kitchen, the two women scurrying behind him—as if *he'd* caused it all—leaving her sitting alone in the kitchen, barefoot and afraid to step on the splinters of glass, as a thin line of blood still trickled down the side of her face.

She'd waited, dabbing at it with a towel, hoping someone would come back for her. When no one did, she climbed over the kitchen counter to a spot where she could safely step down, then tiptoed upstairs, washed her face and put on three band-aids across the cut. The next day, she went to school and told her teacher that the cat had scratched her—although they didn't have a cat.

When Bennett returned that afternoon, she saw an ambulance pulling out of the space in front of their house. She rushed up the steps and found Aunt Mary standing in the front hall, ashen faced.

Your father's dead.

Bennett slung her arms around her aunt's waist and hid her face. Her aunt pushed her away.

Your mother's inside. Her voice was cold.

That's when Bennett knew—as surely as she knew her name and that she was five years old—that her father had died because of what she'd done. She'd broken the glass and lied to her teacher. She wiped her nose on her sleeve. She had no right to cry.

All these years later, Bennett's hand rose to the scar on her face. Though she could barely feel it anymore, it had always been the unerasable reminder of her guilt. Overcome now by both anger and pity, she wondered if it had been her father's shame, not hers, that had made him down pills with his whiskey, without a thought of what effect it would have on his daughter and his wife.

Bennett slipped the documents back into their envelope, got up and opened the back door. She needed air and stood outside for several minutes before returning to the kitchen table to look at the last of the box's contents: an unmarked, overstuffed white envelope sealed with layers of cellophane tape. Slicing carefully through them with a small knife, she found at least a dozen smaller envelopes inside, neatly addressed to her from a street in Baltimore she didn't recognize. Each small envelope had been ripped open, its contents removed and then sloppily refolded and replaced.

Bennett's hands began to shake. There was no mistaking who had written them. She would have recognized Stephen's handwriting anywhere.

One by one, she laid the letters out on the table, and as she read, her tears smeared the words into little blue splotches.

We found a place where my father can spend his last days near his sister ... I want so much for him to be happy so I will be the best son I can possibly be ... It is bittersweet knowing that it won't be long before we are together again.

You would like it here, he wrote on a postcard of Fort McHenry, *won't you please come and visit? I miss you and my father would be so pleased to see you.*

Then a letter: *...I'm sure you are busy with work but please write ...*

And another: *...Have I done something wrong? Why haven't you written?...*

And the last: *...Just let me know you are all right and I won't bother you anymore.*

"Damn you, Mary," Bennett muttered. "Damn you, damn you!" Again and again, her voice growing louder as the the full implications of the cruel deception sank in.

She remembered eagerly checking the mail when she came back from work. *Any letters for me?* she'd ask. *You know what they say,* Aunt Mary would answer, *out of sight, out of mind. I told you men were unreliable.*

As time went by, with no word from Stephen, Bennett had let her dreams go, and with them any hope for happiness. Meanwhile, Aunt Mary and Bancroft and Co. made demands she had to meet. She told herself that she was needed. Her obligations gave her strength.

She didn't let herself think that Stephen never would have broken his promise. It had been both unbearable and inevitable that he would have found someone else. Now it seemed unbearable that perhaps he hadn't.

Bennett pounded her fist on the table.

"Oh God! Stephen must have thought that I rejected him!"

She finished the rest of the bottle of wine, then, exhausted from thinking, stumbled upstairs and fell into bed, where she stayed, in her clothes, for two days.

14

When Bennett finally rose from bed, her head splitting, her hair matted, she made her way back down to the kitchen, poured milk into a bowl and dropped in a handful of cereal. Ignoring the letters still scattered on the table, she leaned against the refrigerator and listlessly lifted a spoonful of cereal to her mouth, letting the milk dribble down her chin and onto her shirt. Losing interest, she abandoned the unfinished cereal in the sink and returned to bed.

For two more days she alternated between tortured sleep and restless visits to the kitchen, unaware of time and deaf to the phone and the repeated knocks and muffled voices at the door. When she ran out of milk she ate the cereal dry, no longer bothering with a bowl and spoon.

She might have let herself drift into madness, had the police not pounded so violently on her door.

"Miss Hall?" a young policeman asked when Bennett cracked open the door." Are you all right, ma'am?"

"Yes ... Why?"

"We received a call from your employer that you might be in trouble. You sure you're all right? You don't look very well."

Bennett saw the officer glance quizzically at her bare feet and stained shirt, and then past her to get a look inside.

"I'm fine," she said. "She needn't have disturbed you."

"All right then. You might want to give her a call."

Bennett nodded.

"I will."

Not ready for Maria's questions, she returned to the kitchen and gathered up all the papers on the table and replaced them in the inlaid box before she picked up the phone.

"You shouldn't have worried, Maria," she began.

"I had to. When you didn't come in three days in a row I called Mama and she said she hadn't seen you, but your car was still there. So I called Joe and he said you had dinner with them and seemed to have things on your mind and maybe just wanted some time to yourself. But then another two days passed and you still didn't call which isn't like you so I called Joe again and got really worried when he said he'd knocked on your door several times. I didn't know whether you were lying unconscious on the floor or were being held hostage by some crazy person. So I called the police."

"The crazy person was me. I'm sorry, Maria."

"Never mind. All that matters is that you are all right. Make sure to give Joe a call; he was worried. He'll be home alone tonight. Isabella is having her first slumber party so I'll have the kids with me."

"What day is it?"

"Saturday."

"And time?"

"Five-thirty."

"Evening?"

"Yes, Bennett, I'm about to close up. Are you sure you're all right?"

"I am and I'll be even better as soon as I take a shower and put on fresh clothes. I'll see you Monday."

∼

At six, Bennett looked out the window and saw Joe drive up and start unloading groceries. She hesitated, then opened the door and asked if he needed help.

He shook his head. "I'm so glad to see you. Have you been away?"

"In a way, but I'm back now. I'm sorry you were worried."

"I was, especially since your car was here. Did you go by train? Have you eaten? Juanita left me with something I'm sure is good. It'd be nice to have company."

"Are you sure?"

Joe laughed. "Of course, I'm sure."

"I'll bring some wine then."

Over dinner Bennett avoided questions, and steered the conversation to the new pediatric wing of the hospital that was opening, a good mechanic Maria had recommended, and how well Juanita was working out.

"I forgot to ask, Bennett, did you find anything interesting in that mystery box?"

"A few things …"

"Genealogical stuff?"

"I thought you didn't—"

"Think it was important? I guess, I didn't, but after you left that night I thought how little I know about my own family's history—and now there's no one left to ask. That made me think about the kids. I want them to be proud of who they are, and I can tell them about Uganda and that their parents were good people, but I can't tell them stories about their grandparents and the people who came before them. Is that why you did your genealogy, to know all those stories no one ever told you?"

Bennett looked down at her plate, so as to avoid his eyes.

"Not exactly," she said. How could she admit that she'd only started the genealogy to keep busy? And her way of keeping busy was to do what she already knew how to do—create reports and file them.

"You must have known your aunt pretty well, at least," Joe said, breaking into her thoughts.

Bennett lined up her knife and fork on her plate, making sure they were parallel, before she answered.

"I thought I did. She was not a pleasant woman, but she took us in when my parents were going through hard times. So I figured that deep down she was a good person."

"You are a kind person, Bennett."

Bennett felt tears welling.

"Not always," she said, remembering how gratitude had turned to guilt after the accident, and often to resentment. And now to anger at her aunt's cruel betrayal.

"It must have been lonely for you."

"It was…" Bennett began to roll her paper napkin into a long thin cylinder, tearing off bits of paper, gathering them into a pile. "She lied to me."

"About what?"

If Bennett told him about the hidden letters, would he blame her for not believing in Stephen enough the way Mrs. McElroy had?

"Everything," she said. "They all did. No one even told me my father was a pianist."

"Does that matter?"

Agitated, Bennett rose from her chair and began to pace.

"Yes! The truth matters. I should have been told. He was somebody until he had an accident and couldn't play anymore."

"The poor man."

"Yes, so I should feel sorry for him, shouldn't I?"

"Don't you?" Joe said, turning his head to follow her as she walked behind him.

"I don't know. He could have done *something!* Beethoven composed when he was deaf. Bach played when he was blind. My father could have taught, or sold pianos or sheet music or shoes, for God's sake. Instead he stayed home and did nothing. I didn't question it at the time—"

"Of course not. You were little and children accept things as they are because they don't know they could be different."

Bennett pounded her fist on the back on Joe's chair. "I didn't even know until now that he killed himself! It didn't matter to him that he left me."

"Your mother—?"

"Never said a thing. Nor Aunt Mary."

Joe reached over and clasped her hand in his.

"I'm sure they were trying to protect you. Feeling abandoned can be terrible for a child. You are an adult. You don't have to view your father that way now. For whatever reason, he lost his ability to cope.

Desperation can make one blind to the effect one has on others. But don't you believe most people do the best they can?"

A sudden ring of the telephone made them both jump. Joe released her hand and went to answer.

"Yes. Yes. Of course. I'll be there as soon as I can."

Joe shrugged and looked at Bennett.

"I'm sorry. A patient. I have to run."

"Of course," Bennett said, yet she felt dismissed. Discarded. Unloved... And childish again.

15

Winter arrived without warning that night, the temperature dropping from unseasonable heat to a penetratingly damp chill as a rainstorm swirled through the city. When Bennett looked out the window the next morning the last of the autumn leaves had blanketed the sidewalks, and broken branches littered her backyard.

The world looked like Bennett felt. Bundled up in a sweater and winter jacket, she brought a shovel up from the basement and started digging up her faded flower beds. She'd get to the debris later.

People do the best they can, Joe had said. But only some people.

All her life she'd been a plodder, quiet and reliable, believing that if she did her job properly she would be appreciated. At work, she'd dreamed of climbing the company ladder step by step, maybe even reaching the level of division head one day. When Bancroft, Chandler and Co. welcomed a new CEO, opportunity knocked to perhaps skip a step or two. The company launched an intensified effort to increase profits for the banks that the company advised and serviced in the region. Subprime lending on mortgages would be strongly promoted.

Steady, reliable Bennett was awarded the responsibility of analyzing, collecting and reporting financial data on the lending history of their banks. She was assigned an assistant analyst, Charlie Moore. They worked well together, even going out for an after-work drink once or twice, as if they'd became friends. It was the happiest Bennett had ever been at her job. She began dreaming she was on a path to the upper levels of management, maybe even Chief Financial Officer.

After months of investigation, analysis, and data collection, she presented top management with a disturbing report: encouraging subprime mortgages to borrowers with flawed credit histories risked harming rather than helping them. And, although those loans might provide lenders with higher returns, the practice also risked creating instability in the housing market. A collapse could lead to a more widespread economic recession..

Bennett's warnings were received and reviewed.

"You must be kidding. We can't publish this. The government is pressing us to promote these loans."

"Then it's a crazy policy!" Bennett blurted out. "It's much too risky."

A man Bennett had never seen before laughed.

"We service a bunch of small banks. Who's going to notice?"

"They'll notice when it all collapses and people get hurt! Numbers don't lie, you know," Bennett said, her face red.

"We really thought you had the company's interests in mind, Miss Hall."

"I can't change the truth."

"All right. We get it. Thanks for your contribution."

The next day, she was transferred to the insurance division's demographic statistics and analysis desk. Financial data was assigned to someone more amenable.

Charlie Moore revised the report, adjusting and deleting unwanted data. He was soon promoted to mortgage services branch head.

There were no more after-work drinks at the local bar. No more opportunities to be betrayed by a friend.

The truth matters, she'd said to Joe, though when it really did matter, she didn't fight for it. She accepted the transfer and let the report be buried. She could have quit and reported it to the press, or her congressman. Would it have changed anything? Probably not—but she should have tried. Joe would have. Maria would have. Maybe even Juanita.

She was weak, like her father. She had no standing to sit in judgment of anyone.

And if truth really mattered, what about Stephen? She wasn't the only person who'd been deceived. Didn't he deserve to know that he hadn't been rejected?

Bennett dug into the flower bed until the last dying plant was yanked out and a stabbing pain in her back replaced the voices in her head.

"Hi, Bennett. What are you doing?" a voice piped up from behind the vine-covered fence.

Bennett could barely see Medi through the tangle, but there was no mistaking the fresh young voice.

"I was cleaning out my garden, but I'm finished digging now."

"My sister likes to dig."

"No, I don't," Hope's voice piped in.

"I didn't mean you," Medi said. "I meant her."

"Is she your imaginary friend?" Bennett asked, looking over the fence. "I had one once. His name was Reggie."

Medi scowled at her.

"No. She's real she's just not here."

"I think we lost her," Hope said, quite undisturbed.

Unsure whether or even how to follow up on this strange bit of conversation, Bennett changed the topic.

"No school today?" she asked,

"No, silly, it's Sunday," Hope giggled as she climbed over the fence and flung her arms around Bennett's legs. Bennett picked her up and held her tightly against her chest. Hope curled her arms around Bennett's neck and put her head on her shoulder. For a moment neither of them said a word.

"Where is your father?" Bennett asked.

"Out front picking up sticks," Medi said.

"That doesn't sound like fun. Let's go rescue him" Bennett suggested, lifting Hope back over the fence. "I'll meet you there."

They found Joe at the sidewalk filling a trashcan with twigs and leaves.

"Oh, good!" he said. "Have you come to help?"

"Yes, but then we're taking you to Joanie's," Bennett said.

"Great idea. In fact, let's go now. I've had enough of this and I'm starving."

They walked the four blocks to the 1950's style luncheonette with its turquoise vinyl booths, black and white checkered floor and child-friendly game room in the back.

"Everybody wash their hands," Joe said, taking Hope's hand and nodding at Medi to follow Bennett.

They ordered two macaroni and cheese, two BLT's, and a pitcher of lemonade. Medi and Hope colored their paper placemats with crayons, and played songs on the tabletop juke box until the food arrived.

After they'd finished eating, the children asked if they could go play ping pong, which, Bennett noticed, was a matter of hitting the ball and then running around trying to find where it had landed on the floor.

"They are happy here, aren't they?" Joe asked, unexpectedly.

"With you? Of course," Bennett replied. "Why wouldn't they be?"

"No, I meant being in America. Sometimes I worry I did the wrong thing, taking them away from their own country."

"I've never heard them say anything like that," Bennett said. "How did it all come about? You've never told me."

Joe turned to see whether the children were still in the back room.

"You know we ran a clinic. Their parents were among our AIDS patients. Their father died when Hope was less than a year old. Their mother was too weak to work. One of the big problems in much of Africa is that even if the patients are given medication, they often don't have enough food to keep them strong. Thankfully, the children were not infected, but their mother could barely feed them, so they came to stay at the clinic."

He brushed some crumbs off the white Formica tabletop.

"She died soon after. There were no relatives to care for the children so they were sent to an orphanage. It broke our hearts to see them go, so Laurie volunteered to work at the orphanage part-time so she could watch over them. We had promised their mother that her children would go to school."

"How was the orphanage? One hears such bad things."

"It was a strange place. It was started by an American woman who felt a calling to work in Africa—which I shouldn't criticize since we had also. She arranged for an American ministry in California to help fund her and started the orphanage. She hired local women to take care of the children, but also found volunteers—mostly Americans—who paid their own way to work there. Some stayed as long as a year. She called it *Loving Arms: A Home for Sick and Destitute Children*. She felt she'd been called to take care of these children and make them feel loved; and if they couldn't be saved, they would *pass on to a better life in Jesus' loving arms*. That's how she put it, but we could never shake the feeling that she was more interested in their peaceful deaths than in saving their lives. She prayed for them but she rarely interacted with them. That was left to the staff."

"Did the children get medical care?" Bennett asked.

"We helped when we could, but mostly it was left to the volunteers. It was very basic. It was hard to know whether they couldn't get the medicines and supplies, or whether it just wasn't a priority."

"It sounds awful."

"No, it wasn't. Very sick children were taken to the hospital, though Ugandan hospitals left a lot to be desired. Everyone on her staff was kind. The children were kept clean, and had enough to eat, even if it was mostly rice. But there wasn't much stimulation. Lots of toys had been donated, but they were rarely played with. The children were never alone, yet whenever there were visitors, they clung to them, hungry for any sign of real affection. Maybe that's not unusual in an orphanage, but that's why we decided we couldn't leave Medi and Hope there."

"And why you adopted them?"

"That's one of the reasons ... " Joe answered. "Laurie had a miscarriage when we first got to Uganda. It led to a serious infection. She almost died, and after that we couldn't have children of our own."

Joe picked up his glass to take a last sip of lemonade, but it was empty.

"It wasn't easy for us to adopt. We were over forty. Both Uganda and the U.S. have endless restrictions and requirements. We were lucky to get everything completed before ... before ... the accident."

He took a deep breath and looked away. Bennett put her hand over his and held it. Joe was usually so calm, so positive. What a selfish idiot she'd been not to have seen past his brave façade before.

"I didn't mean to upset you," she said.

"I know." He smiled at her. "It's hard for me to talk about, but sometimes, I need to get it all out—so thank you for listening."

"Was there another child?" Bennett asked after a moment.

"Why would you ask that?" he said, pulling his hand away.

"Because Medi mentioned a sister and he didn't mean Hope."

Joe looked stricken. Bennett wished she could take the question back.

"I had no right to pry," she said.

Joe shook his head. "Poor Medi, so he does remember her."

Not everything's about you, Bennett.

"I thought maybe he'd forgotten." he went on. "He wasn't even four the last time he saw her. He never mentions her to me."

"I think he talks to Hope about her."

"Oh God, they must think I just left her behind, but we didn't know about her until it was too late."

"I don't understand," Bennett said. "Wasn't she with them at the clinic?"

Jo glanced at the doorway separating them from the game room. Medi and Hope were still busy playing a noisy game of foosbal.

"Before the children's parents came to the clinic, when they realized how sick they were, they sent their oldest child to live with an elderly aunt. The aunt couldn't take the little ones, too, so there was no choice but to bring them along to the clinic."

"What do you know about the older girl?" Bennett asked gently.

"Only that her name is Grace and she is seven years older than Medi ...I didn't know about her, Bennett. I swear. I would never have left her behind had I known. When Laurie died I didn't want to stay in Uganda without her. I decided to come back here. Everything was arranged: tickets, passports, visas for the children. Everything, even bringing Laurie's body home. Then, when we were already in Entebbe about to leave, our friend Hilda called and told me about Grace. Even she hadn't known about her until then."

"So you've never met her?"

"No, and that's what makes it so difficult. On one hand, she should be with Medi and Hope, and I would take her in a minute. But I'm torn. She's her aunt's only family, and Uganda is her home and all she's ever known. I don't know if it's right to rip her away from that. And even if I decided to do it, would they let me without Laurie? And then there's the question of money. The adoption costs are high, and I can't afford for all of us to go over, especially since there's no way to know how long we'd have to stay there, or whether I would even be allowed to bring her back."

"Maybe ..."

"I don't even know if she'd want to come," Joe interrupted. "She doesn't know me from Adam, and may not know that Medi and Hope are here with me. I did do one good thing, though. I arranged for her to go to school. Her parents would have wanted that, and I was afraid the aunt couldn't afford it."

"How did you manage that?"

"Hilda, our friend, has a nephew Isaac who lives in the same village as the aunt—that's how she even found out about Grace—so she asked him to tell the aunt that I would pay. The aunt didn't want to let Grace go at first. She's old and relied on Grace to take care of her—like your Aunt Mary relied on you—but Isaac convinced her that letting Grace go to school was important for her future, so eventually she gave in."

"Does Grace know you did this?" Bennett asked.

Joe shrugged.

"I don't know.'

"You've had no contact with her?"

Joe shook his head.

"I wanted her to think her aunt arranged it. I have written to the school a few times and they always say she's doing well, but I worry what will happen if her aunt dies. She's quite old. Where would Grace go?"

Joe reached for the empty glass again, so Bennett wouldn't see the tears in his eyes.

"How did you end up in Wilmington?" Bennett asked, not knowing what else to say. "Is this where you grew up?

"No, I grew up in Philadelphia, but my aunt and uncle lived here. They were very good to me when my parents died. I tried to keep in touch with them—and with her, after he died—but it was harder from Uganda and I feel bad I didn't do it enough. They had no children or any other relatives, so when she died, the house and the furniture came to me. It was a godsend, almost as if she knew what I needed when I returned with two children and no money. I only wish I could have thanked her."

"Mrs. McElroy was your aunt?" Bennett asked, shocked at this unexpected revelation.

"Did you know her?"

"A little."

There was no way she could tell Joe how kind she'd been without admitting that she'd ignored the thump against the wall. He could never forgive her for that. She cleared her throat, as if she could dislodge her shame that way, and was relieved when Medi and Hope rushed in from the game room, asking excitedly if they could have money for the pinball machine. Joe dug into his pocket for some coins and the children ran off again.

Bennett paid the cashier for lunch, then followed Joe into the game room to watch the children play, shaken again by the recognition of her own weaknesses.

"Listen, Joe. I'll see you later. I have to get something. I'll meet you back at the house."

~

Bennett ran the four blocks back to her house, and was waiting for Joe and the children when they got back.

She handed Joe a small bundle wrapped in tissue paper.

"Your aunt gave me this sweater for safe-keeping. She must have known that one day I would have the chance to give it to you."

16

*J*oe was moved to receive his aunt's sweater. Bennett was relieved to have given it to him, hoping it absolved her a little bit for what she had failed to do—though she didn't tell Joe the whole story.

She couldn't make sense of the jungle of feelings she found herself in. Regret, anger, and shame enveloped her, each pointing to her failings, her weaknesses. Did she have no strengths at all?

Why was Joe so different? He'd suffered losses much greater than hers, yet he strode through life with purpose and compassion. What a pitiful contrast to her own feeble, pointless crawl.

As if to prove her point, she spent the next day meandering aimlessly through the neighborhood, lingering at stop signs as if she expected them to tell her when it was time to go, until she found herself on a short street that ended at a tall wall, on which a ten-foot high rose had been painted. As her eyes traveled down the one side of the street and up the other, she realized that she'd been there before, and that all the chain link fences once enclosing the front yards of the row houses had been removed.

She threw out her arm and punched the corner stop sign with her fist.

It had been her duty, she'd told herself, to care for Aunt Mary—but thirty-odd years behind that fence had been too long. She could never atone for her unlived life— not through genealogy, and not by hanging out with the likes of Lola. But she could find Stephen and undo her aunt's deception.

She shook the pain our of her hand and started walking faster, and was almost running by the time she reached her house. She rushed upstairs and turned on her computer. No more whining. It was time to act.

Her hand still smarting, she googled Stephen Bannister, irrationally hoping he'd pop up and smile at her with his soft blue eyes.

There were several Stephen Bannisters, but most of them were too young, posting silliness on Facebook. Two were on ancestry.com, born a century ago in places far from Wilmington.

He could be anywhere. Even overseas. She'd never find that on the internet but this was no time to give up. She had to correct the injustice her aunt had foisted on them.

But if she told Stephen she never received his letters, she'd also have to confess that she thought he'd found someone else and she had been too weak to fight for him. What would he think of her then?

Would he even care? He might have forgotten all about her.

But what if he'd never recovered from the hurt of her rejection? Would he resent her intrusion or would he think she'd searched for him because she wanted him back? Or would he think she was crazy, a demented stalker? She couldn't bear the thought of that.

She pressed her temples hard with the heels of her hands. Why was this so difficult? All she wanted was to know that he was happy—that his aunt hadn't ruined both their lives. But did guilt or curiosity give her the right to disturb Stephen's life?

She shut the computer down and went to bed. She'd sleep on it and decide in the morning.

When she opened her front door to get the newspaper the next morning, Bennett looked out on the oak trees lining both sides of Spring Street. Bereft of leaves and dormant now, they looked dead. But instead of dying, they'd conserved the sun's energy and suspended their growth so they could survive the winter and prepare for the glorious growth of spring. Could she reawaken like that—or had she been dormant so long that she had no resources left?

She felt a deep shudder of fear that her time for living had run out and not a soul could ever say she'd done her best.

For her own sake if not his, she had to find Stephen.

His letters might hold a clue to his whereabouts. She had read them so quickly she hadn't thought to look for an address, overwhelmed as she was by the realization that he had waited in vain for answers to letters she'd never received.

She read each letter again, one by one. It was in the fifth one that she read:

We bought a place where my father can spend his last days near his sister. It's a big corner row house on Butchers Hill, a neighborhood close to Johns Hopkins in case of emergency. We have a nice little walled garden to sit in but we can also walk to Patterson Park nearby on days Dad is feeling stronger. We're living on the ground floor, and the top two floors are rented out. The rent covers the mortgage, so we are very lucky. It's also a comfort knowing that someone is in the house at night. We could have rented a place but Dad wanted to make sure I had a roof over my head without him.

I won't be earning enough on my own until I finish some sort of schooling, which I haven't even started yet.

At the bottom, he'd neatly printed the address—the address where he had waited for her answer. She'd go there first.

She resolved to drive to Baltimore on Sunday when the shop was closed. Saturday was the shop's busiest day and she didn't want to leave Maria in the lurch again.

17

Sunday morning brought charcoal skies as wind and rain broke off a large branch of the oak tree in the side garden, barely missing Bennett's roof. Leaf-filled gutters overflowed, spilling their debris onto the back patio.

Bennett called Joe and told him she was going out, and not to worry. She would take care of cleaning up as soon as the storm passed. Then under cover of an umbrella, she ran to her car. Rain or not, she was going to Baltimore.

She was itchy to leave but afraid if she took the interstate she'd get to Baltimore much too early. She didn't want to arrive at Stephen's house until afternoon. Route 40 was only interesting if she were looking to buy cheap liquor or used cars; but if she took Route 1 south, she could meander a bit and even save on tolls.

She decided to stop at Longwood Gardens. Nothing was in bloom outdoors, but its conservatory was filled with gardens she could explore. As she entered the tropical garden, lush and heavy with jungle perfumes, she wondered if Uganda was like that. Or was it more like the desert garden, dry and hot and prickly? She'd have to ask Joe. A visit to Longwood might be a good geography lesson for Medi and Hope.

She bought two garden ornaments, four packets of wildflower seeds, and a bird feeder at the gift shop; and had a sandwich and coffee in their café before continuing on.

When she finally reached East Fairmont Avenue on Butchers Hill in Baltimore, it was three o'clock. The rain had stopped and she found a parking space directly in front of the address Stephen had written her.

Was this a mistake? She could still change her mind.

She sat in the car with the motor running for several minutes, staring at the door of the corner unit and hoping no one was looking out the window.

A young boy, dribbling a basketball on the sidewalk, snapped Bennett out of her inertia. She retied the scarf around her neck, brushed imaginary lint off her coat, walked up the front steps, and rang the doorbell. She was grateful another minute passed before she heard a sound coming from inside.

The door opened, and there he stood: Stephen. His once thick hair had thinned and turned to silver, making his soft blue eyes lighter than she remembered. His thickened waist was hidden behind an apron stained across the middle. In his arms he held a large green ceramic mixing bowl.

For the second that preceded recognition, he smiled. Their eyes met and then looked down as the bowl fell noiselessly, endlessly downwards until it shattered noisily, spilling its buttery, chocolaty contents onto the marble floor.

Instinctively, he caught Bennett's arm lest she fall too.

"Bennett," he whispered, as time returned to its normal speed, "I didn't think .,."

"Sorry, I'm … I…" she stammered.

"I'd better clean this up," he said, freeing her arm. "It's my first attempt at baking."

Stephen left Bennett waiting, motionless and trying to remember the words she'd rehearsed. When he returned he had a wet rag in one hand and a towel in the other.

"Let me help," she said, but he shook his head and bent down to wipe the spill. He gathered the green shards, folded them into the towel and laid the bundle in a corner.

"There," he said, and wiped his hands on his apron before taking it off. "Now we can go in." He nodded in the direction of the living room.

Stephen sat down on one sofa and gestured for Bennett to sit on the other. A leather armchair and footstool stood between them. On one end of the room, overflowing bookcases filled the space on either side of a large flat-screen TV. In the corner by the window there was a grand piano with a songbook open to *Stardust*; in the other, an antique mahogany display case she remembered from their house in Wilmington. Walls not covered by built-in bookcases were covered with art—paintings, etchings, collages, framed batiks, and a carved wooden Madonna. A sign of the cultured life she might have led. And a room Joe would feel comfortable in.

"It's been a long time," Stephen said.

"Twenty-seven years," she answered, precisely but inadequately, hoping he would say something more.

Stephen sat at the edge of the sofa, his back straight and his hands clasped together between his widespread legs.

Not like Joe, she thought, who liked to sit, leaning back, with his legs straight out, feet crossed at the ankles.

"I never expected to see you again," he said. "What brings you here now?"

She cleared her throat. "To explain ... that is, I found out something I want you to know ... about your letters."

"The ones you never answered?"

She felt herself redden. "That's just it. I never received them ... my aunt hid them. I didn't know until—."

"I promised I would write. You should have known I would." He spoke softly, but Bennett sensed the hurt behind his words.

"You're right, I should have, but I convinced myself that you must have met someone else. Someone better." It was because of her aunt's low opinion of men, and of her, but she couldn't tell Stephen that. She was a grown woman and it was time she accepted the consequences of her own weaknesses.

"I should have," she said again. "And I am truly sorry."

He waited a moment before answering.

"It was long ago, Bennett. We were different people then."

And with that he smiled—only a half-smile, but a smile nevertheless, and Bennett saw the gentleness of the boy she'd once loved. She hadn't broken him, just his heart a bit.

"Did you marry?" she asked.

"Yes. I met Annie when my father was in hospice. She was one of the nurses there ... but we didn't marry then. I wanted to finish college first. I became a teacher—I've been a high school teacher for more than twenty years now."

"English?"

"Of course," he laughed, "after all those years of reading to my father, what else could I be?"

"I'm surrounded by books, too, but in a used book store. Books and antiques."

"That sounds nice," he said, but asked for no details.

"Did you have four children as we, as you planned?" Bennett asked.

"No, only three. One is working in New York. One's in college, and the youngest will be off soon, too. How about you?"

She shook her head. She wanted to tell him how attached she was to her neighbor's children, but that wasn't the same, and he'd probably think her pathetic for making the comparison.

"Not married, no children, not even a dog, I'm afraid."

"Too busy traveling and doing all kinds of exciting things, I'm sure. Our youngest wants to backpack around the world. You could tell him it's not as simple as he thinks."

Bennett saw him sneaking a glance at his watch.

"I've kept you too long," she said, rising. "I didn't realize how late it was. I hope you don't mind that I—"

"Oh no. I'm glad you came … It's always good to know the truth of things."

Stephen walked her to the door, and kissed her lightly on the cheek.

"Your scar has almost disappeared," he said.

"Yes. Time will do that."

"It was good to see you, Bennett," he said. But he didn't ask whether she still lived in Wilmington or how he could reach her. And she didn't offer.

She wouldn't see him again, but he was fine and she felt strangely relieved, as if he too had been locked behind a fence and was now free.

18

When Bennett opened the door to the shop on Monday morning, the phone was already ringing. Too early for customers, she thought as she ran to answer it.

"I'm so glad you're there," Maria said. "My car didn't start so I'm running late. But I should be there within the hour."

"No problem. No one's here yet and I have several things I want to get done today."

She walked back to the front door, turned on all the lights, shook out the welcome mat, and replaced the books that had been left on the counter. The shop was bright and inviting and well organized—so much better than the first time she saw it. Maria and she had done a good job.

She was on her way to the back room when the bell over the front door tinkled. Probably a browser. Browsers far outnumbered customers even on the best of days. Bennett turned around and saw a man holding the door open, one foot in and one foot out of the store, as if he were afraid he wouldn't be able to escape.

"Any chance you got any garden gnomes?" he yelled. "I'm looking for one of those heavy old German or Swiss ones, none of those damn plastic things made in China."

"I'm afraid we don't get too many garden ornaments, but if you would like to leave us your name, we can call you if we come across any."

"Just tell Maria Fred was here. She knows me. I've been coming here for years. This is my favorite place."

"Glad to hear it," Bennett said, and wrote down his name and put it by the cash register.

"What was Fred looking for this time?" Maria said when she arrived.

"Garden gnomes."

She laughed. "He's a funny guy. Comes in every few months and asks for something we don't have—giant bird houses, street lamps, ping-pong tables, aquariums. Once he came for a samovar and we had it. I guess that gave him hope. Which reminds me—has Meyer Gold called?"

"No. That name doesn't sound familiar."

"You'd like him. He's a wonderful old man—Viennese, like Mr. Schimmerling, though they didn't know each other there. He comes in every year at the same time, the second week of November, and buys a bunch of travel books. Not just guides but stories. Travel literature, I guess you'd call it. Some are out of print and have to be specially ordered. I'm starting to worry that he hasn't come in ... I should call him."

Bennett nodded and went to the back room to enter their previous week's receipts. She had almost finished when Maria came in and asked her to do her a favor.

"Mr. Gold didn't sound good when I called and said he probably wouldn't be coming in anymore. Do you think you could go over and check on him? Tell him he doesn't have to come to the shop. He can tell us the places he's interested in and we can do the search for him. Then you or I could bring him whatever we find. He doesn't live too far."

"You're much better with people than I am, Maria. Don't you think you should go?"

"I can't. The electrician is coming to fix the wiring in the basement. It kept shorting out and now it's out completely. I'd really appreciate it if you went."

Maria wrote down Meyer Gold's address and handed it to her.

An hour later, Bennett pulled up in front of the middle one of three old red-brick row houses with four apartments each, bordered on one side by Speedy Cash Payday Loans on one side and McLorie's bar on the other. She was checking the names over the buzzer when the door opened and a young woman with a stroller asked if she was looking for someone.

"Yes, please. Mr. Gold. Meyer Gold."

"Upstairs, on the left."

Bennett turned on the hall light and walked up the narrow stairs—it smelled of unfamiliar spices. She knocked on the door of Apartment 2A. After a few moments, the door opened a crack.

"I would like to help you, but I'm not in the market for anything today," a voice said, in an accent stronger than Mr. Schimmerling's.

Bennett leaned forward, placing her face close to the opening.

"Mr. Gold, I'm sorry to bother you. My name is Bennett Hall and I work at the bookshop with Maria. She asked me stop by and see if there was anything you needed. She was worried when you said you couldn't come for your annual visit."

The door closed, but Bennett heard the unlatching of the chain, and waited until the door opened again.

Meyer Gold couldn't have been taller than 5'4. His back was straight, which was impressive for a man who appeared to begin his eighties. He wore a suit that was well-tailored but had seen better days. His shirt was pressed, and he wore a tie. Dapper, was the word that came to mind—if one looked past the worn corduroy slippers. His gray hair was brushed neatly back, with only a hint of a part just off-center. His small equally neat mustache was still dark and well trimmed, as were his eyebrows. He was a miniature version of one of Bennett's favorite old movie actors: William Powell. Bennett wouldn't have been surprised if she stepped into Meyer Gold's apartment and found everything was in black and white.

"That's very kind of her," Mr. Gold was saying. He looked up at Bennett, who, even in low-heeled pumps, towered over him. "Do come in, your *High*ness!" he said, tickled at his own joke. "It is very cold. I like to make myself a cup of hot cocoa on a day like this. Will join me?"

"I don't want to put you to any trouble. I'm only here because Maria was concerned that you weren't feeling well."

"I'm fine. In better health than I deserve at my age." He turned toward a closet-sized space that now served as a kitchen. "Do join me, please. It really is no trouble. I have the ingredients, a pot, and a stove. And even two cups. Would you prefer to wait for me in the library or the dining room?"

Bennett was puzzled by the question as the apartment was tiny, but then noticed Mr. Gold's eyes crinkling with amusement at the joke he'd obviously made before. He pointed to the two chairs in front of the bookcase.

"That's the library," he said, pointing to the built-in bookcases that completely covered one wall. "And here is the dining room," now pointing to the round table and two chairs that practically filled the remaining space.

"How nice. You don't have to choose between food for the body and food for the mind," Bennett said, as she sat down on the side of the table that faced the bookcase. Mr. Gold looked pleased.

The bottom shelves of the bookcases were full, lined with piles of books with titles like *Hiking Through Carpathia*, *The Journals of Captain Cook*, *Petrarch's Guide to the Holy Land*. The top shelves overflowed with travel souvenirs, most of which were costumed dolls, tiny baskets and pots, and small pieces of jewelry—all things a young girl would collect, not a grown man. A granddaughter, perhaps. One section of one shelf was inexplicably empty, yet diligently kept free of dust.

"Are you a traveller, Mr. Gold?"

"Not this year, I'm afraid. I have run out of strength and money. One of the dangers of living so long."

Mr. Gold briskly stirred cocoa, sugar and hot water in a milk jug and then poured the thick mixture carefully into each cup. It smelled rich.

"It's Spanish," Mr. Gold said. "but still not as good as the one I had at Fargas in Barcelona. That one was so thick you had to eat it with a spoon. Not too milky not too sweet. Perhaps I should try a touch of corn starch in mine next time to thicken it. What do you think? Do you think the Spaniards do that?"

Bennett had no idea. She'd never made hot cocoa at all, except by pushing a button on a vending machine.

"This one is excellent as it is, but I suppose it's always worth experimenting."

"You're absolutely right, Mrs. Hall. One should always be open to new ideas."

Bennett took another sip of the hot drink.

"How did you decide where to travel. Mr. Gold? I have never been anywhere except once to New Orleans, and that was long ago."

"Ah. My destinations were predetermined. I took at least one trip every year—more the first years—each time to a different place. I have two more places to go, but I fear I won't make it to them. I am ninety-eight and a half, you know." He laughed. "Have you ever noticed that old people like me talk about their ages with the same pride that little children do? I'm four! Five and a quarter! Ninety and a half! By the time I reach a hundred and five, I'll probably add the days as well. A hundred and five and fourteen days! But that would be another six-and-a-half years. They could race by, or be painfully interminable. Or worse: interminably painful. One never knows."

He paused, deep in thought. "It's funny about time," he went on after a while. "As you get older you lose your bearings. A decade can fly by more quickly than a year, a day can drag at a snail's pace. Things that happened eighty years ago are crystal clear, but you can't remember what you did yesterday, or if something happened last year or twenty years ago."

Mr. Gold was gazing into his cup. Moments passed. What was he remembering? Bennett wanted to ask, although it was unlike her to ask anything too personal. Yet, when Mr. Gold looked up and his eyes were smiling, Bennett felt her curiosity encouraged.

"May I ask, what did you mean your travels were predetermined?" She was intrigued by what or who had determined them, although she wondered whether this question was any less intrusive than the one she hadn't asked.

Mr. Gold turned around to the bookcase and took down a small photograph of a young girl in a wheelchair, her legs covered with a blanket, holding a scruffy, overloved teddy bear in her lap. Her eyes were upcast, and she was smiling affectionately at the unseen photographer. Mr. Gold traced the outline of her face with his finger before passing the photograph to Bennett.

"This is my sister Elsie when she was twelve and a half, six years after she came down with polio."

"She's lovely."

"Yes, she was a very pretty girl. Very frail yet full of life and dreams. She wanted to be an explorer, she said, and see the world ... She never stopped dreaming, even when she grew so weak she couldn't leave her bed. I told her she should make a list, and when she got stronger we would go to all the places together."

"Did you?" Bennett asked, although she already saw the answer in Mr. Gold's eyes.

"No. She died eighteen months after this picture was taken—in the spring of 1937. She was barely fourteen."

"I'm sorry." Bennett looked down at the photograph, and then the books on the bottom shelf. "Is that why—?"

"Indeed, Mrs. Hall! She made her list, and on the first anniversary of her birthday without her I formulated a plan. I would go for her and I would bring her a little token from each place. The first place on her list was Sweden. I wasn't sure why at first, it didn't seem especially exotic, but after reading about it and seeing a book of photographs, I thought it must have been to see the midnight sun. So I made a plan to go by bicycle that summer. But we were Jews and things were starting to look very bad for us. I told my parents we should leave immediately and try to go to America or Australia, but my mother was sure the bad times would not last long and nothing would happen to us. After all, we were patriotic Austrians and Vienna was our home. America and Australia were much too far. So I said we should go to Sweden at least, for Elsie, because she'd wanted it so much, but they wouldn't. So I went by myself, and that's what saved me. Elsie saved me ..."

"And your parents?"

Mr. Gold shook his head. "They waited too long. When Hitler came they were taken away."

Bennett leaned forward to hear, for Mr. Gold's voice had become almost inaudible. But then he regained his strength and said, "I didn't stay in Sweden after the war. I was restless and anxious to fulfill my promise to Elsie but I had no job and no money. Fortunately, I met an old man who suggested I go down to the docks and see about a job on a freighter; they were always looking for people. Before I knew it I was scrubbing decks on a freighter going to Hong Kong."

"Weren't you afraid?"

"After what people had lived through during the war, it seemed rather safe, actually. Nothing to worry about except doing my job. I switched from one ship to another, choosing them according to where they were going, so I could check off all the countries on Elsie's list—even if I only saw the ports. It took me thirty years."

"It must feel really good to have accomplished that, and to have led such an exciting life, Mr. Gold."

Mr. Gold shrugged, his eyes no longer smiling.

"Yes, it was interesting, and you're right, there was satisfaction in knowing I had kept my promise. I found camaraderie with my shipmates, but I never had a family again. Never had a woman who loved me ... or children. It was a high price to pay— perhaps too high."

"Some people pay that price and have nothing to show for it," Bennett said.

Mr. Gold gave her a sharp look. "You are right, Mrs. Hall. Forgive me for burdening you with my regrets. My story is no worse than anyone else's and better than many."

"No, no, that's not what I meant ... I appreciate your confiding in me, and would very much like to hear about the places you visited. Did you continue traveling after you left shipboard work?"

Mr. Gold smiled at her. "You are kind to be so interested in an old man, but I think I have bored you enough already. What will your husband say when—"

"I'm not married, Mr. Gold. And I have not been bored. Not at all."

"There's not much else to report. When I settled here, about thirty-five years ago, I took a job as a night clerk in a small hotel. It was a lonely job but not demanding, and gave me much time to read. I read about all the countries I had been to. Then I read about the places I still needed to go. That is how I met Mr. Schimmerling. We became friends and I spent many hours in his shop. He found the most fascinating books for me." He pointed to the rows of books behind Bennett. "Once a year I would go to one of the places still on the list. As you can tell, the list was very long, and the only thing I have left from my family. It gave me direction and purpose all my life. I only wish I could tell my sister that."

"I'm sure she knows," Bennett said, though she wasn't sure at all. "What is the next place on the list, Mr. Gold—out of curiosity."

"Ah, Mrs., I mean, Miss Hall, it is the one place you have been: New Orleans. Perhaps when you have time, you will give me the pleasure of your company again and tell me about it. It was high on Elsie's list because of its music, but I kept putting it off because I thought it wasn't as far as the other places and I could go anytime. Now I fear I'm too old and have put it off too long."

Mr. Gold slumped back in his chair, his hands motionless in his lap.

"I'm afraid I've tired you, Mr Gold," Bennett said, rising to leave. "Thank you so much for a wonderful morning. I look forward to coming again soon so we can talk about New Orleans."

They shook hands, and Mr. Gold rose to accompany Bennett to the door. As Bennett walked down the narrow stairs, she heard the door chain being pulled back into place.

19

*B*ennett spent Tuesday afternoon scouring the shelves of the shop for books about New Orleans. She packed a dozen of them into a tote bag to look through at home before determining which of them to take to Mr. Gold.

It was already dark when she left the shop. The strong afternoon wind had cleared the sky of clouds and despite the cold it seemed a perfect time to leave her car and walk home. The next day's forecast was for sun and slightly warmer temperatures, so having to walk back again in the morning would be no problem.

With her tote bag slung over one shoulder and her handbag over the other, she strolled along the river, thinking about Meyer Gold and how he had followed his sister's dream for all those years. Bennett had always envied people who had dreams. She'd never had one, moving from one day to the next, dutifully fulfilling her obligations, not daring to look too far forward—except for that one time with Bancroft, Chandler and Co. Maybe with Stephen by her side it would have been different.

Stephen appeared to be content with the path he'd chosen, content with the choices he'd made—content with his life, in other words—whereas she would have continued on her road to nowhere until she died, had fortune not shuffled things around for her.

She'd only moved to her perfect little house on Spring Street because unemployment had forced her to; only enjoyed Christmas with Mrs. McElroy because she'd insisted. Even her job at the shop—a job she always looked forward to—only came about because Juanita coerced her into helping Maria. And would she have ever gotten to know Joe and the children if the babysitter hadn't had an emergency? She had done nothing to deserve the improvements in her life, so what right did she have to want more? But she did. She hungered for what other people call a Life—if only she could figure out what that meant.

Men her age tried to recapture their youths by running off with their assistants or buying sports cars they could barely get their creaky bodies in and out of. Bennett had no idea what women did. Her mother had died too young to be an example, and Aunt Mary never talked about her youth with any hunger to recapture it. And her own youth was the last thing Bennett wanted to recapture. She wanted a life that had significance, not a jumble of short-lived adventures. Her meaningless socializing with Lola had shown her that.

Her father must have had a vision once of what he wanted, and had been determined and disciplined enough to achieve it. How could he have let it all go because of an accident? He should have held on to at least part of his dream, and taught his daughter how to have courage.

Bennett's stride grew longer, her pace faster, as she tried to outrun the fear that it was much too late to find the answers she needed. People came of age at twenty-five not fifty.

Joe opened his front door just as she was unlocking hers.

"Bennett, are you all right?"

"Yes, why?"

"I called the shop to invite you for dinner and Maria said you'd left ages ago. I got worried you'd disappeared again. And where's your car? Did it break down somewhere?"

Bennett blushed, embarrassed that he might see how his words pleased her.

"I'm fine, it was such a nice evening, I decided to walk home."

"Did you stop to eat, or can you join us for dinner? We've got lots."

She nodded. "If you're sure. I'd like to tell you about someone I met today."

"Of course, I'm sure. So come over as soon as you can. Dinner is about ready. And we can have a nice long chat afterwards."

After dinner, quick baths, and bedtime stories for Medi and Hope, Joe and Bennett settled down with a pot of tea to talk in the living room. Joe listened attentively to her description of Meyer Gold's lifetime mission, probably glad, she thought, that she had something interesting to tell him for a change.

"I imagine you had big dreams when you were twelve, Joe." She watched Joe sit back in his easy chair, his hands wrapped around his teacup, and remembered Stephen sitting so stiffly on the edge of the sofa, wondering why she'd come to see him after so long.

"Oh yes," Joe said, laughing, "I had lots of dreams. Although I loved my parents, I thought their lives were terribly ordinary and small. I was convinced that if my life was going to be different, I would have to do something grand. The saints were my first heroes, and I read everything I could about them and desperately wanted to do something selfless and magnificent like they had. I realized soon enough though that martyrdom and sainthood were probably not routes I was suited for. If I was going to save the world, I had to find another way. How about you? What were your dreams?"

Bennett smiled. "Figuring out how best to keep out of Aunt Mary's way was dream enough, although one day, when I was about thirteen, I was at the library and came across a book that mentioned the Beguines."

"Like the dance?"

Bennett laughed. "Yes, but not as much fun. The Beguines weren't nuns exactly but they were monastic and lived in communities called Bequinages."

"And why would that appeal to you? It sounds grim."

"Not at all. They were revolutionary—especially for then—wanting to control their own lives, and not be controlled by men. They could leave the Bequinage anytime they wanted to, but while they were together their mission was to care for the poor and the sick. And of course they were poor themselves. It may sound odd to you, but to me it seemed noble and cozy and modern all at the same time."

"What did your aunt think of your plan?"

"I didn't tell her. I didn't tell anyone. Then I found out that there were only a few Beguines left and they were very old—and lived in the Netherlands and spoke Dutch, which, of course, I didn't. So that was the end of that plan."

Joe laughed. "Smart decision, I'd say."

"Yes, except I never came up with another plan."

Bennett leaned forward to take off her sweater, but feeling awkward, as if she were taking liberties she shouldn't, she leaned back again, hoping he hadn't noticed. She'd never feel at ease with who she was the way Joe did. And now it seemed hot in the room. Maybe she should have taken her sweater off, after all.

"What made you want to be a doctor?" she asked.

"My mother."

Joe put his feet down, reached for the teapot and poured them each another cup. Holding the warm cup with both hands again, he leaned back and breathed in the cinnamon and clove aromas of the tea.

"One day, it was so hot that a boy in my class actually tried to fry an egg on the sidewalk. When I came home from school I found my mother sitting alone at the kitchen table. The table wasn't set, there was no smell of food in the air, no pots on the stove. She jumped up when she saw me, as if she hadn't expected me, and said she'd lost all track of time, which was not like her at all. She didn't look right and I thought maybe it was the heat, but after that she seemed to grow weaker every day. She was pale and the dark shadows she had under eyes when she was tired never went away anymore. Sometimes I'd see her holding on to the wall to steady herself."

Joe closed his eyes for a moment.

"I told my father he had to make her go to the doctor but she resisted, saying it was a waste of money and the doctor would tell her to take it easy which she was doing already—but, of course, she wasn't. She was still trying to do everything she'd always done. Even when she finally did go to the doctor, she probably didn't tell him how she really felt, because it wasn't in her to complain…It shouldn't have been a shock when the doctor told us there was nothing more he could do, but it was. She had waited too long. I begged her to go to the hospital but she wouldn't. So I stayed home to take care of her as much as I could—just like one of your Beguines would have." He smiled at Bennett. "It must have been like that for you and your Aunt Mary."

Bennett shook her head.

"No. We were never close like that. I envy you."

"The strange thing," Joe said, "is that I probably saw my mother smile more then than at any other time. The only time I ever heard her really laugh was when her relatives came and they talked about when they were young and still in Naples—and that wasn't very often. Only three times that I can remember."

"Mrs. McElroy told me how good you were to her, and how brave you were after she died. "

Joe opened his eyes with surprise.

"I keep forgetting that you knew my aunt. I like that you and I share that."

Joe smiled and touched her hand. The flutter this caused in Bennett's heart was quickly quashed by the rush of shame that followed. Poor Mrs. McElroy. How could Bennett have been so callous as to disregard that thud… She blinked and cleared her throat, muttering something about dreams and Joe's deciding to become a doctor.

"I planned on being a nurse at first," he said. 'My mother said doctors focus on curing diseases when what the patient really wants is for someone to care about them. In many ways she was right—my patients often preferred my wife's care to mine—but I wanted more. I wanted to be the one that found a cure, not just a treatment. So I went back to the library and hung out in the biography section. I was determined to find a doctor I could pattern myself after, someone who would inspire me. I found Albert Schweitzer. The more I read about him the more impressed I was. He was a brilliant student, an author, and a musician but that wasn't enough for him. He wanted to do something that made a real difference, so when he was thirty he studied medicine and became a doctor and a missionary in Africa. That was it! I was going to be exactly like him—at least the doctor-in-Africa part."

"What did your father say to that?"

"I didn't tell him. I liked having a secret plan. It made me feel important. When I finally did say something, it didn't go over too well. At first he just said, that's good, son, but you don't have to decide yet. When I insisted that I had already decided and wasn't changing my mind, he looked crushed, like I was telling him I was moving to the moon. He said there was no chance I could get into medical school. I said I could if I worked really hard, but he said even if I did there was no way he could pay for it. I told him I'd find a way and after I finished I'd go to Africa and help people who were sick and didn't have doctors. That's when he got really upset and said I was crazy and would get all kinds of terrible diseases and I should just forget the whole thing. He stormed out of the kitchen and slammed the door, which wasn't like him at all. The last thing I heard was "I'm not going to lose you, too!"

"He loved you and was afraid," Bennett interjected.

"Yes," Joe said, "I get that now but all I could think of then was that I wasn't going to let him change my plans—so I stopped talking about it. In fact, we didn't talk about much of anything important after my mother died, which I really regret now. But that's the trouble with being young, isn't it? And male, probably. And here I am talking your head off! I didn't mean to tell you my whole life saga. I think you deserve a drink for being such a good listener. Let me see what I have ...."

He opened the china cabinet door. "Well, not much," he said when all he found were a bottle of Bordeaux and an almost empty bottle of whiskey. "Wine will have to do. How about it?"

Bennett nodded and made a mental note to contribute to the liquor cabinet next time she came.

"Wine is perfect, Joe, but don't stop talking. I want to know how you got to medical school."

He poured them each a glass of wine and they sat down together on the sofa.

"My father was right. There was no way we could afford it—although it was a lot cheaper then than it is now—but I was determined. I would work and save, and take out loans."

"I thought your aunt and uncle offered to help?"

"They did, but they weren't rich people. I wouldn't have asked them. Then, in my junior year, my father died in an accident at the factory where he worked. Not only had I lost my only parent, I thought it was the end of my dream. But when I was going through his papers I found that he had taken out term life insurance. And because his was an accidental death, they paid double. He did it to protect me in case something happened to him. So it was ironic that it made it possible to do what I had dreamed of but he'd been most afraid of—my becoming a doctor and going to Africa."

Joe went into the kitchen and brought out two apples and a knife.

"You know, Dr. Schweitzer also married the nurse he worked with?" he said.

"So you really followed in his footsteps., just like you planned. You must be very proud."

"I am, but I wish my parents knew. And I wish they knew Medi and Hope, and that the kids knew them. I miss all the conversations we should have had and didn't. I knew more about my father because of the stories my aunt and uncle told. And I can imagine his life because we grew up in the same place. But my mother grew up in Naples. What was that like when she was young? Where did she live? What was her family like? Did she have friends? Was she happy there? Was she sorry she left? What dreams did she have? I don't know any of those things. One day I'd like to go there and see it for myself. Maybe I should be like you, Bennett, and start digging into my roots."

He handed Bennett a slice of apple and she caught a glimpse of his watch.

"Oh my, I didn't realize it was so late."

"Oh," he said, jumping to his feet. "It's my fault. I've kept you too long."

"No, just the opposite, I've kept you and you have to work tomorrow."

She would have liked to tell Joe how much she enjoyed listening to him, but there was a sadness to his smile that made her think it wasn't the right time. His thoughts were on the past, a past in which she had played no part.

20

Bennett's clock ticked off its phosphorescent minutes as she flitted restlessly from dream to memory to regret. Barely in their teens, Joe and Mr. Gold had overcome their losses and focused on their goals—goals that gave them purpose.

Not she.

Not Bennett Mary Hall.

She sat up in bed, reached over to turn on the light, almost knocking the lamp over, and glared at the wall in front of her. Bare. Anonymous. No clue to the room's inhabitant's age or gender, to its passions or interests. Nothing to distinguish this room from a random room in a random motel somewhere—except for the stack of books on the night table, which weren't even for her. They were for Mr. Gold.

After making her bed, taking a shower, getting dressed and having breakfast, it was finally eight o'clock.

It was a weekday, not a day to sleep in. Shannon Butler should be awake.

The phone rang three times before Shannon answered.

"I hope I didn't wake you," Bennett said.

"Miss Hall? How nice to hear from you."

"You were away so I didn't get the chance to thank you for giving me that box. You were right. It had some very important papers in it. Some were even life-changing."

"Well, my goodness. That does sound exciting."

"I found out, you see, that my father's parents were Jewish. From France."

"It's the menorah, isn't it? You'd like it back?"

"Yes. I think it must have belonged to them. And other than the piano it's the only thing my father brought to the house with him. It wasn't his house, you see."

"Well, Miss Hall, you must come and tell me all about it. It all sounds terribly intriguing."

"You don't mind then?"

"About the menorah? Oh no. It's only right, isn't it, that it stay in the family?"

"I'll come now then, if that's all right."

"Oh yes, do. I'll pack it up, and we can have coffee while you tell me everything."

21

Most of the books Bennett had collected for Meyer Gold were New Orleans travel guides, but she had also found John Kennedy Toole's novel about New Orleans that had won the Pulitzer Prize. It might never have been published had the author's mother not shown the manuscript to Walker Percy years after her son had been driven to suicide by depression and the novel's repeated rejection.

When Bennett first opened *A Confederacy of Dunces*, her mouth fell open as she saw that underneath the title, someone had written *To Ben - Never give up. You can do it.*

"I won't!" she'd shouted to the world. This Ben wasn't going to let another second of her life slip through her fingers.

Ready to take this important first step into a richer life in person, she had enjoyed telling Shannon Butler about her genealogical discoveries. She even told her about Meyer Gold and what she had planned for him.

It was almost noon when Bennett walked up the worn concrete steps of Mr. Gold's red-brick row house, avoiding the cracks that had caused the edges of the steps to crumble.

Holding her tote bag of books with one hand, she pressed the buzzer marked M.Gold with the other. "Mr. Gold? It's Bennett Hall. I've brought you something." She waited for an answer, then pressed the buzzer again and spoke more loudly into the intercom. "Mr. Gold, it's Bennett Hall. May I come up?"

There was a click and the latch opened. Bennett sprinted up the stairs and arrived at the door to Apartment 2A in time to hear Mr. Gold unhook the chain. The door opened and Mr. Gold greeted her with a smile.

"Please, please. Do come in. Did you have to wait long downstairs? Sometimes I miss hearing the buzzer when the water's running."

Bennett shook Mr. Gold's hand vigorously. "No, not at all. I don't mean to disturb you but I have brought you some books about New Orleans. More than that, I have brought you a plan. I think we should go there. You and I. I will drive. It will take us a few days, but there are interesting things to see on the way. Places your sister might have added to her list had she known about them. I have already worked out a route we can take, but, of course, if you would rather go a different way we can change it. I am open to your suggestions."

The words had tumbled out so quickly that Bennett found herself out of breath. She suddenly realized she was still holding Mr. Gold's hand, and wondered if Mr. Gold could be any more surprised by her long speech than she was herself.

"My goodness, Miss Hall. Please sit down. I'm not a young man anymore. I don't think I can keep up with you."

That made Bennett laugh.

"Oh no, Mr. Gold, it is just the opposite. I am trying to catch up to you."

Mr. Gold indicated that they should sit down at the table and offered her a drink or something to eat.

"I'm too excited," Bennett said, shaking her head.

She pulled out a large map, unfolded it and laid it on the table. Mr. Gold listened attentively as Bennett pointed out all the places they might stop, and described the sights they could see there.

"I've checked them all out online. I've also found several inns with restaurants on the way that sound especially interesting or charming."

Mr. Gold smiled warmly and nodded.

"It is quite a plan."

"If you think the trip is too rushed, Mr. Gold, we can stop more often or stay longer in certain places. In New Orleans, I thought it best if we stayed right in the French Quarter for convenience sake—though not on Bourbon Street—but of course, if you prefer, we could stay somewhere else."

"Miss Hall, Miss Hall. I am greatly tempted," Mr. Gold said, raising his hand to his heart, "and more deeply touched than I can express. It is a magnificent plan, but as much as it breaks my heart, I cannot go with you. My health will not permit it."

"Even if we flew instead?"

Mr. Gold shook his head.

Bennett looked down at the map and silently refolded it. She should have asked first instead of forcing the poor man to admit he was too old and too weak to take the trip. And even if his health allowed, why should he agree to go off with a woman he hardly knew?

Her eyes still downcast, Bennett said, "I apologize, Mr. Gold. I did not mean to put you in an awkward position …"

"Not at all. You have made me a wonderfully generous offer, and if I were ninety-seven instead of ninety-eight I would have accepted it with great enthusiasm. Alas, this last year had crept into various parts of my body, causing them to behave quite badly, so it is they who should apologize to you." Bennett looked up to find Mr. Gold smiling. "I may be too old to travel, but I hope I will never be old to make a new friend. Do call me Meyer, Miss Hall, and I will call you Bennett, if I may. When you have a little time, I would like to hear about your visit to New Orleans."

That afternoon, Bennett called a mason to repair the row house's front steps.

22

When Maria acquired—one could almost say stole, the price was so low— twenty-three cartons of books at a Main Line Philadelphia estate sale over the weekend, Bennett felt the self-doubts of the last few days lessen. Logging in, organizing, and inspecting book collections was the part of her job she was best at. She'd leaf through each volume to make sure nothing of value had been slipped between its pages, often losing herself in the brittle and yellowed book reviews she'd find. Once she discovered almost a thousand dollars in hundred dollar bills strategically placed every thirty pages. She made a point of returning money and personal letters to the estate sale agents to pass on to the relevant families. This conscientious consideration was so appreciated by the agents that Maria was often given a chance to preview their more interesting sales.

At the very bottom of the last Main Line crate, Bennett found an old Russell Stover chocolate box containing two books: *The Illustrated Guide to Mardi Gras* and *Carnival Around the World*, along with a handwritten volume entitled *Recipes handed down to me in September of 1883 by Madame Begue of Begue's Restaurant on the corner of Decatur and Madison*.

As she flipped through the pages of both books, she recalled how, as a child, she had crammed herself so full of baseball information that she'd almost felt as if she'd actually been to a game. If she gave Meyer Gold these books he might feel the same about New Orleans.

But why stop there? New Orleans was more than just words in a book. Food was meant to be eaten, and music to be heard. And if Meyer couldn't go to New Orleans, why not bring New Orleans to him? Mardi Gras in autumn might seem odd, but there was no point in putting it off. As Meyer himself had pointed out, he was ninety-eight and a half.

Bennett pulled out a sheet of paper and divided it into three columns: *Music, Food, Decorations.* Under each she made a list of things they would need.

There were numerous Mardi Gras supply places on the internet, and a party store that carried beads and masks was conveniently located in a strip mall a short drive away. Even finding a Dixieland band was less of a challenge than she anticipated, thanks to *www.gigbookies.org* with their all-encompassing slogan: *Any music. Any function. Anywhere. No group too small. No crowd too big.* She should be able to afford one afternoon of their time.

When she showed Juanita the old recipe book and told her about Mr. Gold, Juanita said she'd love to put together a menu for the occasion. Bennett offered to pay her but she refused.

The biggest challenge was deciding whom to invite. Bennett worried that she, Maria, Juanita, Joe, and the children wouldn't be enough to make it really festive. She asked Maria if she knew any of Meyer's friends.

"I don't think he has many. And the few I knew about have died. Mr. Schimmerling was probably his closest friend. But I wouldn't worry, the musicians will take up half the living room already, and at his age, Mr. Gold probably wouldn't like a crowd—unless you want to invite

Lola, of course. She's a party girl. Think of all the people she could bring."

"They'd probably all be her exes," Bennett said, cringing at the thought. A small party was definitely best.

Following Joe's advice—he thought that a total surprise might be too much excitement for a man of Mr. Gold's age—Bennett told Meyer that she was having a small gathering at her house and would like him to come.

"Can I come pick you up on Saturday around four?"

"That would be lovely," Meyer said. "Is it a special occasion?"

"I hope so," Bennett replied.

The day before the big day, there was a short fit of weather hysteria with radio and television forecasters threatening a massive snowstorm and consequent run on supermarkets and gas stations. After multiple calls to gigbookies, Bennett was reassured that the musicians could be counted on. In the end there was only a dusting of snow on the sidewalks, which melted before noon.

When Bennett and Meyer arrived at the house and walked up the steps, Bennett pointed to the *Welcome to New Orleans* sign the children had made.

"When Mohammed can't go to the mountain, the mountain must come to Mohammed."

The door swung open to reveal a room festooned with hundreds of beads, feathers, and masks. Hope and Isabella were in full Mardi Gras regalia, in their tutus, feathered masks and multiple strings of traditional purple, gold and green beads. Medi, in a purple velvet robe, mask, and a few strands of beads of his own, held out a large purple turban encased in a jewel-encrusted gold crown.

"The king has arrived!" he said, making his voice sound as deep as possible, and holding the crown up to Meyer Gold.

"Let's let poor Mr. Gold come in out of the cold first, Medi," Maria said, holding out her hand for support. "It's wonderful to see you, Mr. Gold."

Bennett took the older man's arm and led him to a gold lamé draped easy chair in the living room which, like everyone and everything, was bedecked with beads.

"You have been crowned King of the Mardi Gras and we are your subjects."

Maria introduced her mother and Isabella. Bennett presented Joe and the children.

"And now let the festivities begin!"

There was no immediate response to this announcement, but after a few hasty whispers and rustling about, three men in black suits and bow ties who called themselves the Riverside Strutters marched out of the kitchen playing *When the Saints Go Marching In*—one on trumpet, one on trombone and the third on clarinet.

As the song came to an end, Bennett saw Hope holding Meyer's hand and heard her whisper, "Don't cry, Mr. Gold. Bennett said this music was going to make you happy."

"Oh, it does," Meyer said.

Thanks to Bennett's recipe finds and Juanita's cooking skills, their feast of gumbo, jambalaya, fried oysters and étouffée could have been served in the best of New Orleans' restaurants. And for dessert Juanita had baked a splendid King Cake decorated with gold, green and purple icing, and a string of gold beads. Following Mardi Gras tradition, a tiny baby figurine was hidden inside, promising luck and prosperity to the finder.

The Strutters played every jazz melody young Elsie Gold could have wished for. At the end, the children must have thought Muskrat Ramble was a lullaby, for each of them fell asleep nestled in someone's arms.

When Meyer's eyes began to droop as well, Bennett asked if he would like to go home.

"Forgive me," Meyer said. "I was only closing my eyes so I could fix the memory of this special evening in my mind. Thanks to all of you, and most especially you, my dear Bennett, I've had the opportunity to see and hear and taste the very best of New Orleans. With a full heart I can now cross it off the list."

Bennett accompanied Meyer home, and as they entered the small apartment there was a whiff of something—of remembered adventures perhaps—as if one could still smell the complex aroma of the oolong tea Meyer had drunk in China, or the intoxicating scent of jasmine that had filled the air of India or Catalonia.

As Bennett was about to take her leave, Meyer took her hand firmly in his. His hands were surprisingly strong, and his eyes bright.

"You are a lucky woman, Bennett, to be surrounded by friends and children who think so highly of you." Still holding Bennett's hand, he leaned forward and whispered, "And if I may say so, I believe I spied a look of special affection in Joe's eyes."

23

*B*ennett lay on her back, her arms crossed above her head, her eyes tracing and retracing the white streaks of streetlight reflected on the ceiling. It was already three in the morning but she was still too exhilarated to sleep. She had finally accomplished something she was proud of. She had made someone happy. And Meyer had called her a lucky woman, highly thought of by her friends. Especially Joe. It couldn't get much better than that.

Eventually, her eyes, more tired than her mind, gave up and closed. She drifted off into a deep, untroubled sleep, and did not wake until the phone rang the next morning.

She picked up the receiver and groggily mumbled hello.

"Bennett?" It was Joe. "Did I wake you?"

"No, no," she said, looking at the clock and seeing it was almost ten. "I'm awake. Where are you?"

"Home. It's Sunday. I just wanted to thank you for last night. It put us all in such a festive mood, the kids and I thought we should all be together for Christmas, here at our house—unless you've already made other plans. What do you say?"

"I'd like that very much. What can I do?"

"Could you call Meyer and invite him? And I'll call Maria."

Bennett had just finished speaking to Meyer when she heard repeated knocking at her door. She opened it to find Medi and Hope asking to come in.

"Did you write to Santa, Bennett?" Medi asked.

"Not yet. Do you think I'm too late?"

Medi gave it some thought. "No. Probably a lot of people write late, but I wrote early. I want him to read my letter very carefully. Papa says we can't have everything we want, so I thought I'd give him lots of choices. I wrote Hope's letter too.

"'Cause I can't spell so good, " Hope explained. "Juanita says it doesn't matter. She says sometimes she sees Santa sitting on the windowsill writing things down."

"What kind of things?" Bennett asked.

"Well, I know he writes down if you are good or bad. And he probably writes down what presents you want in case you don't know how to write or don't know his address."

"That's very good then, because I didn't know his address."

Presents. Bennett would definitely have to buy presents—but what? She used to buy her aunt poinsettias—except once, the first time she was promoted, she'd bought her a blue raincoat, only to have her say "I hate blue." So she'd returned it and went back to poinsettias—until Aunt Mary decided she hated red flowers. After that Bennett bought chocolates, which Aunt Mary wouldn't open in front of her lest she had to offer one. A few days later Bennett would find the empty box in the trash.

Aunt Mary never bought Bennet anything after her mother died.

She knew Medi was desperate to have a bicycle but Joe might think she was usurping his role if she bought it. On the other hand, maybe he'd appreciate it, but she didn't want to ask. She'd have to get something for Maria and Juanita and Isabella and Meyer. She wanted to give Joe something special, but nothing that would embarrass her because it was too much or too little. She could ask Maria, but she'd tease her or suggest something far too personal. Besides, this was something she should be able to figure out for herself. How difficult could it be? Other people bought presents all the time. This was America after all. The economy depended on it.

It was a busy time at the shop, so Bennett couldn't look for anything until after they closed. Except for very occasional trips to buy clothes, she had little experience shopping. Malls were too intimidating. She knew people shopped online but it would be hard to judge the quality of something you couldn't touch.

One couldn't go wrong with books, she thought at first, but realized she didn't know anyone's taste in books. After twelve days of increasing panic that she would never find anything anybody liked, and the realization that Christmas was only two days away, she bought seven bathrobes in the neighborhood Body and Bath Boutique, practically wiping out their stock.Then she stopped at the drug store and, afraid she might not have enough wrapping paper for all the oversized boxes, she bought a dozen rolls of paper and Scotch tape. On impulse, she also threw a velvet Santa hat into the cart.

Unaccustomed to wrapping presents, she tried to devise an efficient system by rolling open the various wrapping papers on the floor and spacing the boxes so that each would have enough paper to cover it. Forgetting to leave enough room for her to maneuver between the long strips of paper, she found herself stepping on and tearing several of them and having to start over again. She precut pieces of tape and stuck them on the sides of the end tables for easy access, but ended up with little transparent flaps in random places on her pants and sleeves. She stepped on one roll of tape and broke it, and lost another when she unknowingly kicked it under the sofa. Nevertheless, each present was wrapped eventually, the ends neatly folded and taped, with gift cards clearly addressed and signed. Torn papers were discarded, leftover rolls put away in the closet. By then it was long after midnight. Her back and knees ached and she fell into bed exhausted. Next year she would start this process much earlier and buy things that were easier to wrap. No one needed or would even want a new bathrobe every year anyway.

At noon on Christmas day, Bennett carried her presents to Joe's front door two boxes at a time, and put on her Santa hat before she knocked on the door. Medi and Hope answered immediately and pulled her in, one grabbing her left elbow, the other her right.

The radio was playing Christmas carols and the room was a jumble of crumpled wrapping paper and open boxes.

"Look, Bennett!" Medi said, jumping up and down with excitement, "Santa got me everything I wanted! Except a parrot. I guess he couldn't find one. But I think it's OK for me to be a pirate without one, don't you think?"

"And I got lots and lots and lots of crayons and paints and papers and pens so I'm going to make you lots and lots of pictures," Hope chimed in, her hands already striped and dotted in all her new marker colors.

"And what did Santa get you, Joe?" Bennett asked.

"It's a bit hard to explain. I'll show you all later. Let's clean up a bit and then we can have some egg nog and a piece of Panettone before others arrive. My mother always had Panettone Christmas morning. I couldn't get it in Uganda so it's a special treat this year."

Maria, Juanita and Isabella arrived soon after they'd finished, their arms laden with presents and mysterious cloth-covered bundles, which turned out to be an extravagance of colorfully decorated cakes and cookies Juanita had spent days preparing.

Bennett left to pick up Meyer. By the time she returned the table had been set and dinner was ready.

"Everything smells wonderful," Meyer said.

"Mama has outdone herself," Maria said. "I think we'll be eating all afternoon."

Bennett looked at Juanita with affection, remembering the year she had brought a complete Christmas dinner to her and her aunt when she saw that the refrigerator was empty and they would order fast food as they did every other day. "I'd rather have fried chicken," her aunt had said, not even bothering to get out of bed. Bennett apologized to Juanita and took a plate to her room and watched a Christmas special on TV. The leftovers lasted her until Juanita came back to clean a few days later.

When dinner was over, the non-Santa presents were brought out to cries of delight and appreciation. Bennett waited until the last gift was opened and then nervously distributed hers. One by one the bathrobes were put on, making the room look like a Turkish bath bathed in color —from the vibrant earthen hues of hair and skin to the rainbow of terrycloth.

"Your turn, Papa," Medi said. "Show us what Santa brought you."

"I got three presents," Joe said. "I told Santa that I was looking for a hobby because I'd never had time for one before, but I couldn't decide what it should be. So he brought me this very big box."

"What's in it? Is it a puppy?" Hope asked.

Joe laughed. "No, honey. No puppy."

He opened the box and pulled out a notebook.

"This is in case I want to write a book about a little girl who wants a puppy, or a boy who wants to be a pirate."

Then he pulled out a smaller box filled with paint, and a canvas.

"Or maybe I'll want learn to be an artist like Hope, or…"

Joe pulled out the last of the items.

"…or I can learn to play the piano by trying out this keyboard. But I'll have to take lessons or watch lots of YouTube videos."

"Can I try?" Meyer asked softly. "It's been a long time and my fingers are stiff."

"That would be great! I even bought a songbook that has Christmas carols in it," Joe said, handing him the book, and turning the voice selection on the keyboard to Grand Piano.

Meyer began to play. His surprisingly resonant baritone blended harmoniously with Juanita's rich alto and Maria's lyrical soprano And the others joined in as best as they could.

"I will definitely have to learn," Joe said."And *then* I'll paint."

"And write," Bennett said.

24

The New Year found Bennett settled into a comfortable routine of work and time with her small circle of friends. She was busy and content. That was enough. Life remained on an even keel, until one morning in February when Joe called.

"I'm sorry. I know it's terribly early," he said, "but the kids are still asleep and I need to talk to you. It's about Grace. I don't know what to do."

"I'll be right there."

Bennett bolted out of bed, splashed cold water on her face, and slipped on the first clothes she saw. In less than five minutes she was at Joe's door. He opened it before her hand even touched the doorknob.

"I don't want to wake the kids," he whispered. "We can talk in the kitchen. I made coffee." He pulled out a chair for her. "Come sit down. I didn't get a chance to look at yesterday's mail until I woke up this morning so I didn't notice the letter from Grace's school. She hasn't been there for over two months. Sometimes girls drop out for a few days to help their families and then return when they can. But two months is much too long for that. They couldn't get hold of her. I'm really worried that something has happened to her—and really upset that they didn't tell me sooner!"

"Would your nurse friend know anything?"

"Hilda? I emailed her right before I called you, but she probably doesn't and her internet doesn't always work so I don't know when she'll get it. I would go there if I could, but I'm very much involved with the new pediatric oncology wing, and the kids are in school ... and I don't really have the money ..."

"I'll go," Bennett said. "I'll go and find Grace."

The words came out before she had a chance to think.

"That's sweet of you, Bennett, but it's complicated. You've never traveled ..."

Joe was right. What did she know about travel? Or Africa? She'd never even crossed the border to Canada. She'd need a passport. And where exactly was Uganda anyway?

Joe frowned. "I'll have to wait for Hilda's answer," he went on, no longer giving Bennett's offer any thought. "I don't have the school's phone number ... I didn't think to ask Hilda for that."

He put his elbows on the table, and held his head in his hands. After a moment, he said, "I never should have left Uganda once I knew about her. But I wanted to get home and so I let myself assume she'd be all right. Now she's gone and it's all my fault."

It pained Bennett to see him so upset.

"You mustn't blame yourself, Joe. Besides, you don't know anything definite yet. Maybe nothing's wrong. Maybe her aunt just needed her at home. As soon as we know, we'll do whatever is needed."

There must be something she could do. She would ask Meyer. He knew the world. He would know.

25

Meyer Gold was waiting on the stoop, holding a square white box tied with string, when Bennett pulled up in her car.

"It sounded like you had something very important to discuss," Meyer said. "I thought we might need nourishment while we talked so I bought us some chocolate babka from Weissman's Bakery. They make the best. Not many of those old bakers left, you know. Now all you can find are scones and muffins."

Meyer stood up and unlocked the door. Holding on to the railing, he switched on the hall light and led the way up the stairs to his apartment.

"I made coffee already and kept it warm, so we can get started immediately. Tell me everything."

Bennett proceeded to tell Meyer about Joe and Laurie's time in Uganda, the adoption, Laurie's death, the discovery that there was a third child, and the news that the child was now missing.

"Perhaps not actually missing," Bennett said, "we just don't know where she is. So I was thinking of going there to find her because Joe can't, but I don't know if I can manage it ..."

"Of course, you can. It's an excellent idea."

"I don't know where to begin. I've never been anywhere."

"It is not so difficult. Don't worry." Meyer pointed to a basket on the floor by his telephone. "Take a piece of paper and a pen and write this down. First and most important, you will need a passport. Go to the office in Washington and tell them it's an emergency, otherwise you'll have to wait for weeks. You'll probably need a visa from the Ugandan Embassy, but you need the passport first. Maybe inoculations, too. You can ask at the passport office ... but you have a computer, you can find out today. Then you book your flight and go. Nothing to it."

Bennett burst out laughing.

"For you. I've never even seen a passport. Maybe you should be the one to go."

Meyer didn't answer. He got up from the table and walked over to the night table next to his narrow bed. He opened the top drawer and took out a leather folder filled with passports.

"These are mine. I still have all of them ... but that is not what I want to show you."

He pulled out a piece of paper and unfolded what had been folded and refolded hundreds of times. A small corner had torn off, and the paper was full of erasures and smudges and little brown stains, as if someone had sprinkled it with coffee.

"This is my list. Elsie's list. You will see that every place but one has been checked off. You gave me New Orleans, now the last one is for you."

He handed the fragile, treasured piece of paper to Bennett. There, on the bottom, in a neat and measured cursive Elsie had written: Uganda (Pearl of Africa).

"It was meant to be, Bennett. You must go for Joe and Grace—and for Elsie and me."

26

She had to go. Meyer was right.

Bennett had always chosen passivity over action, so if she made that choice again no one would think it was unlike her. In reality, no one had ever given her much thought at all. When she blurted out that she would go and find Grace Joe hadn't taken her seriously, clearly considering her offer no more substantial than one Medi or Hope might have made. So he wouldn't be surprised or disappointed if she reneged on his offer merely by never mentioning it again.

But this was Bennett's chance, her chance to do something that could make a difference in someone's life. It was her chance to prove herself; one might even say redeem herself.

She turned on her computer and googled traveling to Uganda. One click and there it was: Bureau of Consular Affairs, U.S. Department of State: Uganda—background information, entry and exit requirements, safety and security, crime, health, transport.

Too much to know. She almost turned the computer off again. She'd never figure it out. Or worse, she'd think she'd figured it out and get it all wrong and end up a failure once again, ridiculed and rejected.

Failure! She could hear Aunt Mary snarl the word, shocking her with the venom of her tone—but not the substance of her accusation for Bennett had often made the same assessment of herself.

Stop. She wasn't totally incompetent. She'd held a job for almost thirty years. She could do this. She'd known nothing about retail and had been overwhelmed by the thought of a massive inventory at the shop, but they'd done it, and she'd easily put the shop's financial affairs in order. Fear not incompetence was her problem, and it was time to defeat it.

Everything she needed to know was on the computer screen. If she took it one step at a time she could overcome her fear. She pulled out a clean sheet of paper, took a deep breath, and glancing back and forth from screen to paper, she wrote out a list. Lists always made her feel she had things under control.

BEFORE LEAVING:

1. *Download passport application from the internet. (Need certified birth certificate, driver's license, and photocopies of each; passport photos, and fee) Go to passport office in Washington, 600 19th St NW.*
2. *Apply for visa to Uganda online.*
3. *Get required vaccinations. Bring medicines. Check medical insurance.*
4. *Book flight.*
5. *Buy a suitcase with wheels. Check weather and pack appropriate clothes. (Shop as needed)*
6. *Make list of everything to be done in Uganda.*
7. *Money (how much?)*

IN UGANDA

1. *Tell U.S. Embassy she's there.*
2. FIND GRACE

3. *Make and follow list of Ugandan and U.S. requirements.*
   4. *Bring Grace back.*

She could manage this. Just follow the lists. But quickly. This was urgent, not a report due next quarter.

She continued scrolling through the State Department website.

Threats to Safety and Security: hazardous driving conditions, inadequate emergency medical care; risk of incursions by armed combatants, attacks by bandits, smugglers, cattle rustlers, carjackings and armed robberies; possible protests resulting in closures, strikes, electric outages, riots; danger of malaria, TB, Marburg and Ebola hemorrhagic fevers, pneumonic plague, meningitis, and other infectious diseases.

Her hands felt damp and fear had turned the sweat trickling down her sides cold. Was she crazy? What if she succumbed to some terrible disease, or was kidnapped? She could be killed. What if she lived but used up all her money on a wild goose chase and came home humiliated and broke?

She didn't have to go. She could chicken out and Joe wouldn't even realize. But what if he did? She didn't mind so much that he considered her naive and inexperienced, but she couldn't bear for him to think her a coward. He wouldn't understand. He'd never been afraid of anything.

Show some guts, Bennett. Grace could be in danger.

She looked down at her list again and underlined FIND GRACE three times. Go. Find Grace. Bring her back. Done.

Done? How done? She had no idea where to look, or how to look. And even if she did manage to find her, wouldn't she have to convince her to come back with her? Joe would blame her if she failed. Rightfully so. When had she ever persuaded anyone of anything?

It was all so complicated and risky but this was her chance. Her one chance maybe, to do something important. Something she could legitimately be proud of. What would Meyer think if she didn't at least try.

~

Deep into the night, Bennett read everything she could about U.S. and Ugandan adoption requirements. Soon she filled a loose-leaf notebook with multicolored dividers and neatly written notes. The orderliness of it made it all seem possible. Controllable and straightforward, the way her work had been at Bancroft, Chandler and Co.

Thinking of work reminded her that there had been an analyst a few cubicles over whose brother was in the Foreign Service. She pulled out the folded sheet of phone numbers she still kept in her wallet and placed it by the phone. She would call first thing in the morning.

She brushed her teeth and dropped into bed, dreaming briefly of lists before falling into a deep sleep. It seemed only minutes later that the sun streaming in her window woke her.

Did the African sun feel like this, bright and warm even on a winter's day?

She picked up the phone.

"Bancroft, Chandler and Company," a young, unfamiliar voice answered. A new receptionist? Had old Myra been laid off, too?

"I'd like to speak to George Barnes, please."

Mr. Barnes was quite surprised to hear from her, having exchanged less than a dozen words with her over the years, but must have found the idea of quiet, diligent Bennett tracking down a missing Ugandan child and bringing her to the U.S. so intriguing that he agreed to give Bennett his brother's email address.

"Sounds like your life has taken an interesting turn, Miss Hall."

"Yes, it has."

"All right then," George Barnes said, after waiting for details that didn't come.

Bennett spent the next hour composing an email explaining the Grace situation and asking what she should or could do.

The next day she received the following reply:

Dear Ms. Hall,

I do not normally work with consular affairs and can offer only a few facts, insights and opinions.

Adoption and visas are complex under U.S. law and probably under Ugandan law as well, as you probably already know.

If the girl is still a minor under Ugandan and U.S. law, then she might very well be adopted by your friend, if the girl wanted to be adopted and if she wanted to go to the U.S. The fact that her two siblings were adopted by your friend would, in the eyes of the U.S. consular officials, mitigate in favor of the adoption. Also, the fact that they were adopted under Ugandan law would indicate that the girl is also an orphan and equally eligible for adoption.

There would be much preparatory work to be done, probably starting with the Ugandan embassy in Washington, and/or an Ugandan consulate. And possibly also with private organizations that facilitate such adoptions, for a fee, perhaps a quite substantial one. There would be costs in Uganda also—some legal fees, but probably also a fair amount of "facilitation payments" to Ugandan attorneys, officials and who knows who else.

The adoption would have to be completed before the girl could leave Uganda. Without the adoption you would have great difficulty getting a legitimate visa to the U.S. since the intention is clearly to have the girl stay permanently in the U.S. Once the girl has a passport, do not do anything clever like taking the girl to an adjacent country to try to obtain a visa there. Suspicions would immediately be aroused about slave trade or exploitation.

The solution: once the adoption is done legitimately, the girl being a minor, I would think that you, being provided with a raft of official papers, would be able to bring the girl to the U.S.

That's the best I can do.

Best regards,

Douglas Barnes

Bennett hadn't expected Mr. Barnes to respond in such an elaborate and informative way, but supposed that the ability to do that must be a prerequisite in his profession. By facilitation payments, Mr. Barnes must have meant bribes. Bennett wondered what the cost of them would be.

P.S. the email went on, *You will be pleasantly surprised at how beautiful Uganda is. Churchill called it the Pearl of Africa.*

The Pearl of Africa. Just what Elsie had written on her list. Bennett liked the sound of it. She'd never been to the pearl of anywhere. It was high time.

27

Bennett thought it strange how memories linked disparate things—the sound of worry in Joe's voice as he called to tell her that Grace was missing with the sight of crocuses sprouting out of the frozen ground in the little flower bed between their front steps. She'd leaped over them to rush up his steps. Now the first daffodils were pushing their way out of the same small space as if to prove to her that time was slipping through her fingers and she had to stop procrastinating. There was nothing more to research. No more websites to take notes on. No more items to check off her list. It was March already and time to go. Steps had been taken.

She would have loved to fly off to Uganda without a word, find Grace and bring her back to a hero's welcome. But, of course, that was impossible. She didn't even know Grace's full name nor where to start looking. Only Joe knew that. She had no choice but to tell him her plan. And now was the time.

Joe had said nothing more since the morning he called, so he must not have heard anything further. Someone else might have assumed his silence meant he'd decided he didn't want Grace after all, but Bennett knew he'd never give up on the child. On any child. He probably saw no point in talking to her about it if he hadn't found a solution—why would he imagine her being any help? Nor had she said anything to him. How could she, if she hadn't mustered up the courage yet to act on it? But now the time had come.

"Joe, I'd like to talk to you about Grace," is how she broke the silence, early one morning.

"I haven't heard anything. Not a word from anyone. Not even Hilda."

"I was afraid you hadn't, but I've been thinking, and I have an idea. Can I come over and talk to you about it?"

She'd imagined Joe's reaction to her plan many times: surprise, elation, gratitude. But reality was not as romantic as her imagination.

"There's no way," he said, slightly irritated.

Bennett held up the notebook she'd brought with her.

"See, I've done a great deal of research."

He sighed, and smiled tolerantly, the way he might have smiled at Hope bringing home an injured creature she knew nothing about.

"You need a passport ..."

"I've already gotten one, and a visa." More confident now she added that she'd even bought a new suitcase, one with wheels.

His laughter made her blush, but she didn't let it dissuade her.

"I know, I've never done anything like this before. You're right that I've never been anywhere. But that was the point of the research. I know what airline to take, what hotel I can stay in when I arrive. In fact, I've done everything I have to except book the flight."

"I don't think you understand what you are getting yourself into ..."

"I think I do. I'll be all right. Meyer has given me all kinds of travel tips." She grinned and added, "Besides, Maria said it's time I had an adventure."

"This is serious, Bennett."

"I know. You said the clinic was in Kasese. I thought I'd go there first. There's a bus I can take from Kampala. I'll find your friend Hilda, and even if she doesn't know anything, she knows where Grace's aunt lives. I'll go there. I won't give up until I find Grace. I promise."

"You can't just bring her back with you. There are rules and requirements."

The more Joe argued, the surer Bennett felt.

"I know that too. Some of the requirements you already fulfilled when you adopted Medi and Hope. The same information would apply to Grace, so I'll need copies of your papers to take along."

"What if she doesn't want to come? She knows even less about me than I know about her."

"I'll tell her everything she wants to know. And you and I will be in touch all the time and can figure out any details we didn't already cover or foresee. I won't do anything crazy."

Her voice was calm and firm.

Joe took a deep breath. "All right," he said, exhaling. His eyebrows eased out of their frown and he nodded. "You'll have to get a cell phone."

"I've already looked into all that. I'll have my smartphone with me for emails or internet, but I'll get an extra phone there for calls just in case. They don't require a contract."

"You need inoculations for …"

"Already done. And I'll take Primaquine against malaria. I didn't relish the possibility of the hallucinations you can get with Lariam."

"You should take along some Doxycycline, in case you have to …"

"I went to the doctor last week."

"The trip is going to cost you a lot of money, Bennett."

"I've been saving for this all my life."

At last, Joe looked at her with the surprise and admiration she'd hoped for.

"You really are prepared, aren't you?"

She smiled, as an unfamiliar feeling of self-worth washed over her.

"It surprised me, too, but it's about time, don't you think?"

28

"Medi, Hope, hurry!" Joe shouted. "We have to leave now, otherwise Bennett will miss her flight."

Joe loaded Bennett's luggage into the trunk of his car. If traffic cooperated they would be at the airport three hours before boarding time, giving her plenty of time to get through security. Joe had checked her in online and she had no luggage to check, just her handbag and her new carry-on. After what she'd read about African airports she didn't want to have to worry about lost luggage.

She bent down to talk to the children she'd so easily and completely grown to love.

"Take good care of your father," she said.

"We will," Medi answered. "Will you send us postcards? I'm going show them to everyone in school."

"As often as I can."

"I'd like a doll," Hope added. "Do you think they have dolls in Uganda?"

"I'm sure they do. I'll look for a very pretty one that looks just like you."

"When are you coming back?" Medi asked, suddenly looking worried.

"As soon as I can. I promise. Meanwhile, make sure Juanita makes you lots of vegetables to eat so you'll get big and strong. Learn some new games so you can teach me when I get back. And Hope, the walls in my house look very bare. Do you think you could draw me some pictures while I'm away?"

She took the children in her arms and kissed each on the cheek.

"Take good care of them," she called out to Juanita, who had come out to wave from the front door.

"Should I park and come in?" Joe asked, when they reached Philadelphia International Airport.

"No, no, you need to get back, and if you come in I might change my mind. I don't like good-byes."

"Don't waste your money on calls, Bennett, it's too expensive, but email me as often as you can."

"I will, I promise."

"And be careful when you use your credit card."

"I know."

"You have all the papers I gave you?"

"Yes. Don't worry. I haven't forgotten anything."

Joe pulled her toward him.

"I'll miss you."

"Me, too," she said inadequately.

"Bennett, you don't have Hilda's phone number!"

"I'll find her, don't worry. I'll talk to everyone in Uganda if I have to until I find Grace. I won't disappoint you. Meanwhile, will you do something for me?"

"Anything."

"Check in on Meyer for me, maybe even invite him for dinner. Maria said she would too. He loved Juanita's cooking."

Joe stroked her face gently.

"You're a wonderful woman, Bennett."

Not yet, she thought, but she was trying.

Concerned that Bennett would find the long trip difficult, Joe had given her a neck pillow and a sleeping pill to take, but Bennett wanted to use the time to think, to review in her mind all that she needed to accomplish. She placed her suitcase in the overhead compartment and her oversized handbag at her feet. As the airplane doors closed, she was relieved to find that no one was sitting next to her. Once the plane had taken off she removed two manila envelopes from her handbag. She emptied the first one onto her lap and looked with satisfaction at the mass of papers she'd assembled: a guidebook to Uganda, a stack of printouts from the internet, a list of useful Ugandan addresses and telephone numbers, certificate of inoculations, emails confirming flight and hotel reservations, copies of all of Joe's papers, and his power of attorney.

The second envelope held an album of photographs she'd put together for Grace. It might help her to see Joe and the children; to see where she would live and go to school. Inside the front cover she'd stuck three letters. One from Joe, about Grace's parents and why Medi and Hope were in America with her; the second a neatly printed letter from Medi telling her about school; and the third from Hope, a stick-figure drawing of a mother and three children holding hands surrounded by a scattering of misshapen little hearts.

This was a big moment in a life that until then had only been filled with small ones. Yet, in the past year, it had been the small moments with friends that had given Bennett the most joy. She closed her eyes and memories floated gently through her mind. She felt herself drifting off. Maybe a little sleep wasn't such a bad idea.

Bennett's foray into her first big moment was not conducive to staying asleep after all. There were movies to watch, magazines to read, announcements to listen to, customs forms to fill out, fellow passengers to look at. Many of the passengers appeared to be Africans. Some of them had the same smooth, round faces and cropped hair that Medi and Hope had. Maybe they were Ugandans too—but which group? Did they look different from each other? She had forgotten to ask Joe about that, but it was probably a silly question. She pulled out her guidebook and read—again—that there were four groups of Ugandans: Bantu, Luo, Nilo Hamites and Sudanic, each with different tribes within the groups: Baganda, Basoga, Bagwe, Bagisu, Acholi, Lango, and each of those with a different language. She'd never remember the names let alone learn any of the languages. Thankfully, English was one of the official languages—but what if the people she had to speak to only spoke their own, or Swahili, which she didn't know either? Too late to worry about it now. She'd just have to manage.

All around her the plane was dark and people were sleeping. She shut off her overhead light and closed her eyes again. Lulled by the low hum of the plane's engines she fell asleep, and woke only when the flight attendants began serving breakfast.

As the plane started to descend, and arrival at Entebbe airport was imminent, she reached into her handbag and pulled out the confirmation email from the hotel in which she would spend her first night and slipped it into her passport case. Joe had insisted on making that reservation.

"I don't want you staying someplace unsafe or way too expensive," he'd said. "I know a place in Kampala, right by the American Embassy that is attractive and quiet, and the staff is very helpful. It's not cheap, but it's not as expensive as the big hotels. And don't forget to wash your hands often and avoid uncooked foods or cooked foods that have been left out. Even if you are in a good hotel. Watch out for prickly heat and pink eye. They're very common. Wear 100% cotton clothes, you'll be much more comfortable. Beware of bugs—especially brightly colored ones. Use insect repellent wherever you go."

"Yes, doctor," she'd answered with a smile, pleased that he was concerned. She wasn't sure she owned anything that was 100% cotton, so she'd added it to the list of things she needed.

She would have liked to visit Lake Victoria and the Botanical Garden in Entebbe, or go to Ninja and dip her toes in the source of the Nile, but she hadn't come to see the sights. She had a reservation in Kampala and would go straight there.

As per Joe's explicit instructions, Bennett hired a taxi to take her to Le Petit Village Hotel on Ggaba Road. She would face the prospect of an Ugandan bus in the morning.

The hotel was as Joe had described it and yet not at all what Bennett had imagined. Its thatched roof and grounds were what one would expect of a grand safari lodge, yet it was up-to-date technologically with wi-fi and flat screen TVs. She'd send a quick email to Joe saying she'd arrived safely, then go for a swim in the pool. For dinner she'd treat herself to a French meal in the hotel restaurant. This was exciting. Why had she waited so long to travel?

As Bennett glanced around the restaurant that evening, her eye caught sight of a well-dressed woman sitting alone in the corner of the dining room, her feet crossed demurely at the ankles. She looked quite serene as she watched a young man playing the piano, which made Bennett think of her father. Bennett would have liked to have seen him play. Instead, she could only picture her Aunt Mary sprawled sloppily on the sofa next to empty soda cans on their never-played piano, her swollen feet barely fitting into her stretched-out slippers.

Bennett shook the image out of her head. How easy it was to pass judgement over her aunt's defects, even now that she had come to recognize parallels to her own.

"A table for one?" the maitre d' asked.

"Yes, please. Near the piano. And a cocktail menu."

29

Concerned that her lack of sleep on the plane combined with the time change would cause her to suffer jet lag of overwhelming proportions just when she had to face the unknown dangers of her first adventure, Bennett was tempted to take a sleeping pill—but decided that a pill on top of two martinis might keep her asleep for a week. She was relieved when she awoke the next morning rested and alert. Having set her alarm and unpacked only the little she needed for the night, she was ready to depart the hotel by dawn, giving her plenty of time to fortify herself with a cup of coffee in the lobby before leaving. She'd heeded the desk clerk's suggestion and ordered a taxi to take her to the bus stop a full hour before the 7:30 departure time.

Several buses took passengers from Kampala to Kasese. After investigating all of them online, Bennett had chosen the Post Bus. It had won the most recent Uganda Transport Safety Award, which was comforting, and its drivers followed the well-paved Fort Portal route rather than the far more congested Masaka-Mbarara road. It looked as sleek and modern in person as it had in the online photo. Another fear allayed.

Bennett found a line of people already waiting to board when she arrived. She assumed the majority were locals, although she had no way of telling. Two men looked to be Southeast Asians, and one Chinese. One couple was white, presumably tourists, given they had cameras with long lenses slung around their necks. She wondered if they could tell that she'd come with quite a different purpose.

She was puzzled that people were lined up on the wrong side of the bus, then remembered reading that in Uganda people drove on the left—a remnant of British colonial rule. Again she was glad she'd limited herself to her handbag and a carry-on, for there were an extraordinarily large number of giant bags being squeezed into the baggage hold. She managed to find a window seat toward the back of the bus, next to a somewhat scruffy, sandy-haired young man, wearing khaki shorts, a khaki vest with multiple pockets, and a red bandana around his throat. The young man let her slip in, then sat down again and placed his large knapsack on the floor, squeezed between his sandled feet. Bennett felt suddenly foolish in her blue suit, white blouse, and flats; though the suit had been purposely chosen as a sign of the seriousness of her task. The flats were a concession to the expected poor condition of country roads.

"Are you going to the Mountains of the Moon too?" the young man asked.

"What do you mean?" Bennett raised her eyebrows, thinking the question odd.

"That's what they call the Rwenzori Mountains National Park," the young man explained.

"Oh. No, I'm not going to there. I suppose you are going on safari," Bennett added, looking at the binoculars hanging around the young man's neck.

"No, just trekking. Beautiful place, the Rwenzori Park. I've been there twice already."

"To see the gorillas?"

"No, you'd have to go the Mgahinga Park to see them—or Rwanda—and even then you'll only see them if you're lucky."

"Or unlucky. I wouldn't want to get too close."

The young man laughed. "Yes, that could be a problem. They are huge. Are you going on safari somewhere else then?

"Afraid not. I'd like to but I'm here for another reason."

"Business?"

"Not exactly."

The young man looked intrigued and Bennett was tempted to satisfy his curiosity, but the bus had started its engine and Bennett turned to look out the window. Joe hadn't talked much about Kampala, but after all that she'd read about it, she didn't want to miss anything.

Had Grace ever been to the capital? Did she know that, like Rome, the city was built on seven hills, and its name meant Hill of the Antelopes because the Buganda kings once grazed impala there?

If she was interested, Bennett could tell her what she'd learned—that in December of 1890 a British explorer named Captain Lugard hoisted the Imperial British East African Company flag and established a small fort. Out of that little administrative post, a small township developed which in time grew into modern Kampala.

Bennett was surprised at the variety of neighborhoods she passed—first by taxi and then on the bus—from sleek concrete and glass high-rises and hotels, to tree-lined streets with up-market houses, to large areas of potholed and unpaved congested streets overflowing with street markets, hustlers, and tin-roofed shanties. And everywhere, people walking, people on bicycles, people crowded into minibuses and motorbike taxis. The bus' progress was so excruciatingly slow at times that she feared they'd never make it out of the city let alone to their destination.

"I wonder if those are the bicycle taxis called *boda-bodas*," she said aloud, as they came to yet another stop. "I've read about them."

"Yes, that's right," the young man answered. "And those minibuses are called *matatus*. They're not the safest, but they're cheap and they'll usually get you where you want to go."

The greenness of the capital gave way to an even lusher and more verdant countryside. Bennett was struck by the rich redness of the soil that defined the unpaved roads and paths leading off the paved road they were on.

Round houses with wooden frames, mud walls, and grass-thatched roofs were scattered over the land on either side of the road, joined intermittently by clusters of roadside markets selling vegetables.

"I wonder why it still reeks of fish," Bennett whispered, after they'd long passed the markets.

The young man nodded in the direction of a woman sitting diagonally opposite. On her lap lay a large fish, its head and tail sticking out from its paper wrapping.

"Can't believe I didn't notice." Bennett laughed. "And what are those large piles of red bricks on the road? Are they for sale?" she asked. Happy the young man was so willing to satisfy her curiosity, she quickly lost her usual reluctance to ask questions.

"Probably not. Parents get together and make them out of mud, fire them in crudely fashioned kilns, and then use them to build village schools."

"What are they like, the schools?" Bennett asked, thinking of Grace.

"Depends. Most of them are one-story brick or cinderblock buildings, sometimes with only one room. Some are even more basic than that —tin roofs on sticks. But there are also some grander ones where the students can board. They all cost money, even the most basic."

Bennett hoped Grace had been to a good one.

"Where do you think they are going?" she said, pointing to people walking along the long roads with no obvious destination in sight.

"To work, probably. They come out of those huts ready to walk miles, dressed in spotless white shirts. If you look at the farmers, or the children, they are covered with red dust from the soil, yet somehow they can get their shirts completely white when they need to. I don't know how they do it."

"Are those plantains or bananas?" Bennett pointed to four men riding bicycles piled miraculously high with giant bunches of fruit.

"Those are matoke. It's the national food. They're cooked slowly, so they can be left to simmer while the people are out working and then they're served with sauces, or in stews or curries with other vegetables"

Bennett leaned back and looked at the young man with admiration.

"You certainly know this country well."

"Not really, but like you I ask a lot of questions."

"Oh, no, not like me at all. I don't usually," Bennett said, although she was pleased that the young man thought of her as someone who was curious. It made her feel interesting. But then, wasn't she already more interesting than before by being on a bus in Uganda?

She suddenly realized that the young man was still speaking.

" ...mostly, I know the Rwenzori and Queen Elizabeth Park, where you can see the animals, and I've stayed in a couple of towns. Are you going to Fort Portal? That's a rather pretty one."

"Is it? I read that in my guidebook, but I have to go to Kasese. I am looking for someone."

"Really? Who? I am going there, too."

"You're not familiar with the clinic there, by any chance?" Bennett ignored the young man's question. It didn't seem right to tell him about Grace.

"I'm afraid not. They have a couple of clinics, I believe, but thank goodness I haven't needed them."

"Where are you staying?"

"In a trekkers hostel. A bit primitive. You might prefer the resort outside of town. They have a swimming pool ..."

"Thanks, but I already have a reservation. A small hotel in the center, on Stanley Street."

"There's an internet cafe near the post office, in case you need that."

"I definitely will, the hotel doesn't have WiFi, at least not for their guests. I appreciate the information."

"No problem."

Bennett turned to look out the window again. Should she have booked the resort, after all?

A young boy leading a small herd of cows with incongruously long horns crossed the road, bringing the bus to a halt.

"They're so skinny," Bennett said, thinking out loud.

"They may look skinny, but they are a true measure of wealth here, and an important part of a bride's dowry."

As the bus pulled into Kasese in the early afternoon, a large sign indicated that they had crossed the equator. In the distance loomed the green Rwenzori Mountains. Bennett realized she'd dozed off after Fort Portal, and hoped she hadn't missed too much.

Unpaved streets and flat-roofed buildings greeted them as they disembarked.

"Reminds you of the Old West, doesn't it?" the young man said." You won't see any gunfights though. The people are very friendly and helpful. You just need to ask."

"Thank you," Bennett answered with a little laugh. "I must look worried. I guess you can tell I'm new at this. Traveling, I mean. I might not have come if it hadn't been for a friend—two friends, really—both much more daring than I. One has been around the world. A few times, probably... oh God, I'm babbling, aren't I? It's because it's my first trip out of the country, you see—not like you. You seem to have traveled a lot. I admire that."

"My parents would have preferred me to get a job but I wanted to see the world before I settled down. I spent a few months backpacking in Europe before I came to East Africa."

"By yourself?"

"Not for long, usually. You always meet people traveling. Two Australians I met in Prague are joining me in a couple of days. Hey, listen, would you like me to help you find your hotel? It's a bit of a walk from here."

"I don't want to impose ..."

"I'm glad to do it. I have nothing planned."

"Maybe you could show me the internet cafe on the way. I'd like to buy a phone, but I think I'd better check in first, and then go back."

"No problem."

"If you really don't have plans, would you like to meet for dinner later?"

"That'd be great. I know a little local place that's quite good." He extended his hand. "I'm Peter, by the way."

"I'm so sorry," Bennett replied, shaking Peter's hand. "I should have introduced myself. My name is Bennett. Bennett Hall."

"Glad to meet you, Bennett. How about 7:00 then? Give you time to settle in."

By the time Peter returned, looking washed and with a clean bandana around his throat, Bennett had acquired a mobile phone, and sent an email to Joe.

"I'm all set." Bennett grinned, feeling rather proud of herself. "The desk clerk even told me where the clinic is that I need to find tomorrow."

Peter laughed.

"You're doing pretty well for your first day as a traveler. Soon you'll be ready to try matoke stew and banana beer."

30

Bennett woke to the sound of voices outside her window. She pulled aside the curtain, as two women passed by, each balancing a basket of fruit on her head. The sun was bright and a wind rushed through the tall grass below. She was in Africa.

Eager to preserve every detail of her adventure, she unwrapped the leather-bound journal she'd bought for just that purpose and began to record the minutiae of her first day. But as she glanced over to her handbag, stuffed full with Joe's documents and adoption information, she took a deep breath. This trip was not about her. It was about Grace and Joe and Medi and Hope. No one cared what time her plane landed or her bus departed. She ripped the first page out of the journal and on a fresh page wrote: *Finding Grace.*

It should have taken her only fifteen minutes to walk the dusty path from the hotel to the medical clinic but, distracted by the unfamiliar sounds and smells, Bennett couldn't help but linger in the local market. The vendors were mostly women, dressed in long, colorfully printed cotton dresses, or T-shirts over long cotton skirts. Some had kerchiefs wrapped around their heads. Some stood chatting and laughing behind long rickety tables laden with local fruit or goat carcasses, while others sat quietly on straw mats next to their displays of patterned baskets. A few, with babies strapped to their backs, sought shade under cotton canopies from which a variety of African garments and hand-dyed cloths hung.

Should she buy one of the short-sleeved, elephant-print shirts? It was hot and Bennett could feel her long-sleeved button-down blouse beginning to cling to her back. Joe had warned her to only wear cotton. Or would she look foolish in an elephant shirt, when what she needed was to make a good if not imposing impression?

"What color?" a woman asked, stepping toward her, a half-dozen shirts in her hands. "Blue? Red? Green? Or stripes? I have stripes."

Bennett shook her head and hurried on. She was wasting time. What if Joe's nurse friend left before she got there, or wasn't there at all? Where could she go then? What if the nurse had bad news? What then?

"You're welcome," the receptionist said when she finally arrived at the clinic, sweaty and out of breath.

For what, Bennett wondered, then remembered that the desk clerk at the hotel had said the same thing. It must be a greeting, not a response. You are welcome here is what they must mean. She hoped it was true.

"Are you injured or ill?" the receptionist asked.

"Neither. I am looking for Hilda Muwango. I understand she is a nurse here. Joe Muir sent me."

The young woman's face broke into a delighted smile and she reached out to grasp Bennett's hand.

"Doctor Joe? You know him? Is he back? We have missed him. How is he, how are the children? You must tell us everything."

"He's very well, and the children are healthy and happy. I will tell Nurse Hilda all the details if you could tell her I am here."

"Hilda is not with us anymore. She has transferred to the new maternity clinic on Stanley Street. Do you know Stanley Street?"

Bennett nodded. "I just came from there. It's where my hotel is."

"Good. Then you will find her easily."

"I hope so. That is, I'm sure I will. Thank you."

Bennett shook the receptionist's hand and started to leave but then turned back to ask. "Will she be working today?"

"Yes, yes, I am sure of it. You must tell her we will want to hear all the news!"

Bennett smiled.

"I will. Thank you."

She wound her way back the way she'd come, passed her hotel, and walked on to the sand-colored, one-story building that held the maternity clinic.

"May I speak to Nurse Hilda Muwango?" she asked at the desk.

The receptionist looked puzzled.

"You have a patient here?"

"No, this is personal. Please tell her I am Joe Muir's friend. From the United States."

The receptionist gave Bennett one last quizzical look before she walked down the hall to one of the recovery rooms.

"She is busy with a patient," she said when she returned moments later. "She said I must tell you she will be most pleased to converse with you when she is finished. You will wait here?"

Bennett nodded and sat down on a nearby bench. Time seemed to stand still under the receptionist's unrelenting gaze, but in reality only ten minutes had passed when she saw a small, plump woman in a neat blue nurse's uniform hurrying down the hall in her direction, a small white cap wobbling precariously on her close-cropped hair.

"I am Hilda," she said, clasping Bennett's hand firmly in both of hers as she tried to catch her breath. "I am very sorry to keep you waiting."

"And I'm Bennett. I believe Joe emailed you that I was coming."

"Yes, finally I was able to receive it, and I am so pleased to meet you, but he did not tell me why you have come—only that you would explain. Is everyone well?"

"Oh yes, Joe and the children are doing very well. It's because of Grace that I am here. You remember, the older sister of the children?"

"Yes, I remember. Is there a problem with the school? Have they not received their fees?"

"No, the problem is that Grace left school. They said that it is not uncommon and usually temporary, but she never came back and no one has heard from her. Joe has been very worried and was hoping you might be able to help me find her."

"I have not had news of Grace for several months," Hilda said.

"Joe thought perhaps you might ask your relative—the one who lives in the same village as Grace's aunt."

"My nephew. I'm afraid he is no longer there and so I have had little news of the village. But Saturday is my day off so I will go there and see what I can learn."

Bennett could not hide her disappointment. "That's three days from now."

"I'm sorry, I cannot go before. Is it too late?" Hilda asked. "Do you have to leave before then?"

"No, I can wait ..."

"Good. Then on Saturday, I will take the earliest bus."

"No, please, let me hire a taxi for you."

"Then we will go together," Hilda said. "That would be best. If Grace is there you will be able to talk to her yourself. What will you do until then? There is nothing of great interest in Kasese ... perhaps you would like to go to Queen Elizabeth Park? Are you staying at the resort? They offer excursions from there."

"No, I'm in the little hotel down the street, but I'm sure they can—"

"I will arrange a driver for you. That would be best."

"I can do that. I don't want to impose."

"No, no, they will charge you a month's wages and then ask you to pay for their children's school fees. I know a driver who will be a good guide for you. The hotel can arrange your accommodation at the park. There is a very fine lodge there. I will also arrange for my friend to drive us on Saturday. We will meet at your hotel after breakfast. Now forgive me but I must return to my patients."

31

"I have arranged for you to stay at the Mweya Safari Lodge for the night," said the Indian desk clerk, who, it turned out, was also the hotel manager and concierge. "I have been told that Jacob will be your driver. He will come to take you to Queen Elizabeth Park tomorrow morning at seven. He will also take you on a safari drive in the evening, and again early the next morning, which are the best times to see the animals. Jacob is a very fine driver and very knowledgeable. He will explain everything. Then he will return you in the late afternoon and your room will be ready. Please let me know if there is any luggage you wish to leave here during your absence."

Bennett thanked him. She was relieved to have more time to steel herself for the visit to Grace's village. She knew that no matter how many times she rehearsed their meeting in her head, the reality would be nothing like what she'd imagined. It never was. Although she hadn't intended this to be a pleasure trip she had to admit she didn't mind having this unexpected diversion.

Jacob and his freshly washed but well-used Toyota Land Cruiser arrived promptly the next morning. He wore the traditional prerequisites for a safari: a khaki vest with several pockets, a white short-sleeved shirt, and khaki pants. Bennett was glad she'd thought to bring a casual skirt and top. A suit would certainly have been out of place.

An image flashed through Bennett's mind of sitting alone in the balcony of the old Odeon Theatre, watching a movie with Clark Gable as a big game hunter. She could almost hear the whirr of the 16mm movie projector, and see the sudden melting of Gable's face as the film got stuck and burned—something that happened far too frequently in the old theatre. She'd gone to the dollar movies most Saturdays when she was a child, until they tore the Odeon down and replaced it with an auto parts store. How long ago that was. Sometimes she had memories so vivid she could almost believe that, if she tried, she would be able to remember everything that had ever happened to her, though most of the time she tried not to remember. Why be reminded that she'd sat out of most of her life?

"Miss Hall?" Jacob said, breaking into Bennett's thoughts. "If you have finished breakfast, it will be my pleasure to introduce you to the treasures of Queen Elizabeth National Park." A broad smile brightened his dark, smooth face, a face that once again reminded Bennett that Medi and Hope had their roots here.

"And it will be my pleasure to see them," Bennett answered, returning the smile.

"I have brought along a pair of binoculars," Jacob said, "in case you do not have any, for we will see many beautiful birds in the park—over 600 species, more than in any other park in Africa."

Bennett walked to the right of the car and then again remembered that the passenger sat on the left.

"Are you a professor?" Jacob asked.

"No, why?"

"Your shoes. They are not the shoes of someone who goes on safaris."

Bennett laughed.

"No, you're right. I should have planned better."

"My father was a professor," Jacob went on, "at Makarere University in Kampala. It was known as the Oxford of Africa then."

"But not anymore? Why did it change?"

"Dictators don't like professors, Miss Hall, and we suffered some very bad years under two of them. You will have heard, I'm sure, of Idi Amin, and Obote, who followed him?"

Bennett nodded,

"My father lost his position—but not his life, as many others did. He had a family, and children who had to eat, so he became a driver. Sometimes a minibus or taxi, at times even as a chauffeur for those who flourished under the regime."

"I'm sorry." Bennett said.

Jacob shrugged. "Yes, it was sad, but that is life. You make the best of what you have, and do what you have to do. In time, my father was able to buy his own taxi. When he died it came to me, as the eldest. I would have preferred to be a professor myself, but I have children who like to eat also—so here I am." He turned to smile at Bennett. "It is not so bad. The sun is shining and there are many beautiful birds to admire. After all these years, I've come to know most of them. One could even say I've become a professor of birds."

Bennett felt a pang...of what? Embarrassment at how trivial her troubles had been compared to theirs? Or was it envy of their courage and resilience? Maybe if she'd been put to the test, she might have risen to...no, she knew she wouldn't have. Not then. And now? Would she be different now?

"I would like to see and learn as much as possible, Jacob, even if I only have two days," she said.

"Every moment counts. My father always said that knowledge is what makes life interesting and since I have a feeling you are not my usual tourist, we will begin with a visit to Katwe Village—not to be confused with the Katwe neighborhood of Kampala."

A foul smell filled their nostrils when they entered the village. Bennett held her nose. "It smells like rotten eggs."

Of all places, why would Jacob bring her here?

"It's the hydrogen sulfide from the salt ponds," Jacob explained. "Katwe Villagers have been harvesting salt from Lake Katwe for hundreds of years. Do you see those ponds along the side of the lake? Those are the salt gardens where the salt is produced by evaporation. The women work there, scraping the bottom, crushing the crystals with their feet, and washing them. The crystals then dry in the hot sun, and that is the salt we eat. The men extract salt from the salt rock in the lake. That is used for animals. One man can extract 1000 kilos a day. I hope one day it will be done by machines because the salt makes people sick. That and the mosquitos. Malaria is a continuing problem, as I'm sure you know."

"Is there no other work for them?"

"There is fishing, of course, but since there is a good market for the salt it is their main source of income, though now some of the women are also selling crafts to tourists. Are you interested in crafts?"

"I did promise to bring some dolls ..." It was the least she could do.

"I will take you to the market then," Jacob said. "You have a daughter? Or a granddaughter?"

"No, they are the daughters of friends."

"Of course, these are Ugandan dolls, made of cloth ..."

"Yes, that's exactly what I want. My friend's little girl Hope is Ugandan—from this part of Uganda, in fact."

"Hope? You don't mean Dr. Joe and Nurse Laurie's Hope?"

"You knew them?"

Jacob laughed.

"Do not be surprised. This is not Kampala. Everybody knew them here. It was a great loss to us when Nurse Laurie died and Doctor Joe left so soon after. Is it because of him that you have come? Did he speak well of our country?"

Bennett didn't know whether to tell Jacob about Grace. She didn't want news of her looking for Grace to get out before she had a chance to speak to her herself. It was best to say nothing for now.

"Yes, Joe often spoke of his time here and how much it meant to him."

"We must look for an especially nice doll then. I know just the right woman to ask."

The market turned out to be a field where large pieces of tie-dyed cloth were laid on the grass to dry. A group of children dressed in blue and yellow school uniforms sat cross-legged on the ground, weaving together mats of straw. Nearby, under a large striped umbrella, a barefoot woman was seated next to a large basket filled with hand sewn dolls. When she stood up, Bennett noticed that she had to support herself with a roughly-hewn cane.

After Jacob introduced her, Bennett picked out a brown cloth doll dressed in a green and white print dress, tied at the waist with a blue-striped strip of cloth, and then a second one for Maria's Isabella. The girls could play with them together. She picked out another one for Meyer Gold's collection and was about to ask how much they cost when she noticed a boy doll in an elephant-print shirt. Medi would like that.

"These are perfect," she said. "I'll take all four."

She pulled out a wad of Ugandan bills and handed them to Jacob.

"I hope that's enough."

～

It was a short drive to Mweya Lodge, which was perched picturesquely on a peninsula overlooking the Kazinga Channel and Lake Edward. Bennett had enough time to check in, wash up, and make reservations for dinner before Jacob returned for their evening drive.

Jacob followed one of the well-established animal viewing routes and pointed out the bushbucks, Defassa waterbucks, banded mongoose and warthogs hiding in the scrub.

"Kobs are the lion's favorite food," he said as a herd of the Uganda antelopes leapt across the savanna.

When a family of elephants made its way out of a clump of acacia trees, Jacob explained how so many of their number had been decimated during the Obote and Amin eras, and were still at risk because of poaching.

"We made great efforts to restore their number but the Chinese desire for ivory is a great threat," Jacob said, shaking his head with regret. "There are efforts to limit the demand, to stop illicit trafficking, but I'm sure you have heard of the mass slaughters that have taken place all over East Africa. It is a great tragedy."

At that moment, a mother elephant pushed her way out of a clump of trees and flapped her giant ears to warn the intruders not to come too close to her calf, a motherly gesture Bennett found deeply touching.

In the water and along the shore of the Kazinga Channel, Bennett recognized hippos, crocodiles, water buffalos, pelicans and giant egrets, but needed Jacob's expertise to identify saddlebills, storks, fish eagles, cormorants and kingfishers. The birds Bennett found most fascinating were the weavers who, with incomprehensible skill, built and balanced their nests on the thinnest blades of grass.

As they continued on their drive, Jacob's practiced eye identified an infinite number of other birds that Bennett could barely catch a glimpse of and whose names she'd never heard before and couldn't possibly remember.

Dinner in the dining room was tasty and enlivened by a demonstration of African dance, but Bennett retired to her comfortable room early so she could write down her impressions of the many things she'd seen and learned on this remarkable day. Writing of her experiences would help her tell the children about the beauties of Uganda when she got back. Unable to remember all the names she'd heard, she determined to buy a book about the wildlife that she could show them.

It was rainy season and early morning showers made the grass green and the air smell fresh. When she awoke shortly after sunrise, Bennett opened the patio door to find a half dozen warthogs sprawled on the grass under the jacaranda trees. Startled, she slammed door shut and walked out the front instead, where Jacob and his Land Cruiser were already waiting.

"I'm glad you're early," Jacob said. "The lions are out this morning and if we go now we can see them."

Again they passed herds of graceful Uganda kobs grazing on the savanna.

"They're eating peacefully now," Jacob explained. "but they'll run like the wind when the lionesses get hungry and start chasing them."

For now the lionesses were content to perch on termite hills, or lie in the grass with their cubs. An old male lion that Jacob called Abraham lay quietly nearby.

"I guess, he's not as dangerous as the young males," Bennett said.

"Just the opposite, my friend," Jacob laughed. "Old lions who are too weak to chase a kob might find *you* quite tempting."

Also walking through the grass were the regal crested cranes. One of the craftswomen in Katwe had made miniature cranes out of straw and grasses and bits of wire. Bennett had bought one but had assumed they were creatures from her imagination. How little she knew about this world.

Baboons raced across their path, monkeys screeched in the distance. The sounds and sights left Bennett with a sense of wonder that only increased when they repeated the drive at dusk and again at dawn the next morning. She envied Jacob his intimate familiarity with this magical world.

She knew these two short days would be slow to fade from her memory.

32

"I hope I am not late," Hilda said, as she hurried into the hotel lobby where Bennett was waiting.

"Not at all. Jacob's not here yet so we still have time for a cup of coffee. Or chai? Joe told me you might prefer that."

Hilda laughed. "Doctor Joe was always good about learning our customs. Have you tried it?"

"Not yet. I'm not sure I'd like milk and spices in my tea, but I'll try it if you're having some. When in Rome and all that ..."

"Actually, nothing for me, thank you. Before Jacob comes: I hope you do not mind, but I have told him about our search for Grace. You can trust him."

"I was thinking of doing it myself today."

Jacob arrived a few minutes later and they began their bumpy forty-five minute drive over dusty, unpaved roads to the little village where Grace's great-aunt lived. A cluster of round, grass-roofed mud huts on one side of the road contrasted with the tin-roofed mud bungalows on the other. A handful of old women squatted on the ground watching a half-dozen children kicking around a hard-shelled fruit of some kind. A young woman with an infant strapped to her back washed clothes in a basin on the ground, hanging them to dry on a rope strung between two trees. Five goats nibbled lazily on a clump of grass, while two chickens pecked at fallen seeds.

"Why are there so few people?" Bennett whispered.

"The others are working in the fields," Hilda replied. "This is a poor village. They eat what they grow. They do not even have a well, as you can see, only that muddy stream. It is the reason my nephew left. There are no opportunities here."

"Where is he now?"

"In Fort Portal. He is an apprentice in a garage."

Hilda got out of the car, walked over to the old women and squatted down to talk to them. Bennett stayed back with Jacob, catching only a few unintelligible sounds as one of the women shook her head. The others nodded in apparent agreement.

After a few minutes, Hilda gestured for Bennett to join her.

"Bad news, I'm afraid. Grace's aunt died about three weeks ago. Grace had been taking care of her for several months, which must be why she left school."

"Where is she now?"

"I will ask, but they may not know."

Hilda addressed the old woman again, and listened patiently as the woman spoke in a tired voice and pointed down the road. Hilda thanked her and gently put her arm around the woman's shoulder. Bennett nodded and mouthed her thanks.

"She said," Hilda explained, as they walked back to Jacob and the car, "that a man has been going to village funerals looking for orphan girls and widows, and offering them jobs. They warned Grace not to go with a man she did not know, but she said she had no choice. She had no family left and needed to work."

"Do they know where she went?"

"They heard the man say something about Fort Portal."

"That's where we'll go then," Bennett said, opening the car door.

"We don't know know where to look," Hilda said, putting her hand on Bennett's arm. "For now it's best we return to Kasese. I will call my nephew. He may know something that will help us find her."

Bennett sighed. She should have known her rescue mission could not succeed so easily. Grace was missing, not just absent from school. Ignorant and completely reliant on others, Bennett had no clue as to what to do next.

They drove back to Kasese in silence.

After dinner in the hotel dining room, Bennett recorded the bare facts of their failed journey. She would wait until morning to email Joe. She'd tell him that they were following a lead, and that she would let him know when they knew something more definite. Afraid anxiety would make her toss and turn all night, swelling into full-fledged panic by dawn, she took a sleeping pill and went to bed.

She woke early the next morning, worrying about what to write Joe, when she heard a knock at her door.

"Miss Hall, you have a visitor downstairs. She says it is important."

Bennett flung on her skirt and top and rushed down to find Hilda sitting in the lobby in her nurse's uniform.

"I am sorry to bother you so early, Bennett, but I am on my way to work. I spoke to my nephew last night. There is a man in Fort Portal, he says, who has been bringing young village girls to work in bars. He tells them they will be well-paid waitresses in fine restaurants but he has something else in mind. My nephew does not know yet where the bars are or if Grace is in one of them, but it is a possibility."

"My God, she's only thirteen! We have to get her away from there. I'll leave right away. Is there a bus that goes there?"

"There should be one this morning. You can ask at the desk. They will know." Hilda glanced down at her watch. "I wish I could go with you but I must go to work and I am already late. I have written down my mobile number as well as my nephew's. Call him when you arrive in Fort Portal. Perhaps he can find out where the bars are—but you must not go there yourself. I have given you Jacob's mobile. He is a good man and will come and help you if you need it. Please call me as soon as you know anything."

Bennett clasped Hilda's hands in hers.

"Thank you. Joe said you were a good friend. I'll call as soon as I can."

Bennett asked the desk clerk for the bus schedule and told him she was checking out. The local was leaving in an hour, the clerk said. That gave Bennett barely enough time to pack and send a message to Joe. Despite her fears, she felt energized by this sudden call to action.

33

Only after Bennett found a seat on the crowded bus did she consider how completely unprepared she was for this sudden change of plans. Except for Peter's comment that Fort Portal was a pretty town, she knew little about the place she was now racing toward, so she pulled out her guidebook and started reading. Fort Portal, it said, was the only Ugandan town with an English name, and was named for Sir Gerald Portal, the British Special Commissioner. Bennett noted that they hadn't renamed it after independence, so Portal must have been an Englishman they liked. The town was known for its fine tea, which was grown in the high green hills just outside of it, beyond which loomed the Rwenzori Mountains. All this was of no importance, of course, to the search for Grace, but reading it soothed her nerves—until she started worrying whether and where she would find a room. Flipping anxiously through the guidebook, she was reassured to read that there were several reasonably priced possibilities in the center of town. When the bus made a stop she called and reserved a room in one of the guest houses that had internet.

Bennett's confidence in the guidebook was somewhat shaken when they entered the town. The book had clearly stated that there was not much traffic and it was safe to hire a boda boda to get around, yet the streets were crowded with bicycles, motorcycles, trucks, and cars. Lining both sides were rows of garages and long stretches of open air markets selling food, tires, and clothing piled up on blankets on the ground. After they crossed the river the streets became more orderly, with shops in what Bennett would now describe as proper buildings. She smiled as she looked out the window. Amazing how one's views of what is proper could change in a few short days.

The room she'd reserved was as described in the guide—sunny and pleasant, overlooking a patio, with private bath and mosquito netting over the bed. She took not being disappointed as a good omen.

After checking in and ordering a cup of the famous Fort Portal tea, Bennett called Hilda's nephew Isaac.

"I believe your aunt Hilda explained the situation to you," Bennett said, after their initial hellos and introductions. "I'd appreciate any help you might give me in finding Grace."

"I will do anything I can. Grace's aunt was of my village and I have known Grace since she was a small child and came to visit with her parents," Isaac replied. "When my aunt told me about the man who came to the village, I asked the other mechanics if they knew of him. They hear things. Men who have good cars and money to spend like to talk. My friends say there are two bars where those men go, and where sometimes foreigners go—foreigners who like African girls, especially young ones. I think we might find her there."

Bennett's heart sank.

"One bar is in the center of town, near your hotel," Isaac went on. "We can go immediately. I will explain to my boss."

"It is tempting to rush over, I agree, but it's not enough to find her. We have to have a way to take her with us. We have to have a plan. I will figure something out."

"You will need a car. My garage will rent you one."

"Yes ... no, how would I get her to Kampala?... I will call Jacob. He will help. Will you come to my hotel after work? I will have a plan by then."

Bennett's hands felt damp and shaky, as if her body knew how unfounded her confidence was. She had no plan, no idea for one, but she knew that whatever they came up with might be their only chance to find Grace.

She wiped her hands on her jeans, pulled out her phone and called Jacob.

"Thank God, you're there, Jacob, I—"

"I've been expecting your call. Hilda told me you went to Fort Portal. What hotel are you in? I will meet you there as soon as I can."

Bennett hung up, and ignoring the heat of the midday sun, took a long walk to think. By the time she returned, she had developed a plan. The only detail missing was the essential one—how to get Grace out of the bar once they found her.

Isaac and Jacob arrived at almost the same time. They agreed it was best to talk in Bennett's room where no one could hear them.

"I was thinking I could say I am her teacher and I have come to take her back to school," Bennett said.

"They won't care," Issac said.

"Oh. Then I will tell them I am looking for help in my hotel."

"They will say that you cannot steal their help, you must find your own," Jacob said. "But I can say I am her father and she must come home with me."

"They know she's an orphan," Isaac said.

"Then I will be a customer," Jacob said. "They will believe that."

"You will have to bring a great deal of money," Isaac said. "Only rich men go there."

"Let's hope it won't get that far," Bennett said, swallowing hard, her stomach churning at the thought of Jacob asking for that poor child as if she were a piece of merchandise. "But if it does, I will give you the money." She suddenly felt she'd stepped into an old gangster movie. "But are you sure it is not too dangerous, Jacob? I do not want to put you in danger."

"It is the child that is in danger, Miss Hall. I have a young daughter and it makes me sick to think something like this could happen to her. I am also concerned for Grace's health. Too many of our men refuse to use condoms. They are foolish and one of the reasons we have so many people with AIDS….Isaac, you will come with me."

"They will never believe I am a man who can afford to go to a bar like that."

"But without you I won't recognize Grace."

There was silence as Isaac pondered this. Then he smiled. "I know! You can say I am your driver and you want to buy me a drink. Then I will look for Grace and tell you which one she is."

"That's good," Bennett said, "but if she reacts when she recognizes you, it might get her into trouble."

Again there was silence.

"No, she is a quiet girl and she will be careful. I will too, but I must talk to her and tell her who Jacob is. Then when he asks for her, she will not be afraid."

"We have to decide what we do once we have found her. And we have to work fast," Bennett replied, now more worried than ever. "It's after six o'clock already."

"I cannot go like this," Isaac said, looking down at his grease-stained mechanic's uniform. I will change and be back as soon as I can."

Jacob loaded Bennett's bags into his car, while they discussed where they should go after they got Grace away from the bar.

"Kampala is too far," Jacob said. "We would arrive there in the middle of the night. I think we must stop in Mubende. While we wait for Isaac, I will call a friend there who has a small resthouse. I'm sure he will put us up. It is a simple place, but clean and safe."

Isaac arrived shortly before seven, wearing a khaki vest, white shirt and khaki pants. He looked over at Jacob and smiled proudly.

"Do I not look like the driver of a rich tourist?"

Jacob laughed, while Bennett smiled back distractedly, her mind occupied with making sure they had considered and resolved every possible obstacle to their plan. Once she was confident they had, she called Joe.

"I was going to email you after we got to Kampala," she told him, after explaining the details of their plan, "but although I think we have everything covered I thought you needed to know exactly what we were doing, just in case."

"I'm really grateful, Bennett, but are you sure you should go right to Kampala? It may be too sudden. Who knows what the poor child has been through already? She needs to feel safe. Don't you think you should take her to Hilda's first? She'll feel much safer with a woman, especially a nurse. There's so much she doesn't know about us and will have to understand before you change her life again."

"I'm an idiot ..." Bennett stammered. "I should have realized."

"God no, Bennett, I didn't mean that. You've been wonderful and your plan will work, I know it. I was only concerned about afterwards ..."

"I understand, Joe, and we'll call Hilda. Everything will be all right." She wiped the perspiration from her brow and hoped her voice did not betray her, for she was not sure at all that they could do this.

"Be careful, Bennett. You don't know what kind of people you are dealing with."

"Jacob and Isaac are doing the hard part. I'll be in touch tomorrow. Try not to worry."

Bennett said goodbye and repeated Joe's concern to Jacob and Isaac.

Jacob nodded. "He is right. But first we must get her away from where she is."

"All right, then," Bennett said, feeling her determination return. "Everything stays the same, except that we will drive to Kasese instead of Mubende when it's over."

"I will call my aunt and tell her to expect you," Isaac added.

"And I will cancel our rooms in Mubende," Jacob said.

"I'll call my hotel in Kasese and make sure they still have a room for me. What would we do without cell phones?"

34

Jacob pulled into the parking lot of a small restaurant close to but not visible from The Victoria Bar. Bennett suggested they order something to eat. It was eight o'clock.

"Isaac will drive you around the corner to the bar," Bennett said, "and leave the key under the passenger seat. Whoever is looking will see that he was your driver, and that you are walking into the bar together. I will wait here in the restaurant until you or Isaac call me. Then I will meet Grace and Jacob at the car and we will leave for Kasese immediately. Isaac, you will stay in the bar until they have left, in case you need to distract anyone."

They nodded in agreement, and there was a momentary silence. They still had almost two hours to kill. Jacob asked Isaac how he liked his job at the garage. Isaac asked Jacob how his children liked school. Bennett tried to listen but was startled and distracted every time the door opened and someone came in or went out. What had she gotten them into? Why had she involved these men? She had no right to put them in danger. Jacob had a family and Isaac wasn't much more than a boy himself. What if the poor girl refused to go with Jacob? There was no way he could just drag her out. It could escalate into a shoot out. Or did people not have guns here and used machetes to chop off limbs instead?

"Are you all right, Bennett?" Jacob asked. "You don't look well."

Bennett took a handkerchief out of her handbag and wiped her face.

"I'm fine, just hot. It's muggy, don't you think?"

"I brought some cards." Jacob said. "We can play poker. It will make the time go faster."

Between hands of seven and five-card stud, Bennett looked at her watch until at last she saw it was almost time to set their plan in motion.

"Let's go over it one more time. Isaac, remember, don't attract attention to yourself. You don't really know Jacob and are only with him because he insisted on buying you a drink. But don't drink, stay alert. And when you leave, go directly home, unless you think someone is following you. Then go to where there are a lot of people and stay there until you feel safe."

Bennett handed Jacob enough money to pay for drinks and Grace, and watched through the restaurant window as Isaac parked in an unlit section of the bar's parking lot but near enough to the entrance that Jacob and Grace could leave quickly.

It took some moments for Jacob to adjust his eyes to the Victoria Bar's smoke-filled, dimly lit room. To the right of the door, pairs of gold carved chairs with leopard print upholstery huddled together in contrived intimacy. Opposite, in front of a gold-flecked, mirrored wall was a long, ornately carved bar. In the center of the room, placed at different angles, were four love seats upholstered in red velvet and trimmed with gold braid and fringe, each with its own small, candle-lit, marble-topped table. Women of various ages and shapes, clad in short, tight-fitting skirts or shorts that would have seen their like in any red light district in the world, were strategically placed around the room.

"Do you see her?" Jacob murmured, as he sat down at one of the small tables and blew out the candle.

Isaac shook his head. "They are all much older. Should I ask for her?"

"No, it's better I do it. You go sit at the bar."

Jacob felt a hand stroke his neck as a woman leaned seductively over him, her low-cut blouse providing a generous view of her ample breasts.

"Buy me a drink, won't you."

"What would you like?" Jacob asked.

"The whisky is very good. For you too?"

"Yes, I'll have the same."

"Wait for me, I'll be right back," she said and smiled, her eyes expressionless.

"No hurry," he said, as calmly as he could. "I'm not going anywhere."

As Jacob watched her amble toward the bar and back, he saw Isaac slip off his bar stool and take two drinks to a woman seated at a table in the corner, but it was too dark for him to make out what she looked like.

Moment later, the ample-breasted woman was back.

"Here's your drink. My name is Lucille, what's yours?"

She sat down next to him, and put her hand on his thigh.

"Moses" he answered. "But I was looking for someone younger. Very young, if you know what I mean."

She pulled her hand away.

"This is not that kind of place, we do not have children here. But do not worry, I can do anything a young girl can do, only better."

Jacob glanced over at Isaac and saw him put something in the unseen woman's hand and then nod in the direction of the door.

"I'm sure you can. Perhaps another time. Enjoy your whisky."

Jacob put some money on the table next to his untouched drink and walked briskly out the front door.

"Why were you talking to that woman?" Jacob asked as Isaac came out.

"Because she was old and I thought she might be sympathetic if I told her I was looking for my sister. I gave her some money and she said to look in The Gentleman Bar. They like young girls and we might find her there. It's a bad place, though. She said she heard they drugged the girls if they resisted."

Jacob felt his heart drop into his stomach.

"Hurry, let's get Bennett. Do you know where the bar is?"

"Yes. It's not far. It's the other one my friends mentioned."

Again, Isaac drove, this time with Bennett in the back seat. He positioned the car in a dark corner of the parking lot adjacent to the bar, as far as possible from the rusty cars and trucks already parked there. As soon as the two men entered the bar, Bennett moved to the front seat, and slouched down, to make herself as invisible as possible.

The Gentleman Bar was a misnomer. Inside of what was once a small warehouse, squeezed between a supermarket and tire shop, its small sign lost among larger, brighter signs pointing to hotels in town, the bar attracted a rougher clientele than The Victoria. Bare light bulbs hung from the ceiling, giving the interior a dim yet harsh look. The furniture was similar to that in The Victoria except that the gilt had long worn off the chair frames, and the upholstery was stained and threadbare. The bar was made of crudely varnished plywood, and the girls who stood around it were young and gaunt, as if they hadn't eaten a proper meal in a long time, reminding Jacob of the scraggly cats he often saw foraging for food in the garbage cans behind hotels. He felt his stomach knot.

"Do you see her?" he whispered to Isaac.

"No. What should we do? Will you ask for her?"

"Not yet." Jacob feared that Grace would appear with a client, having returned from whatever bug-infested place she would have had to take him. The thought made him ill, but it might make it easier to leave with her if they thought he was her next client. He picked out a table in the center of the room and gestured to Isaac to sit down. He leaned over and whispered, "I'll go get us drinks. You keep your eyes open."

Jacob sat down at the bar, put down some money, asked for two whiskies, and carried them back to the table.

At the next table, a girl who looked no older than fifteen sat with an older white man who was clearly drunk and had tattoos up and down his arms and all along his neck. He tried to support his head with his hand, but his elbow kept slipping off the edge of the table, finally causing him to spill his drink on the girl, which caused her to jump up and cry out.

"Grace!" the bartender shouted. "Get in here and clean this up."

A narrow stream of light streaked across the floor as the door to the kitchen opened, illuminating a slender young girl with short, cropped hair. Rag in hand, she rushed to clean up the spill.

Jacob grabbed Isaac's leg under the table and nodded in the girl's direction.

Isaac rose from his chair.

Jacob grabbed his hand and pulled him back. "Not yet," his voice barely above a whisper.

They sat motionless as Grace wiped the table and then the floor. As she stood up and was about to return to the kitchen, Jacob knocked over his whisky.

"Come over here, girl, and clean this up," he said roughly.

Her eyes downcast, Grace walked toward their table. Only then did she notice Isaac. Her eyes filled with tears.

"Don't say anything, Grace," Isaac murmured. "You trust me, don't you? We're going to get you out of here. Is there a back door to the kitchen?"

She nodded.

"Go out that way, but don't run. Pretend you have to spill out some dirty water. We'll meet you there." Gesturing toward Jacob, he added "He's a friend."

Grace wiped their table, and slowly walked back to the kitchen.

"I feel sick," Jacob said loudly, slurring his words and stumbling as he stood up. "You'd better take me back."

Isaac held him by the elbow and led him out the door.

As soon as the door closed, Jacob rang Bennett, then ran behind Isaac down the dark alley behind the bar. It took them a moment to find Grace, who was cowering, trembling, behind a stack of empty liquor cartons. Seconds later, Bennett arrived with the car. There was a loud rumble of thunder and a streak of lightning just as Isaac helped Grace slip into the back seat.

Bennett opened the front car door to move to the back. In the window she saw the reflection of a man yelling, lunging toward her, a knife in his hand. Bennett whirled around, swung her oversized handbag, and with a loud noise she took for another crack of lightening, felt it land on the side of the man's face. A sudden downpour made the man's feet slide from underneath him and he fell, giving Bennett, Jacob and Isaac enough time to get into the car. The wheels squealed in protest as Jacob pressed down hard on the accelerator and careened around the corner.

"We're taking Isaac home first, Grace," Bennett said, barely able to breathe. Never in her life had she felt such a rush of adrenalin. "Then we're going to Kasese to your mother's friend Hilda. It should only take a couple of hours."

She patted Grace's leg and was dismayed to see her wince.

What must she be thinking, forced into a car with two strange men, and a white woman who had just knocked a man to the ground? She was probably terrified. But Bennett couldn't explain everything to her now, not in the car, in the dark. Why would Grace believe her anyway? She was a complete stranger. Joe was right. It would have been disastrous to go to Kampala like this. She was an idiot.

She had no idea how to comfort the poor child. And her shoulder was throbbing.

She turned and saw Jacob looking in the rearview mirror and knew that he could see Grace. Her back was straight and stiff, and she sat as far from Bennett as she could. Her hands were in her lap, her right tightly clutching her left, as if to give it courage and support.

"Do not worry, my child," Jacob said. "You are safe now. We are taking you to Nurse Hilda's house. She was a friend to your parents when they were ill. She will take good care of you."

After a while Grace's shoulders relaxed and she stopped staring out of the window. Leaning back, she closed her eyes.

"Thank you, Jacob," Bennett whispered softly after she was sure Grace was asleep. "Oh, and Jacob, what does *muzungu* mean?"

Jacob smiled.

"Did that man call you that? It's what they call white people, but it means a man who wanders aimlessly."

Not so aimlessly anymore, Bennett thought.

35

"It's good to have you back, Miss Hall," the desk clerk said as Bennett passed through the Stanley Street Hotel lobby on her way to breakfast.

"And very nice to be back," Bennett replied. "Almost like being home."

What a silly thing to say. How could a small hotel in Africa she'd only stayed in a couple of days feel like home when she'd never felt at home in the house she'd lived in most of her life?

She sat down at a table for one by the window. Lulled by the warmth of the sun on her back, she ate breakfast and read the morning paper, putting aside for a moment the knowledge that getting Grace out of The Gentleman Bar was only the beginning of what she'd come to Uganda for. What she had imagined and hoped for was real now. With a lot of help, she had found Grace, though they had barely spoken on the drive from Fort Portal to Hilda's house. Not knowing how to break the silence, she'd been relieved when Grace fell asleep, her head coming to rest on her shoulder. Isaac had told her only that Bennett was a friend. Today she'd have to explain the rest.

She wondered if the poor girl realized how lucky she was that the man hadn't taken her to some bar in Kampala. They might never have found her there. Even so, she must be frightened. Bennett hoped she could prepare her for all the changes still to come. It would be a mistake to underestimate the effect that leaving a place that had always been her home would have on her. And there was still the devastating possibility that she would convince Grace and then her efforts to make it happen would fail. What then? Would it be better not to say anything yet? No, that wasn't possible. There was no way she could proceed without Grace's agreement. The authorities—neither Ugandan nor American—would ever allow her to take the child to the United States without her permission. Bennett had to make it work. She'd promised Joe.

Bennett walked up to the mosquito netting hanging loosely in the doorway of Hilda's small cinder block house. Nervous perspiration trickled its way down her sides. This was it. This was the moment she would have to talk to Grace in the light of day and tell her everything Joe and she had planned for her.

"Hello?"

"Come in, Bennett, I'm glad you're here." Hilda pushed the netting aside. "Grace is washing up so we have a few minutes to talk."

"How is she?"

"Thanks to God, she seems all right. We had a long talk when she woke this morning. I explained to her that I am Isaac's aunt."

"Did she ... was she forced to ...?"

Hilda lowered her voice to a whisper. "The good Lord watched out for her. Grace had injured her thigh when she was at her aunt's, and when she arrived in Fort Portal the man saw that her wound was oozing. He got angry, she said, and slapped her and told her that she was useless to him like that. But, it meant that she was sent to work in the kitchen until it got better. Of course, it didn't get better because no one took care of it."

"And now?"

"I have cleansed it with antiseptic and will bring some antibiotic cream from the clinic today. It is not as bad as it looked at first. It will heal quickly now."

"Does she realize what kind of place she was in?" Bennett asked.

"I do not think she fully understood, but I am not sure. She doesn't want to talk about it."

"Does she know about Joe, and why I'm here?"

"Not yet. Her aunt told her nothing, it seems, only that her parents had died. Grace thinks it was her aunt who paid for school. When her aunt died Grace thought her school days were over, which is why she didn't go back."

"Poor child. Has she asked about Medi and Hope?"

Hilda shook her head.

"She doesn't realize we know anything about them."

Hearing the soft sound of footsteps, Hilda turned to see Grace standing in the doorway. She had changed into a fresh T-shirt and long, dye-tied skirt. Beads of water glistened on her short, cropped hair.

"Come in, child," Hilda said, taking her by the hand. "Bennett has much to tell you."

Bennett stood up and smiled.

"Good morning, Grace, you look refreshed. I hope you slept well."

Grace nodded but did not return her smile.

"You know something about my brother and sister?" she asked, looking first at Hilda and then Bennett. She had overheard them.

"They are well," Bennett replied.

Hilda patted the chair next to hers.

"Come, let us sit. You sit by me, child, and Bennett will explain everything."

Grace listened intently as Bennett faced her across the table and recounted, as simply and gently as she could, how Joe and his wife had cared for her parents; how, having taken Medi and Hope into their hearts, they couldn't bear to see them living in an orphanage; how they went and got them, and adopted them so that they would always have a home; how, when Joe's wife died, Joe felt it was time to return home to America and begin a new life there with the children.

Grace turned away as a tear trickled down her cheek.

"Oh, my dear, don't be sad."

"I am not sad. I am happy they are well. I am big so they did not want me. I understand."

"Oh no, Grace, that's not how it was at all. I didn't explain it right. Joe didn't know about you. He would never have left you behind had she known."

"It's true," Hilda said. "I didn't know myself until another nurse who knew your mother well told me that you were living with your mother's aunt. When she told me the name of the village I realized it was the one my nephew Isaac lived in. Joe and the children were already in Kampala and were leaving for America the next day when I found out. There was nothing Joe could do."

"He didn't forget you—ever," Bennett broke in. "Even from so far away, Joe kept the promise he had made to your parents, that their children would go to school. Once he learned about you, he arranged to pay your school fees until he could arrange for you to join him in America."

"He paid for my school?" Grace asked, as she wiped her tears with the back of her hand.

"Yes, and the school told him you were doing well. When you stopped going they didn't tell him right away and when they did he didn't know how to reach you. That's why I have come—to find you and bring you to America so that you can be with Medi and Hope. I am going to do all I can to make that happen as soon as possible."

Hilda took the girl's hands in hers.

"It's true, Grace. I have talked to Joe myself."

"And look, I've brought some pictures to show you," Bennett said, passing Grace the album she had so carefully put together in preparation for this moment.

Grace turned the pages and looked with wonder at the photographs of Medi and Hope in their room, in their garden, in school, at an amusement park, on the lap of a strange man with long white beard and a red suit. Silently she let her fingers trace the outlines of her siblings' faces.

"They have grown. Do they have a picture of me?"

"Not yet," Bennett said, reaching into her pocket for her phone. "But I can take one of you right now and send it to them with my phone. They will be so happy to see your face."

Grace straightened her back and looked with great seriousness at the phone.

"May I see it?" she asked.

"Of course," Bennett said, turning the phone around. "You know, Medi told me all about the time you helped him catch a really big frog."

"He remembers me?"

"He certainly does, my dear. He certainly does ... here, let me take another picture," she said, this time capturing Grace's smile. "I will send them when I return to the hotel."

Barely an hour had passed since Bennett walked through the curtained doorway of Hilda's house, yet she knew that for Grace everything had changed.

36

"When are you leaving for Kampala?" Hilda asked, once it became clear that Grace was eager to join her siblings.

"I'm not sure," Bennett answered. "I've gone through all my notes and the first thing we have to do is to go to the Probation and Social Welfare Office. I was thinking that that might be easier to do here than in Kampala."

"Let me talk to our priest first. Father James knows his way around the Department of Youth and Child Affairs and he'll know who you should talk to. It might even be best if he made the appointment for you."

Bennett nodded and rose to leave.

"In that case, he may have to see all the documents. I'd better go get them."

Hilda turned to Grace and asked if she would mind going with Bennett while she tracked down Father James.

Bennett noticed a flicker of fear in Grace's eyes.

"Will we come back?"

"Of course," Bennett reassured her. "My hotel is not far. We won't be long at all."

"Neither will I," Hilda added.

Bennett and Grace set off for Stanley Street a few minutes later.

"This must all be very confusing for you," Bennett said. "If you have any questions, you mustn't be afraid to ask me. I will answer everything as honestly as I can."

Grace considered this offer for a few moments and then asked, timidly, "Will I be able to go to school in America?"

"Of course. All the children go to school."

"Even the girls? My aunt said girls must learn to do a woman's work at home, not go to school. Was it wrong what she said?"

Bennett hesitated. "Things have changed since your aunt was young, especially for girls. People know now that when girls go to school it's good for everyone."

Grace looked down and kicked a pebble out of her way.

"Will Dr. Joe still pay my fees?"

"There won't be any. Public schools are free. Until university anyway, but you don't have to worry about that yet."

"Can I become a nurse like Hilda?" she asked, after she'd given Bennett's words some thought.

"You can be anything you want to be."

Grace's face broke into a grin and her step quickened.

"Did you come to Uganda in an airplane?" she asked, now more curious than anxious.

"Yes."

"Were you afraid?"

"I was the first time I flew, but it's not so different from being on a bus."

Grace's eyes narrowed. She was skeptical.

"Except that you're in the sky and not on a road, of course, " Bennett added, "but it's beautiful to fly over the clouds, and when you are lower to the ground you can see the countryside and towns and villages just like a bird sees them."

"How many days will it take?" Grace asked, her interest growing with every word.

"Only one," Bennett explained. "Then when we get to the U.S. Joe will meet us at the airport and drive us home in his car."

"Do you live with them?"

"I live next door. That is, it's one house but it has two parts, and they live in one part and I live in the other."

"Is it beautiful like Hilda's?"

"I think you will like it," Bennett said, thinking how small and plain Hilda's cinder block house was, and how unfinished many Ugandan houses looked to American eyes.

As they reached the hotel, Hilda called her.

"Father James said you should talk to Cedric Bisikwa because he's honest; he called him an island of integrity. He's made an appointment for you for tomorrow afternoon at two. You will need all your documents. And he will want to talk to Grace."

"Of course. I will tell her."

"What will you tell me?" Grace asked.

"That we have an appointment tomorrow. Will you be happy to go to America, Grace? When we talk to the officials about the adoption, they will want to know how you feel about it."

"I will tell them," she said, "that my family is waiting for me."

Bennett hooked Grace's arm in hers and patted her hand.

"You're right. It's as simple as that."

Yet Bennett knew that to be as brave as this child was not simple at all.

Longing to hear Joe's voice, Bennett decided to bring him up to date by phone this time.

"She's a lovely child, Joe."

"Do you really think they'll let her come?"

"We have all the documentation we need, and we're meeting with an official the local priest thinks is honest. I think that bodes well, don't you?""

"It's not always that simple ... oh my God, Bennett, I just realized that you don't have Grace's birth certificate. You will need that. How could I have forgotten?"

As his words tumbled out, she could picture Joe pacing back and forth, switching the phone from his left ear to his right and back again as he always did.

"I'll take care of it. Don't get upset. I'll go to the records office where she was born."

"No, that would take too long. It took me a month to get Medi and Hope's. Go to the school. They should have one from when she enrolled. I should have made sure I had a copy."

"OK, will do. I'll keep you posted ... Joe? I'm losing the connection."

Afraid the school wouldn't give her the birth certificate, Bennett called and said she was the headmistress of Grace's new school and needed the certificate to complete her registration. She was told that they would have it ready for her courier to pick up in the morning.

Clearly a headmistress wouldn't go herself, and they'd never believe she was the courier, so she asked Jacob to stop at the school the next day before taking her and Grace to Cedric Bisikwa's office.

They arrived early. With the hope that it would be merely a matter of checking all the necessary forms and papers and asking Grace if she was in agreement—none of which should take too long—Bennett asked Jacob if he would mind waiting for them.

There were several people in the waiting room but, apparently, they were all there without appointments, for Bennett and Grace were shown in ahead of them at precisely two o'clock.

"Is your husband with you, Mrs. Hall?" Mr. Bisikwa asked, after the initial introductions were made.

"I am not married, but I'm not the one who is adopting Grace. I am here as a representative of Dr. Giordano Muir, who is the adopted father of Grace's siblings and would like to adopt Grace as well."

When Mr. Bisikwa did not respond, Bennett pulled out her folder of documents.

"Yes, I see, you have documents," Mr. Bisikwa said, scowling, "but it is most irregular and, I must say, inappropriately nonchalant, for the parents not to be here when requesting an adoption—especially a foreign adoption. We are not handing out prizes, you know."

"I understand," Bennett said, "but it is difficult for Dr. Muir to come with his children at this time, and Mrs. Muir is no longer with us." When Mr. Bisikwa did not respond, she added, "She died here in Uganda, because she was serving selflessly as a nurse to your countrymen."

Mr. Bisikwa glared at her.

"That's all well and good, but if it is too difficult for Dr. Muir to present himself, perhaps it is also too difficult for him, a widower, to support another child."

"No, you ... I didn't mean ... if you would just look at the documents."

Mr. Bisikwa raised his open hand.

"There is no need for me to see them. I'm afraid, I cannot approve this petition at this time." Ignoring Bennett's protestations, Mr. Bisikwa stamped REJECTED on the application. "Good day, Mrs. Hall."

Stunned, Bennett did not move. How could she have misstepped so badly?

"You may go, Mrs. Hall. I have other people waiting. We will find a proper place for the girl, here in her own country."

Bennett put her arm around Grace's shoulders. She was trembling. In silence, they walked toward the elevator, barely aware of the short, wiry man sidling up to them.

"Come into my office," he whispered. "There's always a way."

Bennett hesitated but seeing Victor Kizito, Assistant Probation and Social Welfare Officer on the door she was somewhat reassured. Perhaps...

"Mr. Bisikwa is a very busy man," the man went on. "Sometimes a small detail is misinterpreted so that the more relevant facts of the case are obscured. I am sure we can find a way to ensure success for you."

"That's incredibly kind of you," Bennett replied, pulling Grace closer to him.

"Adoption is a family matter, and I understand what it is to have family—parents, siblings, nephews, cousins. I myself have six children I must send to school, and, of course, for their sake I want to send them to the best schools. That is a great expense for a lowly bureaucrat, as you can imagine. And it is not only my children that concern me. As head of a large family I am responsible for everyone. These burdens are heavy sometimes—my mother's medical bills, my brother's debts, a widowed sister—you know how it is."

Bennett nodded sympathetically, as she let go of Grace and opened her handbag to pull out the documents.

"I have documents that show—"

"I'm sure they are in order," Mr. Kizito said, peering into Bennett's eyes. "You look like an upstanding woman, a woman who understands the value of things. There are fees and court costs."

"Yes, of course," Bennett said. "I am prepared."

"You would be very wise to act immediately. With inflation being what it is, the costs are constantly increasing." His voice dropped to a conspiratorial whisper. "I find my foreign clients prefer to pay in their own currency without the hassles of bank conversions. Twenty thousand dollars should cover everything."

Bennett stiffened. What a fool she was not to see this coming. If Bisikwa was an island of integrity there had to be a sea of corruption, and here it was.

"I see. I will have to…"

Mr. Kizito smiled and moved to open the door.

"Immediate action is very persuasive …"

Bennett gave him a sharp look and took Grace by the hand.

"I'll be back in the morning after I've made arrangements."

"Come at nine, and come directly to me, Mrs. Hall. There's no need to bother the receptionist."

Mr. Kizito held out his hand but Bennett walked out without taking it, her arm around Grace's shoulders.

"Is it too much, Bennett?" Grace asked, her eyes welling up with tears as she looked up at her.

"Nothing is too much. You mustn't worry about that."

37

Bennett made do with a lukewarm gin and tonic when the hotel bar ran out of ice, though what she really wanted was a bottomless bottle of straight alcohol to dull the pain of the last few hours.

Rescuing Grace from The Gentleman Bar had given her a rush of unwarranted confidence. The rescue hadn't been her doing, and when faced with Mr. Bisikwa, she'd blown it. Why would the next day be any different? Because it had to be. The thought of failing Grace and Joe was unbearable.

Her only chance to succeed was to acquiesce to Kizito's demands—but how realistic a chance was it? The man hadn't even pretended to review the documents. For twenty thousand dollars he would have sold Grace to any man who wanted her. What if Kizito took the money and didn't keep his word? What recourse would they have then?

Or should they go to Kampala and try there? If they acted quickly would anyone even know that they'd already been rejected?

Kizito must have done this before, many times before. It was time someone stopped him. Bennett could finally show some backbone and refuse to bow to such moral corruption. But at what cost? Did she have the right to risk Grace's future just to make herself feel good?

She had spent the hours after the meeting reassuring Grace that these were merely bureaucratic details she needn't worry about. Facilitation payments, Douglas Barnes had called them. If that's how it was, was it up to her to fight a system in a country that was not hers—to be David against their Goliath?

No. She was no David. Kizito expected her at nine the next morning. She would be there.

Bennett set her alarm for six. That would give her time to go to the bank for money before she picked up Grace.

Exhausted, she lay down and pulled the sheet over her head. In minutes, she was asleep.

At midnight she awoke with a start, determined to go to the police and have Kizito arrested for corruption, or blackmail, or whatever they were willing to charge t with; then fell asleep again.

At two-thirty she sat bolt upright, dripping with sweat, terrified the bank would deny her the twenty-thousand dollars and Kizito would rescind his offer.

At four a.m. she lay chilled and shivering, staring into the darkness, convinced that whatever she decided would be wrong and Grace would be lost to them forever.

At five forty-five she turned off the alarm. There was only one thing to to be done.

38

Bennett looked at her watch. 8:59. She and Grace had been in the waiting room for fifteen minutes. Without a word, she stood up, patted Grace on the hand, marched past the receptionist and planted herself squarely in front of Mr. Bisikwa's desk.

"You have made a grave error, sir," she said, her words slow and deliberate, her voice as resonant as possible.

"My decision was final, Mrs. Hall." The senior Probation and Social Welfare Officer barely looked up from the stack of papers in front of him. "Unless circumstances have changed ..."

"You mean, circumstances such as paying you a twenty thousand dollar bribe, Mr. Bisikwa?"

"How dare you!"

The left side of the official's face twitched as he rose from his chair and glared at his accuser.

Bennett leaned over the desk and slammed her handbag down, spilling out half its contents, and narrowly missing Mr. Bisikwa's fingers.

"You might have at least pretended to look at these documents before you ordered your flunky to reach his grubby fingers into my pocket. You will not get away with this. I am notifying the United States Embassy, and we will take action—and I will inform the BBC and CNN, too," Bennett added hurriedly and unnecessarily, for if she hadn't been so intent on the most effective and intimidating way of making her case, she might have understood that Mr. Bisikwa had collapsed into his chair in sorrow, not defeat.

"Please, Mrs. Hall. Sit down and tell me what happened."

Bennett collected the contents of her handbag, and slowly felt her fury subside. She began to recount the events of the previous afternoon.

Mr. Bisikwa frowned and shook his head.

"I cannot tell you how sorry I am. I take my responsibility to the children in our care very seriously and am distressed to hear this. Mr. Kizito has only been with us a short time and came with the highest references—but I promise you, he will be reassigned immediately."

"Reassigned? What does it take to be fired?" Bennett felt her anger rise again.

"My hands are tied, his uncle is a powerful member of parliament. But I have a friend in the transportation authority. I will arrange to have Kizito transferred there. He will at least be removed from child welfare cases."

"Can't you charge him with corruption?"

Mr. Bisikwa shrugged and opened his hands in a gesture of helplessness.

"Yes, I could report this to the IG, the Inspectorate of Government. You would have to remain in Uganda until your testimony could be heard, which could be months. If we are lucky it would be brought to the anti-corruption court, but I fear that as no money actually changed hands, the charges would be dropped. There always seems to be a way for the charges to be dropped."

Bennett felt a rush of empathy for the man, and for a moment imagined herself nobly joining in his Sisyphean struggle—although she knew all too well the cost of fighting battles one could only lose.

"None of this solves your problem, does it, Mrs. Hall?" Mr. Bisikwa's voice broke into Bennett's thoughts. "I at least owe you the chance of presenting your case in full."

Bennett laid out all the documents she'd brought and recited the explanations she had rehearsed so many times: that Grace and her siblings were orphans, that her siblings had been legally adopted before Joe knew about Grace; that Grace, having no family left, was eager to join her siblings in America and become part of a family again. With no one to protect her, Grace had already been pulled into a dangerous situation that might well befall her again. She needed the protection of a father.

"You appear to have a strong case, but it is necessary I speak with Grace myself," Mr. Bisikwa said.

"Of course. She is waiting in the reception room."

She rose to open the door and motioned for Grace to come in.

"Mr. Bisikwa would like to talk to you. And you can show him the album I brought you."

Mr. Bisikwa asked Bennett to wait by the receptionist while he spoke to Grace alone.

"There's still the issue of Dr. Muir's absence, Mrs. Hall," he said, when he called Bennett back in.

"Yes, I understand your concern and I think there is a way that can be resolved as well. We can arrange a meeting on the internet—a video chat—so that you can see him, talk to him, ask him questions."

Mr. Bisikwa nodded.

"It's unusual, but we will give it a try." He rose and extended his hand to Bennett. "Mrs. Hall, I greatly appreciate your cooperation, but more than that your honesty in coming to me rather than agreeing to Mr. Kizito's demands. I recognize that you took a risk and that it took courage to do so, but courage is what is required from all sides if there's to be any hope of ridding ourselves of the poison of corruption."

Bennett suggested a long walk before returning Grace to Hilda's care. They talked about birds and the weather, and the English books Grace had been introduced to in school. Anything not to discuss what had happened and not happened at the Probation and Social Welfare Office.

"Good afternoon, Mrs. Hall. Have you had a pleasant day?" the hotel desk clerk inquired when Bennett returned. Bennett stared and raised her hand in greeting but did not respond. She took a few steps toward the stairs, and then began to run, her heart racing as if in terror of what was behind her. She'd kept it together until then, juggling righteous outrage at Kizito's corruption with calm optimism for Grace, but now her neck and shoulders ached and her hands shook so hard she couldn't get her room key into the keyhole. She closed her eyes, took three deep breaths, and tried the key again.

If Bisikwa approved the adoption application, there were a dozen more hurdles to conquer. Even if the Ugandans agreed to the adoption, there was still the U.S. Embassy to convince, which meant more interviews, more calls, more forms to fill out.

She was delusional to think she could pull this off.

She threw her handbag and jacket on the chair, and put her hands to her temples in a futile effort to stop the pounding, as the last drops of self-confidence drained away. She felt the remnants of her scar, a reminder of how the littlest things can make everything go wrong.

Once a loser, always a loser. Why would it be any different now?

She had shut the windows but forgotten to close the shutters, so the room was stifling from the lack of air and the heat of the afternoon sun. She switched on the ceiling fan and took off everything but her underclothes, pulled the bedspread off the bed and threw herself face down on the momentarily cool sheets.

Bennett awoke two hours later and groaned as she struggled to get off the bed. Her panic had subsided but her back was stiff from having slept on her stomach.

The sun had set and the room had cooled. The numbers on the alarm clock glowed dimly in the dark. She'd better grab something to eat before they stopped serving. When she reached the lobby she was surprised to see a familiar figure leaning against the front desk, a backpack slung over one shoulder.

"My God, Peter, is that you? You've grown a beard."

The young American turned around.

"Oh, good! I was just about to ask reception if you were still here by any chance. I got back from the Rwenzori about an hour ago and thought I'd check to see how you'd managed with your search. I was intrigued when you told me you were looking for someone. Figured it wasn't Dr. Livingston so it must be a long-lost love."

Bennett laughed. "Not that either, I'm afraid, but I did find the person I was looking for. Have you had dinner? I'd enjoy the company and I can fill you in, if you're interested."

It was almost midnight by the time Bennett and Peter finished telling each other all that had transpired in the few weeks since they first met on the post bus from Kampala.

"Wow, I'm very impressed, Bennett. Rescuing children and fighting corruption— that's more than I expected."

Bennett laughed.

"Or I. But let's not jinx it, I haven't succeeded yet. Let's get back to you. You described your hikes so well I feel like I was there with you. You should write a travel guide."

"Not much chance of that. Too much like school."

"So what are your plans now?"

Peter leaned back and rocked on the back legs of his chair.

"My father wants me to go home and work with him. He arranges deals for people—big deals, like buying businesses. He says I could make a lot of money. That part sounds good, obviously, but wheeling and dealing are not my thing. I wish he'd ask my sister. I'm more a hands-on kind of guy. And I'd rather do something useful like building houses for poor people or digging wells in the desert."

"But your parents don't agree?"

"Dad thinks I'm naive, and Mom worries I'll starve or get sick."

"Sounds like you have normal parents. Not everyone's that lucky."

Peter smiled—somewhat sheepishly, Bennett thought.

"You're right—it's a rich kid's problem which is why I've decided to go home for a while and earn my keep before I go off and dig wells."

"Any ideas of where you'd want to go?"

"I was thinking Central or South America. I've never been there—but it means I have to learn a little Spanish first."

Bennett glanced at her watch.

"It's late—will they still let you in at the hostel?"

"They were full. I thought I'd hang out at the bus station until the bus leaves in the morning."

"Don't do that. We'll ask downstairs. They might have something or at least let you wait in the lobby. I need to get an early start myself, so I'll see you before you leave."

After eating a quick breakfast the next morning, and exchanging promises to stay in touch, Peter left for the bus station, and Bennett returned to her room and called down for an additional pot of coffee. A few extra doses of caffeine were warranted if she was to tackle the State Department's endless adoption requirements.

She tapped her pencil nervously on the table. She was normally a patient person but the uncertainty and waiting filled her with anxiety —first the wait for Bisikwa's decision, then for the Ugandan High Court's. After that, she'd have to register the adoption in Kampala, and wait for the Ministry of Foreign Affairs to be informed. Only then could she schedule an interview at the U.S. Embassy—at which point American red tape and other waiting times would take over.

She must have read the tedious list of required forms ten or twenty times by now, and felt she could handle them—after all, she'd done nothing but tedious paperwork her whole adult life—although nothing quite as redundant as these forms.

First there was an Affidavit of Support if a full and final adoption has been completed in Uganda; then a Petition to Classify Orphan as an Immediate Relative (wasn't that what adoption was?); followed by Child's birth certificate, passport, four passport photographs, court ruling with petitioner's name, adoption order with petitioner's name. (How many more ways would she need to prove adoption?); along with Death certificates of the biological parents (which had already been required and submitted for the Ugandan court to approve Medi and Hope's adoption).

In addition, she would have to bring: the Application for Immigrant Visa Application and pertinent fee; Affidavit Concerning Exemption from Immigrant Vaccination Requirements; and most recent tax returns. She'd foolishly brought hers, when they obviously needed Joe's, so she wrote herself a note to ask Joe to scan and email them.

One would have thought that after the Ugandan adoption was finalized, a U.S. adoption would be almost automatic, but a new "long" birth certificate would have to be obtained at the Ministry of Justice and Constitutional Affairs in Kampala, along with the parents' death certificates (*again—as if, at this point, there was still doubt that Grace was an orphan!*), and possibly a clearance from the Ministry of Gender, Labor and Social Development, so that a passport could be obtained from Ugandan authorities in order to apply for an immigration visa from the U.S. Embassy, which in turn would require Grace to have a medical exam from the Embassy's panel physician, who was a part of the International Organization for Migration, and thankfully also located in Kampala. *Good grief!*

To keep track—and to calm her nerves—Bennett drew up a chart with a the list of required documents on the left, and dates received and submitted on the right.

In addition to the hassle, every delay cost her money. And what was she supposed to do with Grace while they waited? She couldn't leave her with Hilda. The poor woman had a job and her own family to worry about. Besides, Grace had to be in Kampala. They could share a hotel room, of course, but the poor child would feel trapped if they had to stay there too long.

That's what Bennett would have liked to grumble to Joe about when he called, but hearing the worry in his voice she didn't have the heart.

"I'm feeling positive," she said. "I'm sure Bisikwa is going to approve this as soon as he talks to you, and if he approves it I don't think the High Court can object. I'd like to get started on all the red tape but I don't think there's anything I can do yet."

At that moment, she heard a rustling and turned to see an envelope being pushed under her door.

"Hold on, Joe, I think this might be important." She ripped open the envelope and picked up the phone again. "All right! Good news. Bisikwa is going to WhatsApp you tomorrow morning at nine, your time. He asked that the children be there, so he can talk to them, too."

Two days later Mr. Bisikwa called to tell Bennett that he had approved the adoption, and had already sent his report to the High Court, with a request that they expedite their ruling.

"And you will be pleased to hear," he added, "that Mr. Kizito is no longer in our employ."

"I certainly am," Bennett said, raising her fist in a gesture of triumph he couldn't see. They'd rescued Grace from the Gentleman Club and won Mr. Bisikwa's approval. "I can't thank you enough," she added before hanging up.

With two hurdles overcome, victory was achievable!

If all went well.

But at night—every night—alone and in the dark, the terrors returned, filling her with fear that in the end she would fail after all, leaving all who mattered to her shattered and in despair.

When night passed and she awoke, Bennett pulled herself together and walked the dusty road to Hilda's house. Only then, when she saw Grace waiting for her on the front step, eager to ply her with questions, did she feel her shoulders relax again and a smile form on her face.

"What will I wear in America? Does it rain where you live? Do you grow matoke in your garden? Will I have my own bed? When will I start school? What color uniform will I wear? Have you ever seen a movie? Do you have elephants? How many kinds of birds are there?"

Her questions rushed out of her like a waterfall suddenly nourished by the melting of a glacier in spring.

"One day, Grace, when you go to college you can study birds and become an ornithologist. Maybe you'll even discover a bird no one has ever seen before."

Grace looked down at her feet and traced a circle in the dirt with her toe.

"Do I have to? Does it mean I cannot become a nurse?"

"No, of course you can be a nurse, but the world is so full of possibilities you may change your mind. Whatever you decide to do you will do well. I'm sure of that."

Grace looked relieved and slipped her arm in Bennett's.

"I might want to be a teacher. I miss going to school."

"We can do some lessons together, if you like."

"Oh, yes, please!" Grace said.

So the next day, and the days after that, after they returned from their early morning walk to market, they sat down in the shade of the moo-yahoo tree and did their lessons—lessons that included grammar and math but were usually a matter of answering Grace's never-ending stream of questions, which she no longer limited to the basics of her future life.

In return, Grace explained how her great-aunt crushed and boiled moo-yahoo nuts until their special butter rose to the surface, then scooped it into gourds to cool and set. When Bennett looked up moo-yahoo in her guidebook, she was surprised to learn that Grace's special butter was the shea butter she'd often seen in drug stores at home, and the tree she called karite, was known as a shea tree in other countries.

In the late-afternoon Grace often cooked supper for Hilda and her family, and taught Bennett how to make lagalagala pancakes and matoke stew

On the seventeenth day of waiting, they received the High Court's approval. It was time to leave for Kampala.

39

Bennett was waiting in the hotel lobby when Hilda and Grace arrived, followed moments later by Jacob.

"I've put some things together for Grace," Hilda said, pointing to a red, white and blue plaid, zippered plastic bag, the sort Ugandas often used to carry groceries and laundry. "I must go to work, but you will let me know—"

"Of course," Bennett said. "I don't know how to thank you."

Hilda took Bennett's hand in hers.

"May God be with you both," she said. "That will be my thanks."

"We must leave or you will miss your bus," Jacob said. "Are you certain I cannot drive you to Kampala?"

"We will be fine, and I can't take you away from your work again. You have done so much for me already. I will never forget it. I hope one day we will meet again."

"I am certain of it," Jacob said.

～

As a final kindness, Jacob had arranged for Grace to stay with his sister in the Muyenga area of Kampala, and for Bennett he'd reserved a room in a reasonably priced hotel a short distance away. It was only a few minutes walk from the Tank Hill Shopping Center, where she could go for a meal.

"Jacob's sister is funny," Grace told Bennett when she went to pick her up after her first day there.

"Do you mean strange?" Bennett asked, concerned. "She's treating you well, isn't she?"

"Oh yes, and she makes me laugh."

"Well, that's certainly a good thing."

Grace looked up at Bennett.

"Everything is going to be all right now, isn't it?"

"It will, I promise," she said, although she felt her throat tighten with fear that she would not live up to Grace's trust in her. "Come, I saw an Italian gelato place in the shopping center. Have you ever had one?"

"Is it a jelly?"

"No, it's a kind of ice cream they eat in Italy. Remember, we saw a map of Italy when we were doing our lessons."

Grace nodded and asked, "Who are your people, Bennett? I want to know about your tribe."

"We don't have tribes like here, Grace."

"But you must have people ... Didn't your mother tell you about them?"

Bennett shook her head.

Grace looked puzzled. "I know many Buganda stories. Do you not tell stories in America?"

"Yes, but we have many different peoples who have different histories and different customs because they came from different places, at different times, and for many different reasons. So sometimes, instead of their histories, they share their dreams."

"Will there be no one to tell me Buganda stories anymore?"

"There might be. We will see, but if you get homesick for Uganda you can tell Joe. He loved it here and will understand. He might even know stories you don't."

Grace lowered her eyes.

"I did not always love my people. In my aunt's village they said my parents fell into sickness because they did not follow the traditional ways. I felt ashamed."

Bennett shook her head.

"You mustn't. It was not their fault. They were good people and had great hopes for their children. That's why they wanted all of you to go to school so you could have a better life. They would be very proud of you for going."

Grace clasped Bennett's hand and they walked in silence for a while.

"Grace, I think Medi and Hope would enjoy hearing your Buganda stories. Do you have a favorite one?"

"Yes. The one about Kintu. That is my very favorite."

She closed her eyes and for a moment it was as if she were listening for the slow rhythm and cadence of an old storyteller. As she began to speak, her expressive hands accompanied the images the story had created in her mind.

"Kintu was the first man on earth, but Gulu was the creator of all things and lived in heaven. He had many children who came down to earth to play. One day his daughter Namdi saw Kintu. She liked him right away, but her family didn't. Gulu said if Kintu could meet all the challenges set for him, he would allow him to marry Namdi. They didn't think Kintu could do it, but he was brave and clever and so he did."

"And they live happily ever after?"

"They were happy but some sad things happened too," Grace admitted, "but I don't like to talk about them. We don't have to, do we?"

40

> Bennett Hall
>
> To: JMuirMD@gmail.com
>
> Re: update

Dear Joe -

I finally have an appointment at the Embassy. Despite biting my nails waiting for it, time has passed surprisingly quickly. There's been a great deal of running around getting red-tape settled in preparation, but I've also had a chance to explore Kampala with Grace. We saw Lake Victoria, which really impressed her. She enjoyed our visits to the art gallery at Makarere University and the Kasubi Tombs, and we spent several hours at the National Museum. She is intelligent and eager to learn.

I would have taken her shopping for some clothes, for she had only what Hilda gave her, but Jacob's sister is an accomplished seamstress and offered to help her make some dresses. It was a chance for them to do things together, but *you may have to buy her some American-style clothes and shoes too. She certainly has nothing for cold weather.*

Grace said she's been making presents for you and the children but she wouldn't tell me what.

Our appointment is with Glendora Dobbs in Consular Affairs tomorrow morning, and I will call you immediately afterwards to let you know how it went. Her name sounds like a combination of romance heroine and practicality, but her voice was quite mellifluous on the phone so it's hard to know what to expect.

With the seven-hour time difference, Joe would not see the message until he returned from work. By then Bennett would be asleep. Too nervous to eat, she decided to stay in her room and forgo dinner. She reorganized all the pockets of her large handbag again, unpacked the suit and blouse she planned to wear the next morning, and read Kampala's *Daily Monitor* and *New Vision* newspapers from cover to cover.

Bennett and Grace took a taxi to the hillside U.S. Embassy on Ggaba Road, then walked from the guard house to a courtyard ringed by palm trees, where they found a local Ugandan selling espresso from a cart. Guessing a little extra fortification could do no harm, Bennett ordered one for herself, and one for Grace, who was curious to try one. Grace added three sugars to hers and found it very tasty.

Glendora Dobbs was in her early sixties, short and squat, and nothing like her voice. More a Dobbs than a Glendora. But that was not a bad thing, for she soon made it clear that she was not one to waste time.

Bennett presented the pertinent documents, authorizations, and permits, and explained, as persuasively as she could, all the circumstances leading to the adoption request, as well as the reason that she was in attendance rather than Joe. She then waited in the adjoining room while Ms Dobbs spoke to Grace.

"The documents are complete and in order," Glendora Dobbs said when she reentered, her honey-like voice reassuring. "Grace seems very happy at the prospect of reuniting with her siblings and having a father-figure in her life again, so I see no reason, at this point, not to approve your petition. But, I would feel more comfortable if Dr. Muir were here in person."

Bennett was about to plead their case again when Glendora Dobbs broke in.

"No need to go through your arguments, Miss Hall. I am flying to Washington tomorrow and will be back in a week. I'm sure Dr. Muir and I can arrange a meeting while I am there. I have his number. Meanwhile, you may take Grace for her Embassy panel physician exam so everything can be completed upon my return."

Anxious to let Joe know but stymied by a dead phone battery and a sputtering internet connection once they left the compound, Bennett took Grace back to Jacob's sister and then had to wait another two hours before she managed to send her email to Joe.

Bennett Hall

To: JMuirMd

Re: update

Joe - Sorry I couldn't phone (dead battery) or email (dying internet) until now.

Everything went very smoothly. Through a stroke of luck, our timing was perfect for Glendora Dobbs is flying to DC tomorrow and may have already called you. She wants to meet with you. I think you should take Medi and Hope along so that she sees how they are thriving with you and how eager they are for Grace to join them. You probably don't need to stay more than a day. She was very positive. I think we're almost home free. Meanwhile I'm taking Grace for her physical. As soon as we get definite word, I will make reservations for us to fly home. My head is spinning. Knock on wood, we are almost there. I dread to think how slowly these next days will pass.

Tunaalabagana

(Grace says that means see you later)

Joe Muir

To: benniehall@gmail.com

Re: re: update

Ms Dobbs just called me. (You're right about her voice!) We are going down to DC tomorrow and spending the night so that we can be fresh and bright the next morning when we see her. Keep your fingers crossed. I'm a nervous wreck and spend my evenings working on my hobbies. Music has been eliminated as I have no talent. Art is about to be. (Hope is better than I am.) Writing may be my only option. Better start practicing.

Since we'll be there, I want to take the kids around Washington, show them the monuments and tell them about what it means to be American. Might as well make this really educational!

You're a treasure, Benniehall! (Hope says that's what we should call you from now on!)

Weebale, weebale, weebale! (Has Grace taught you that? It means thank you, thank you, thank you!)

I know I don't have to ask, but do keep me posted.

I talked to Meyer and he is doing well. I invited him to dinner but he said we should wait until you get back, so come home soon, Benniehall. You are missed.

Joe

Come home soon, Benniehall. Bennett would never tire of reading that.

With much to do, the days of waiting passed quickly after all. Joe's meeting with Ms Dobbs went well and Grace's physical was successfully completed. With adoption and passport approved and in hand, Bennett and Grace booked their flight. One more day and they would be on their way.

"There are two art galleries I'd still like to see," Bennett said to Grace. "I heard there are some very fine artists working in Kampala. I think I would like a piece of Ugandan art to take home. Will you help me choose?"

In a tiny gallery on the ground floor of an office building they found a small collection of West African masks, a stone sculpture from Zimbabwe, a small painting by a Kenyan artist who had studied icon painting in Russia, and three haunting portraits of young women by Ugandan artist Geoffrey Mukasa, each a collage of magazine scraps embellished with gold leaf. The only decision was which of the three portraits they liked best. Each was more expensive than Bennett had budgeted for, but she knew she would never regret buying any of them. After much thought and discussion, they chose a full-length figure in shades of red and gold.

"You'll have to help me figure out the perfect place to hang it, Grace."

While they waited for the portrait to be safely wrapped for their flight, Grace spotted a carved ebony sculpture of a mother and child.

"Look, Bennett. Isn't she beautiful?"

Grace held the sculpture tenderly in her hands, and then reluctantly, placed the sculpture back on its shelf.

"Does she remind you of your mother?" Bennett asked.

Grace nodded, as two tears trickled down her cheeks.

"Then I think you must have her."

"Shall I pack them up together?" the gallery owner asked.

"No, separately, please," Bennett replied. "The young lady will want to carry her sculpture herself."

The next morning Bennett settled her hotel bill and asked the desk clerk to call a taxi. It was very early but she wanted to have ample time at the airport after she picked up Grace so that they could call Hilda and Jacob for a final good-bye and thank you.

"Your car to take you to Entebbe is already waiting outside, Miss Hall."

"But I didn't—"

As Bennett turned, she saw Jacob, Hilda and Grace standing at the door.

"You don't think we would let you and Grace leave without a proper good-bye. How would it look if we let a stranger take you to the airport?"

Bennett felt the tears pricking her eyes. No regrets this time. Only gratitude for the gifts of friendship and joy she would never forget.

For weeks Bennett had fought and waited, arduously, anxiously, impatiently, for the moment she could bring Grace home to Joe. Yet now, leaving Uganda seemed to have come too soon. The little bit of it that she knew, had come to feel so familiar that she found it hard to imagine no longer being there. A place and time that had changed her would soon be just a memory and she feared that without them she would be no better a human being than the one she'd been before.

As they crossed the skies over the Atlantic, Grace sat motionless, her shoulder resting comfortably against Bennett's. Intoxicated by the excitement of her first flight, she'd lost herself in the magic of watching the images that flickered on the miniature screen in front of her, forgetting, for those moments, all the changes that still lay ahead of her.

Bennett closed her eyes and could still see Jacob, with his kind, broad smile, shaking her hand firmly with both of his as he bid her farewell; and Hilda, her face tearstained, embracing Grace and then her, wishing them both God's blessings on this important journey.

41

It took Bennett only a moment to spot Joe, his freckled face rising above others, distinct in the sea of multiethnic faces waiting for international arrivals. Her observations were quickly interrupted by two children sneaking through the jungle of legs to run up to her, with Joe squeezing himself through behind them.

"Bennie! Did you bring her, did you bring her?" Hope shouted over the din of the crowd.

Bennett took Grace's hand and pulled her in front of her, placing her hands protectively on her shoulders.

"Here's your sister, Hope and Medi. She's waited a long time to see you again."

Hope jumped up and down and yanked at Grace's arm.

"I helped Papa fix up your room. We put balloons ..."

"Don't tell her," Medi said. "You'll spoil the surprise."

"You can show her everything when we get home," Joe said, reaching out to embrace Grace.

Feeling Grace stiffen slightly, Bennett looked into Joe's eyes and smiled, even as she held on to Grace's shoulders.

"Grace, this is Joe."

Bennet saw that Joe understood, for he smiled back and said, "Did you have a good flight, Grace? We are so happy that you are finally here. Come, let's get your bags out to the car. I borrowed a friend's van so we'd have plenty of room. What's the big package?"

"A special souvenir of Uganda. We'll show you later," Bennet said.

She pushed the luggage cart as Joe and the children led the way to the car.

Joe strapped Hope into her booster seat. Medi buckled his own seat belt and showed Grace how to buckle hers.

Hope chattered away, telling Grace about school, her new bedspread, and that Juanita was at their house making them a special dinner.

"Juanita speaks Spanish, do you speak Spanish?" Hope asked.

"Don't be silly, Hope," Medi said. "They don't speak Spanish in Uganda."

"Do you think she is all right with this?" Joe whispered to Bennett. "She hasn't seen them since Hope was a baby. She might not even remember them."

Bennett glanced back at Grace, who noticed and turned to smile at her.

"She remembers, and she'll be fine, but it may be a while before she shows it. She's learned to be cautious."

Joe turned to Bennett. "We've missed you, Benniehall."

Before she could answer, Grace leaned forward and whispered, "Look, Bennett, big buildings just like in Kampala."

When they arrived home the rain clouds that had darkened the sky earlier lifted and the sun shone brightly on Spring Street, showing off the well-tended flower beds overflowing with color in front of each half of their shared house.

"You've been gardening, Joe!" Bennett said, pleased that he'd tended her flowers too.

"It's so beautiful," Grace said. "Do you really live here?"

"Welcome to your new home, sweetheart," Joe replied. "We are so happy you are here."

Hope grabbed Grace's hand and pulled her toward the steps. "Come, Grace! Come see your room."

A harsh caw echoed through the oak tree, followed by a melody of high and low chirps.

"What bird is that?" Grace asked, stopping to turn her head toward the sounds.

"It's a blue jay," Medi explained. "We have robins too, and cardinals and finches and sparrows. And sometimes we have a woodpecker. He's very noisy. Want to see our birdhouses? We've got five of them. I helped Papa put them up."

Grace nodded and let him take her hand from Hope as he led the way.

"I painted the red one," Hope added, skipping along behind them. "Papa says hummingbirds like red but I've never seen one. They're very tiny, you know."

"Hope and Medi are going to make it easy for Grace," Bennett said, once the children were out of earshot.

Joe reached out and embraced her.

"Thank you, Bennie! You don't know what this means to me."

"And to me," she said, but seeing Joe's eyes following Grace, she kissed him on the cheek and reached for her suitcase. "Go on, then, go see what they're up to. I'll take my things over and unpack."

"Don't be long. Juanita has prepared a feast."

"Wouldn't you rather have this time alone with your family?"

"Without you? Don't be silly. You're the hero of the day, and the kids would be crushed if you didn't come. I'll give you an hour to unpack but no more. I put all your mail on the kitchen table."

Joe gave her hand a quick squeeze as he hurried to join the children in the backyard.

Bennett could still hear the happy murmur of their voices as she entered her house. She walked from window to window and raised the shades that had been pulled down to keep out the sun. Everything looked clean and smelled of Pine Sol. A sure sign that Juanita had been there. Smiling, she carried her suitcase upstairs and hung up her suit. The rest could wait.

The mail lay in a basket on the kitchen table, not that there was very much. She had prewritten checks for Joe to pay the few monthly bills that could arrive in her absence, and he had left the receipts. There were no personal letters, only catalogues and accumulated copies of the National Geographic. Now that she'd actually been somewhere, they'd be even more interesting. Grace might enjoy them, too. In fact, she should order the kids' editions for Medi and Hope. There was so much about the world they should know.

"I almost forgot!" she said aloud, as she ran upstairs again, and dug into her suitcase. Under her jeans she found the dolls she'd bought with Jacob her first week in Uganda. A boy for Medi, and three girls. Two for Hope and Isabella, and the third for the child that would never see it—Meyer's beloved Elsie.

Shouldn't she wrap them? Children seemed to like the excitement of that extra little anticipation before the paper is torn off—but she had nothing she could use. It would only take a minute to run down to the drug store. If the car started after all this time. They were bound to have some sort of wrapping paper, and she could pick up flowers for Juanita and a bottle of wine for Joe.

When she returned she wrapped the dolls carefully, marking each neatly with the child's name, and only then realized that she had nothing for Grace to open. She looked around. There must be something she could give her—but of course there was nothing, not a photograph or knickknack. If it weren't for the books upstairs in her office there'd be nothing in the house to indicate who lived there. An intruder might wonder why anyone needed half a house to store a few pieces of furniture.

Maybe one of the books? A novel? Something historical? Certainly not the reference books, so heavy and colorless and hardly appropriate. Then Bennett remembered the Uganda travel guide in her suitcase. It was dog-eared from having been read from cover to cover, but Grace would think it was the right thing. On the inside title page, Bennett wrote:

For my dear Grace -
This is my well-used guide to the country of your birth --
and in many ways of mine as well,
for it is there that I found great joy and friendship.
With deep affection always,
Bennett

Before she could change her mind, she wrapped it and added it to the other gifts.

It was time to go over.

∽

"Look, Bennie. She's sleepy from her trip," Hope said, as she cradled the little cloth doll in her arms. "Our house is a long way from Africa."

"Mine's not tired," Medi said, as he placed his in his G.I. Joe Jeep. "He's going on safari. That's why he's wearing an elephant shirt."

Grace flung her arms around Bennett's neck without a word after she read the inscription. She held her book tightly to her chest as she took in the scene around her. After a while, she put the book down and announced shyly that she had some presents for them, too.

"Unless you want me to wait until tomorrow…"

"No, now, now!" Hope said, jumping up and down. "Where are they? Are they upstairs? Can you get them?"

Grace ran up the stairs and returned with two lumpy bags.

"Jacob's sister helped me make them."

One by one, Grace pulled out birds whose fabric feathers she had painstakingly sewn to their stuffed bodies. Their wings fluttered magically as she propelled them through the air and handed them to Hope and Medi: black and white fish eagles; red-bellied, blue-feathered kingfishers; bright yellow weavers; and polka-dotted guinea fowls. Bennett recognized them all. Then finally, for her and Joe, two regal, orange-crowned, black-and-white bodied, red-necked crested cranes. Bennett's favorite.

"These are all Ugandan birds," Joe explained to the children, "and they're just how I remember them. I've never had a more beautiful present, Grace."

Hope and Medi laughed as they ran around the room, holding a bird in each hand and letting their wings flutter.

"Look, Grace, they're flying!" Hope squealed with delight.

"Grace looks really happy," Bennett whispered to Joe.

"The children and I are taking a week off to get her settled," Joe said. "Medi and Hope insisted on being included, so I've given Juanita the time off, too."

"If there's anything I can do …"

"You've already done the most important part, Bennett," he said, patting her hand.

"Of course. I understand," she said. This was Joe's time, not hers. And he'd not called her Benniehall or just Bennie.

She smiled to hide her disappointment.

42

Bennett asked Maria if she could manage without her for a few more days so she could reorient herself to being back.

"I've been forsaken by you for a long time, but I guess another week won't kill me. I'm so glad you're back, and congratulations, Bennett. You're a real hero around here."

"Not quite, I had a lot of help, but thanks. Have you seen Meyer? I tried calling but a visiting nurse answered the phone and, after a moment of silence, she said Meyer was a bit under the weather and needed his rest. He would call when he felt better. I asked her to please tell him I was successful and brought Grace home"

Bennett placed the little doll she'd bought for Elsie on a shelf over the kitchen counter so as not to forget to give it to him.

After filing away paid bills, and putting the magazines she wanted to read on the night table next to her bed, Bennett wrote emails to Hilda and Jacob, telling them about her and Grace's homecoming. Next, she sent off a short answer to Peter's email, which had arrived a few days earlier with the news that he was working for his father's company after all. Bennett invited him to visit should he ever come east.

Finally, she sent a thank you note to Douglas Barnes at the State Department, telling him his advice had proved invaluable, even when she ignored it.

She sorted through the many papers she'd accumulated in Uganda, and put those concerning Grace aside for Joe. The rest she organized and alphabetized, then filed in the Ikea file boxes she'd once allotted to genealogical research and changed the labels.

The only things missing were photographs of Uganda. She had none. Having had little reason—or desire—to commemorate her life experiences before, she didn't own a camera and hadn't thought to use her phone except to send the photo of Grace to Joe. Her life had been enriched a hundredfold and she longed now for visible proof of the people that had changed her: Grace, Jacob, Hilda; Joe and the children, of course; and Maria and Juanita, and Meyer Gold. Even Lola. Bennett was amazed at how many there were after her long years of loneliness. It had all begun with Mrs. McElroy. With her kindness and gentle conversation, she had broken through a wall Bennett had so long accepted without question. Bit by bit those cracks in the wall had revealed feelings and hopes Bennett never thought she'd have.

Bennett saved the best task for last. Holding Grace's crested crane gently in her hand, she walked from room to room looking for the perfect home for it. It would remind her forever that life was worth living even if only for brief moments of happiness or a short glimpses of beauty.

Having checked every promising spot, she finally hung the crested crane in the window overlooking the garden. If Grace looked up she would see it and perhaps find comfort in the small reminder of home when the changes in her life seemed too overwhelming.

When Grace was more settled, she would ask her to come over to help hang the portrait they'd bought together in Kampala.

With her grand adventure over, and everything in place at home, it was time Bennett returned to work. She'd forsaken Maria and the shop long enough.

"I can't tell you how happy I am to have you back," Maria said. "I've missed your company, and so have our customers."

"I've missed you too, although you seem to have managed fine without me," Bennett said, looking around the well-ordered shop. Furniture had been rearranged to make room for new acquisitions. Paintings, once stacked in boxes, now hung on the walls.

"Oh yes, it looks good, but I am desperately behind on paperwork. Come look at this!" Maria said, leading Bennett to the storage room where a table was piled high with sales slips, invoices, and bank statements. "I'm going to drown in paper if we don't get this in shape again."

"At least it looks like business has been good."

"It has. A local reporter did an article on us that brought in a slew of new customers, some of whom are dealers like Lola and are becoming regulars, so I've spent a few Sundays going up to estate sales in Pennsylvania to increase our stock. The prices up there are better for some reason, and Isabella is becoming a good little traveler."

"You'll have to show me what you've found."

"I even found a few things for you."

"Me? What do I need?"

"Dishes, for one thing. Mama said you only have enough for four, and two of the plates are already chipped."

"I'm only one person."

"You have friends. Don't you think it's time you invited us over? I found a lovely set of blue and white transferware—the English kind you said you liked. Not Spode, but still a really attractive pattern."

Bennett blushed.

"I don't know what to say."

"Thank you is fine. But that's not all I have. I was thinking you need an accent piece in your house, some really interesting piece of furniture. And since I have an antique shop ..."

'I don't want anything too big or too dark," Bennett said, remembering Aunt Mary's ghastly pieces.

"Don't worry, I wouldn't do that to you. I was thinking of an Arts and Crafts piece, at first, but then I found something even better. I know you'll like it. I've kept it hidden so no one else could buy it. It's a Sorrentine copy of a Louis XV secretaire, but it was made so long ago it probably qualifies as an antique itself."

"Sounds a bit too fancy for me."

"No, it's perfect. You'll see."

Maria pushed aside a tall screen to reveal a small sloped-top desk on four curved legs in perfect condition.

"Sorrento is famous for its marquetry, Bennett, and the craftsmanship on this desk is especially fine. I thought you'd appreciate that."

On the front, above the two curved drawers, an intricately inlaid panel sloped to the top. The wood was fruitwood, and had a warm, golden tone to it, making Bennett think of Abraham the lion.

Maria folded down the sloped panel, exposing two small, curved drawers on either side of two shelves. The writing surface was covered in unblemished leather.

"And look how easily all the drawers open," she said, "and the legs don't have a chip on them."

Bennett slid her hand over the smooth, undulated surfaces.

"You're right, Maria. It is truly beautiful, but I don't know if I can afford it."

"You don't have to, and I'm so glad you like it! It's only a little part of what I owe you, but I hope you'll accept it as a down payment. The dishes are a gift too but only on the condition that you have a party and I'm invited."

"It's a deal, and I can't thank you enough."

"Good. I was going to surprise you and have it waiting for you when you got back but I wasn't sure where you'd want me to put it. I have someone coming later to come get it, and then they're supposed to deliver it to you sometime this afternoon. Joe's out with all the kids, but Mama said she can let him in if you can't be there in time."

Bennett spent the day working on the shop's neglected paperwork and didn't arrive home until shortly after six.

"Something came up and they can't deliver until tomorrow," Juanita said, walking over from Joe's house.

"I'm sorry you've had to wait all this time for nothing.'

"I didn't mind," Juanita said. "I could get things done without anybody interrupting me."

"Do you have time then for a cup of tea?"

"That would be nice."

They went into the kitchen and Bennett put a kettle up to boil.

"I was worried you would not like the desk," Juanita said. "I remember how you didn't like your aunt's furniture."

"The desk is beautiful—nothing like Aunt Mary's furniture. I didn't like anything in that house."

"Your aunt called it the house of broken dreams," Juanita said.

Bennett's eyes widened in surprise.

"What dreams did she ever have?"

"Everyone has dreams, Bennett."

"She never told me. And she wasn't interested in mine."

The tea kettle began to whistle.

"Hope Earl Grey is all right," Bennett said, throwing two tea bags into a tea pot.

Juanita nodded.

"Your Aunt Mary had a sad life, you know."

"Maybe because she was so negative about everything. She was always warning me about the dangers around me."

"She had reason to be afraid of the world. Like me, she was a girl from the mountains. Her parents were very poor, like mine. She got involved with a boy and got pregnant when she was still a girl. His parents sent him away, and her parents forced her to give her baby up for adoption. She never even knew if it was a boy or girl."

The shrill whistle of the tea kettle finally caught Bennett's attention, and she poured what remained of the boiling water into the teapot.

"She should have told me."

"She was ashamed."

"But how did she end up in that house? It must have been really grand once?"

"So she really told you nothing?"

Juanita shook her head at such silence.

"Nothing," Bennett said, pouring them each a cup of tea.

"Then I will tell you. Your Aunt ran away after they took the baby, and hitchhiked to New York. It scares me to think of what it must have been like for her—no money, no friends or family. Thankfully, she found a job as a hatcheck girl in a nightclub. A young man from Wilmington who had also just come to New York often went to the nightclub with his friends. He fell in love with her—I think she must have been very beautiful—and despite his parents' objections, they got married. One day, when they were visiting them, he wanted to show off his new car and took them all for a ride. He was going too fast and they had a terrible accident. Only Mary survived. There were no relatives, so she inherited the house—the house you then grew up in. Strange, isn't it?"

Bennett stirred her tea, though there was no sugar in it, trying to imagine that the woman she had known was once young and beautiful.

"It must have been painful for her to liven that house," she said.

"It was, but she had nothing else."

"Yet she took us in. I never knew why."

"Her husband and your father were best friends. And your mother welcomed her when no one else did. Her friendship must have meant the world to her—enough to keep you with her when your mother died."

Bennett, still stirring her untouched tea, could barely process it all. How could she have known so little for so long?

"Did she tell you about my father?"

Juanita nodded. "A little bit."

Bennett's fingers traced the thin scar on the side of her face.

"Well, I wouldn't have known anything about him if the new owner hadn't found a box of papers in the attic. I was Mary's hostage after all."

"What do you mean?"

Bennett flicked her hand as if to swat away a fly. Juanita wouldn't understand.

"Nothing. Never mind."

"It must have been very lonely for both of you," Juanita said.

"It was. But she talked to you."

"Not really me. She was talking to herself, trying to sort out all her regrets. I just listened. Maybe I shouldn't ask, but why did you stay with her so long?"

"I felt responsible for her."

"And maybe you loved her."

Bennett felt the blood rush to her cheeks.

"I didn't stay out of love. I tolerated her because I had to."

"Oh Bennett, no one likes to be tolerated."

"I tried to love her. I felt responsible for her... though maybe I told myself that because I wasn't brave enough to leave," Bennett said, finally taking a sip of her tea. "I should have left. It would have been better for both of us. I almost did once, when I was young and in love —but she deceived me in the most cruel way by hiding his letters— something I didn't know about for almost thirty years, when it was far too late to undo the damage she had caused. I can never forgive her for that." Before Juanita could answer, she went on. "It's too bad that life disappointed her, but her anger made it so much worse. I know it's childish to feel she should have loved me. But feeling unloved and then rejected by Stephen was bad enough. I didn't want to be bitter and angry too, so I tried not to feel anything."

Bennett poured them each another cup of tea, though by now the tea had grown cold.

The woman who had so long overshadowed her life had had, in the end, even less of a life than she, and was perhaps as burdened by Bennett as Bennett had been by her. What a terrible waste of years on both their parts.

Juanita put her hand on hers and said, "You both did the best you could."

There was that phrase again.

"We didn't, and we should have—when it still mattered."

43

The sun was already halfway up the sky the next morning when Bennett was awakened by a loud knocking at the door, and a voice shouting *Delivery! She* slipped on her robe and rushed down to open the door. A burly young man handed her a large box marked DISHES, then returned to the van doubled parked in front of the house. He lifted a large, quilt-covered object effortlessly off the van and onto his back, and carried it up the front steps and into the house.

"Where d'ya wannit?"

"Right here," Bennett said pointing to the empty space between the door and the front window.

The young man unwrapped the object, refolded the quilt, and moved the object into place. Bennett pulled out her wallet and thanked him. She was about to close the door behind him when she heard Hope shouting from the window.

"What did you get, Bennie? Can I see?"

"Give me a few minutes to unpack the box and then come on over, all of you. It's a special gift from Maria."

One by one they came in and joined Bennett in staring admiringly at the Sorrentine desk before they all slid their hands over its smooth surface, as if assuring themselves that it was real.

"It's a lovely piece, Bennett, "Joe said. "Funny, isn't it, how we all had to touch it."

"Maria gave me some beautiful English dishes too. You can go look, kids. They're in the kitchen." She turned to Joe. "My mother had a service for twelve similar to this. It must have been a wedding present, I realize now. She brought it along, but my aunt shoved it to the back of the china cabinet, chipping several of the pieces."

"Where is it now?"

"I got rid of it, but now that I learned what skill it took to produce it, I regret it. For each piece an artist had to create a copper engraving which was then printed on tissue paper. The wet ink had to be carefully transferred from the flat tissue to a curved bowl or plate. The print was then set by firing in a kiln. Early pieces like my mother's were individually colored by hand, making each a small work of art."

"It's amazing how much you've learned working in Maria's shop," Joe said, patting her shoulder.

Bennett blushed. Was his pat affectionate or condescending? She might even have asked him had there not been a loud crash and a shriek from the kitchen, which made them both jump up, certain that something terrible had happened to the children. It turned out it was merely a pot lid that had slipped to the floor.

Feeling foolish, Bennett returned to the living room where Grace was gently tracing the desk's inlaid patterns with her fingers.

"Do you like it?"

"It is perfect."

Bennett opened the front panel.

"This was meant for writing letters, so maybe you can come and use it sometime."

"Oh yes, I would like that. I would be just like the ladies in the English book Joe gave me."

44

"How many stamps do I need for Uganda?" Grace asked Bennett the next evening, as she folded the many pages of the letter she'd written into an envelope. On it she had drawn a tiny but remarkably accurate crested crane.

"I'm not sure. I'll take it to the post office in the morning and have it weighed."

It was only after she'd seen Grace to the door, that Bennett noticed that she'd left the envelope open. She was about to seal it when it occurred to her that she might have left it open for her to read. Overcome by curiosity to know what Grace thought of her new life, she ignored her compunctions and removed the neatly written pages.

 Dear Hilda,

I am like an English girl, sitting at Bennett's beautiful new old desk, and writing you with the new pen and special paper she bought me. How are you and your family? I think of you often and how kind you were to me. Do you see Jacob

and Isaac? Please tell them I think of them gratefully too, and that I will write Jacob's sister very soon.

I am very happy to be with Medi and Hope and to see how well they are. They are so big—not the babies anymore that I remember. I will begin school next week. It is very big, with many rooms and students and teachers. I hope I will make friends there so that I will not feel lonely. Joe says many students there are from other countries. Maybe there will be another African girl.

Joe is very good to me but I am worried sometimes that I am a burden he did not expect. I do not want him to feel I am his duty so I try not to get in the way. I help in the house when I can, but he does not let me do very much. I think he is afraid I will not do it correctly because I am not used to such a rich house. I am learning how to cook American food.

Bennett is kind and generous, as you know, and I dream that she will marry Joe. Then we can be a family, and Medi, Hope and I can have a mother again. I see her look at Joe and her eyes get soft and I know that she loves him, but Joe has so many worries in his head, working in his job and taking care of us, that I don't think he knows it. I must be patient and not be trouble for him so that he has time to think about himself. Then he will realize that he is her Kintu and she loves him.

I miss the songs of our birds, and the feel of our red soil under my feet. Here I have to wear shoes all the time and the soil is grey or brown, and sometimes there is no soil at all, only streets. I hope one day to have a camera so that I can send you photographs of everyone, and of our house and my school and the little birds in our garden. One is so small you can hardly see it. They call it a hummingbird. I have not seen any forests or mountains yet but Joe says America has *many of them. I think there must be many different birds there, even some big ones.*

The city where we live has many big buildings, just like Kampala. Some people live in them but many people live in houses like you, with gardens. We live in a house that has two parts—one for us and one for Bennett. We have a big garden in the back and a little one in front, and there are big trees all around. Bennett says our city has parks and a zoo with many animals from Africa, but it is not big like Queen Elizabeth Park and many of the animals are in cages. I think it would make me sad to see them there.

Tell your children hello hello.

I will write again.

Your friend,

Grace

Bennett's hands trembled as she slipped the letter back into its envelope.

Grace was right. She did love Joe, but loving him wasn't enough. He deserved someone like Laurie, someone with dreams, someone who'd spent her life making a difference, not someone who in fifty years had only stepped up to the plate once.

For all she knew, he already met someone at the hospital. Someone younger—maybe even a doctor like him. Or a nurse like Laurie. Even if he didn't, he had too much to think about now. It was too late. Joe didn't need her.

Sometimes she wanted to tell Joe how she felt, but if she did, she could lose everything. If he already met someone, and they got married, his wife wouldn't want her making claims on his affection or time. Medi and Hope would turn to their new mother for help with homework and chess lessons. His wife might even make them move, leaving Bennett to live next door to strangers. She wouldn't feel Hope's little arms around her neck anymore, or Medi's hand in hers when she challenged him to arm wrestling. Grace might write for a while, but in time, Bennett would fade out of her mind, too. Poor Grace, she thought of her as Namdi to Joe's Kintu. She didn't understand that Bennett was only a bit player in Joe's life, whose only role was to move the plot along. To Joe she was a little moon circling around him, when what she really wished was to be his sun.

Bennett slumped down in her chair, then picked herself up again and shuffled over to the front window. From the corner of her eye, she could see the lights from Joe's living room shining onto the hedge below it. She pictured him sitting in his overstuffed chair, his legs stretched out, his hands wrapped around a cup of hot tea, as he watched his children play.

There had been times when she had let herself hope that bringing Grace home would make Joe see her in a different light, as more than a friend—but it was foolishness to have such romantic dreams at her age.

Even if she did dare to admit her feelings, why would he return them? How could he love a woman who'd never inspired passion in anyone, who had never been anyone's sun?

They were friends, and she should be grateful for that and stop hoping for fairy tales.

Bennett sealed the letter and placed it on the table by the front door where it lay ready to be posted.

One thing, she could do for Joe was to find a way to dispel Grace's doubts about him, to make Grace see that everything Joe had done for her, he'd done because he wanted to, because he was generous and kind and wanted Grace to be happy.

Sunday, Maria was taking all the children roller skating. If Joe wasn't busy with his doctor friend, she would suggest that he and she take a walk along the river. We need to talk, she would say, there is something you need to know.

~

"Poor child," Joe said after they'd talked. "I should have realized."

"I'm sorry …"

Joe squeezed Bennett's hand.

"Don't be sorry. I see now that I've been too solicitous and it made her uncomfortable. I was so afraid that if I asked her to help around the house she'd think she had to earn her keep or even worse, that I only had her come so she could work for me."

"I'm sure …" Bennett began, though Grace's letter had so flustered her that she was no longer sure of what she was sure.

"I'll talk to her tonight. And don't worry, I won't say anything about the letter. I'm grateful you read it, even if you shouldn't have." He smiled at her and linked his arm in hers. "I don't know what I would do without you, Bennie."

Another woman might have grabbed onto those words, slung her arms around his neck, and said, "Nor I without you!"— but she was afraid his words couldn't possibly mean what she wanted them to, even if he did call her Bennie.

~

Once school started, Bennett noticed that Grace seemed more at ease with Joe, and when they invited her to dinner, they were often in the kitchen talking and working together.

"Joe said I could make the main course," Grace explained, as she wiped her hands on her apron, a smudge of tomato sauce on her cheek, a few specks of flour on her hair. "Juanita's been teaching me how to cook."

"Grace is already a better cook than I am," Joe said, winking at her, to show that things had changed.

"Grace lets me set the table," Hope said. "And she said you should sit at the head of the table, opposite Papa."

"She makes me clean up," Medi grumbled.

"Because you are a boy and strong enough to carry the dishes," Hope explained. "Grace says we all have to do our part."

Bennett returned Joe's smile with a nod. Things had definitely improved.

One evening, when she stayed on after the children were all in bed, she helped Joe in the kitchen with the last of the clean up.

"How is Grace adjusting to school?" she asked. "She hasn't said much to me but it must be difficult being the newcomer at her age—as well as dealing with all the academic challenges."

Bennett pushed back a lock of hair that had caught the full force of steam coming out of the dishwasher, as they waited for the dishes to cool enough to remove.

"When I first registered her I had a long talk with the principal about what grade she should be in. Everything is new, but Grace is bright. I figured we could manage the academic part by getting tutors if she needed them. She might need one for math to begin with, but she doesn't seem to mind that."

"How about her classmates? Are they accepting her?"

"I think so," Joe said, as he pulled out the plates and stacked them. "Though she did say she didn't understand why some of them are called African-American when they've never been to Africa. Some of them seem angry, she said, and I had to offer a lot of painful explanations of slavery and the struggle for civil rights, and how things have changed for the better but there are still so many inequities that have to be fixed, and that life is often difficult when you are a minority. And even when you're not. She asked me if it was all right for her to talk to anyone she wanted. I didn't understand at first, but then she said the Black kids seemed to stick together, and so did kids who spoke another language. I told her that sometimes it makes people feel more comfortable to be with people who are just like them, but you can learn so much from other cultures that she should feel free to be friends with whomever she wants. It's important to have friends to laugh with and do things with. You don't have to have many, I told her. Sometimes one good friend is all you need. She said she was glad because she would like to be friends with a girl from Iraq, who was new, too. I told her that that would be very kind of her. It can be hard to be the new one, especially if you speak a different language. So all in all I think she's doing all right."

Not only all right, but light years ahead of where Bennett had been at that age. Or at any age, for that matter. And yet she understood her life had changed. She had changed.

Every spring, under the warmth of the sun, seeds long dormant sprout, and life rises again from the barrenness of winter. Bennett's spring had been late in arriving. Sometimes a tree needs to fall to make room for the sun to shine in. Aunt Mary's death and losing her job were the two great trees that fell for Bennett. Mrs McElroy, Juanita, Maria, Meyer, Hilda, Jacob, Joe and the children were the rays of sun that had nourished her and made her grow.

But even this new Bennett wouldn't be enough for someone as vital as Joe, would it?

45

From: Peter

To: bennielhall@gmail.com

Subj: are you there?

Good morning, my friend -

Are you home or are you saving someone somewhere?

You won't believe this, but one of my father's Australian clients is interested in possibly buying a boat building concern in a river town called Bridgton, which—if google maps are correct—does have a bridge and is coincidentally near you. The company has gone under but the owner says the facilities are still up to par. So I am being sent to check out whether this is true, and if it is then possibly even to negotiate a price. My brother would be much better at this, but Dad wants me to go so he can convince me that business is the right road for me. I guess I should be grateful that he trusts me not to louse things up too much. I will be flying into Philadelphia next Wednesday and renting a car. Could you give me an idea of an interesting place for me to stay? My father says it would be inappropriate for me to negotiate from a bunk in a youth hostel, but I'm just not a Hilton Marriott kind of guy.

After I finish I plan to look for something more socially relevant to do. I thought while I was there I could look around and see if there are some poor people I could build houses for, or delinquent boys I could set straight. If nothing else there must be students who are desperately in need of someone to teach them about African wildlife conservation. I am open to many possibilities and suggestions.

How is Grace adjusting to her new life?

Hope you are doing well and I hope very much that we can get together while I am there.

If you are interested, I will bring my Uganda photos.

Cheers,

Peter

Open to possibilities. What a wonderful philosophy of life! She envied Peter his fearless openness and his ability to be social or alone. But what use was envy? Best to have him come and be inspiring.

From: Bennett

To: Peter4294@thecarringtoncompany.com

re: are you there?

Dear Peter -

I'm here and would be more than delighted if you would be my guest. Think of my place as a small but exclusive B&B, with only one special guest at a time. Warning though, I'm not so good at interesting breakfasts.

Let me know your exact flight information and I will pick you up in Philadelphia. You can rent your car locally. It'll be cheaper than at the airport.

I think I know which boatyard you mean. It was once quite a thriving company. In fact, the company I used to work for did their accounting at one time. Perhaps I can get some information from them that would be useful to you. As the buyer is Australian there will be extra red tape to wade through to close the deal. I would be glad to help with that as well as I've become pretty expert at red tape.

I'm still working at the shop and have a great "boss" so I won't have too much trouble taking time off if needed. On the other hand, you may want to work for her too. She's quite charming. And you could even learn some Spanish.

I can't imagine how an Australian even heard about it, but I hope the boatyard deal goes through and your client can revitalize the business. Bridgton was once a very pretty little town and it would be wonderful to see it come back.

Grace is adjusting well but she will love talking to someone who has been to Uganda—and can even talk about its birds with her. Do bring photos.

We will catch up in more detail when you come.

All the best,

Bennett (the children now call me Bennie, so feel free)

Bennett realized that her second bedroom was still empty, and she'd have to hustle to purchase a bed and whatever else was needed for a guest room. With Maria's help, she chose a dresser from the shop's stock and bought a lamp and chair at Ikea. When everything was bought and delivered, she asked Grace to come and help her arrange it properly, and to finally hang the portrait they'd bought in Uganda.

"I think we should have a welcome dinner," Grace said. "I can make it."

"I don't have enough chairs for all of us."

"I'm sure Joe will let us do it at our house."

Our house. That was a very good sign.

A few days later, a tasty dinner was prepared and ready to eat when Bennett and Peter returned from the airport.

The children took to Peter immediately, listening eagerly to his descriptions of the animals he'd seen on his trek in Uganda.

"You and Joe seem very close," Peter said, when he and Bennett returned home afterwards.

"We're friends, that's all."

"Are you sure? It looks like more than that to me."

Bennett shook her head. Peter wouldn't understand.

"Come on, let's get you settled. Tomorrow we'll talk about your boatyard deal."

Bennett was worried that Peter would be in over his head, arranging an international deal that required municipal, county and state permits, lawyers, bankers, and tax advisors for a client that lived on the other side of the world, but Peter said once he got the Bridgton town council to approve the sale, he could hand over the legal and financial details to his father's staff.

It only took Peter two meetings to convince the town council that nothing would be better for their town's development than to have an absent Australian businessman, represented by a company based in California whose representative in negotiations was a young man who knew nothing about boat building, take over the defunct Bridgton Boat Works. Within a week, Peter's work was done and he was free to leave.

"You're obviously good at his, Peter, don't you want to keep at it?" Bennett said over dinner the day of Peter's successful negotiations..

"No. It's really not my thing. I have a few more loose ends to tie up and then I thought I'd go to Arizona or New Mexico and work on an Indian Reservation, or maybe up north to the Rockies to volunteer in a national park."

"I know you're eager to start on your new adventure," Bennett said, "but do stay a little longer, Peter, I'm enjoying your company. There must be some places around here you'd enjoy visiting."

"I was hoping you'd say that," Peter said with a grin. "I haven't seen where you work yet."

"We'll do that first thing tomorrow."

Maria was struggling to push a dresser to the wall when Bennett and Peter arrived at the shop the next morning.

"Here, let me," Peter said, taking over.

"That's all right," Maria answered, looking questioningly at Bennett.

Bennett laughed. "This is Peter, Maria. Peter Carrington. He jumps into things."

Peter offered Maria his hand.

"Sorry, I didn't mean ... Really nice to meet you. This is a great shop you have," he said, not taking his eyes off her.

"You haven't seen it yet," she laughed, shaking his hand.

"Then you must show me. Bennett told me you were thinking of making some changes. If it involves construction, I'm your man. Ask me anything."

"Go on, Maria. I'll mind the shop meanwhile." Bennett said.

The tour took much longer than the size of the building warranted, and when they returned, Peter and Maria were laughing and talking as if they were old friends.

"I'm sure you both have work to do, so I'll be going," Peter said. "But I'll see you at eight, Maria."

"You have plans?" Bennett asked, as she walked Peter to the door. "When did that happen?'

"When Maria told me what structural changes she wanted to make, I suggested we get together tonight to talk about it. I really do have experience in that, and I even took some architecture classes. I won't give her any bum advice. Don't worry."

Peter looked so pleased that Bennett swallowed the little lump of envy she felt rising in her throat. Her life was better than it had ever been, but she'd have to accept that it was far too late to be young and full of confidence.

When Bennett rose the next morning she found a note on the kitchen table.

Going for a run along the river. I'm meeting Maria at the shop at nine. When you come, we'll tell you what we came up with last night and you can tell us what you think.

Peter.

Maria and Peter were seated at a table in the back of the shop when Bennett arrived.

"Look, Bennett. Here are some of the ideas Peter came up with last night!"

Maria waved a sheaf of drawings excitedly in front of her.

Bennett laughed.

"Oh, no. Have I been replaced already?"

"Not a chance," Maria said. "But do come look. Peter thinks we should reconfigure the whole space, not just open the wall between the shops."

"That sounds drastic," Bennett said.

"No, it isn't actually. It just means using the spaces differently. He thinks we should move the bookshop upstairs. I'd never been up there and thought it was just an attic, but it's a full second floor, with lots of windows, and totally open like a loft. That way, the main floor would give me much more space for the furniture. I've always wanted to display things in room arrangements, with paintings and objects, so that customers would feel like they were walking through a beautiful house. And upstairs will be great for the bookshop. We can put the bookcases we already have along the walls and build low ones to be free standing in the middle, back to back. And I'd like a long table and chairs for people to be able to sit down and look through things. And we have to close Mr. Schimmerling's door. We shouldn't have two doors to the street."

"And we're going to move the office out of the storage room and down to the basement," Peter said.

"Isn't it rather dark there?"

"Maria said you'd say that, but you'll love it. It'll be much bigger, and with the right lighting, and light walls, you'll think you're in the tropics."

"Well, it all sounds very exciting," Bennett said, drawn in by their enthusiasm. "We'll need permits, of course … I can start on them tomorrow."

"Wait. You're too fast, guys," Maria said. "I'm not sure I have enough money. Labor is expensive."

"I'm doing it," Peter said. "You can't turn down free labor."

"I have to think about it. You might get bored and leave me stranded."

"I wouldn't," Peter said, not smiling this time.

"Someone's at the door. I'll think about it. I promise. You just have to give me a little time," she said, and turned to go greet her customer.

"I'll leave you to it then," Peter said. "See you later, Benniehall."

After Peter and the customer were both gone, Maria asked Bennett what she thought.

"I'm really tempted, Bennett—he has some great ideas—but thinking about what it will cost makes me nervous. I'm not sure I'll qualify for a loan. And what if we do all this and then people stop coming? We don't have many young customers as it is."

"I'll talk to Peter tonight," Bennett said. "I don't know him that well but I like him. If he offered to help you I'm sure he means it. He's worked as a carpenter, so he knows what he's doing. But I'll make sure he's not just thinking of this as a lark."

Bennett took Peter out for dinner at an Italian restaurant in the neighborhood that had recently been taken over by a young couple from Sicily.

"White tablecloths, just like in Italy," Peter said.

Lining the walls were black and white photographs of men and women, matted and framed in black.

When the owner came to take their order, Peter asked if the photo behind them was of a relative.

"Si, that is my nonna, my grandmother. The others are my husband's aunts and uncles."

"You look like her. Are you from Palermo?"

"No, no, from Caltagirone."

"That's where that long, beautiful staircase is, isn't it? The one with all the tiles. It was one of my favorite places."

She was so pleased he knew it that she insisted on bringing them an aperitivo on the house, with a bowl of warm olives, fresh bread and a bottle of olive oil.

"The oil is from my family's olives—only for special guests," she said.

After she left for the kitchen, Bennett said, "How do you do that, make friends with everyone?"

"I like people."

"Just in general or specifically, too?"

"What do you mean?"

"Do you like Maria specifically? She means a lot to me and I don't want you giving her ideas you are not serious about, or that will cost much more than she can afford. She works hard, and can't waste money she doesn't have. She has a young daughter and takes that responsibility very seriously. I don't want you taking advantage of her."

"Bennett, I'm hurt. I wouldn't do that. She's your friend, so I wouldn't do that to her—or to you."

"Sorry, I was just being protective, but tell me, what makes you want to do this instead of going west as you had planned?"

"Because I really like the idea of making an ordinary, rather run down place into a place people from all over town would want to come to. And I do like Maria, specifically. I've earned enough money now, thanks to my dad, so I can support myself for a while and help her. It will cost her money because she'll have to pay for the materials, but I won't go overboard. It'll be mostly paint and drywall, and I'll contribute the labor—and as payment she can write me a good reference afterwards."

"All right then. I wanted to make sure. She's worried that this might not be the right business to put a lot of money into. Young people don't seem to be into antiques."

"But they do need furniture, so she could try showing mid-century modern. That's very popular now. It might even be worth importing some. Maria could show those pieces in combination with a nice antique piece to show how you can use them together. Just think how nice it looks at your house, Bennett, a beautiful inlaid desk mixed in with more modern stuff."

After Bennett reported his conversation to Maria and she told him she'd stayed up all night thinking about it and decided that if she had a really good space, she could always change what was in it. It would make a great art gallery or crafted clothing shop. She owned a building and might as well make the best of it.

"But we still have to watch the money we spend. I can't get in over my head. Did Peter say he could do the work himself?"

"Most of it."

"I might know some guys in my apartment building who could help. They're always looking for work."

Updating and enlarging the rest room became the first project, moving the office downstairs the second. The basement was so big, they split it in two—half for the office, the other half for storage and furniture refinishing. With freshly painted walls and updated lighting, the new office looked almost sunny. New and ample cabinets gave Bennett a chance to organize all the supplies and paperwork.

In addition to Mr. Vecchietti's old roll-top desk, which was kept for sentimental reasons and became home to the computer, Bennett now had a long table where things could be spread out and looked at. Not only papers, but collections of small objects that Maria sometimes brought back from estate sales.

"As soon as we can, we'll put down carpeting and get proper heating," Maria said.

"We can manage for now, " Bennett said. "It's dry and insulated. If it gets too cold I can use Mr. Vecchietti's old kerosene heater. By summer, we should have enough money—"

"Summer's good. You should always install carpet in warm weather," Peter said. "I have some other ideas for the summer, too."

"Doesn't sound like he's leaving, Maria," Bennett said, which made her blush.

Upstairs, Maria and Peter rearranged furniture, placed objects, and hung paintings. Bennett was pleased to see them working so well together, bouncing ideas off each other. Peter didn't push her and Bennett could see that she appreciated that. She'd been wary of men after Carlos, she said. But little by little Peter was winning her trust.

When they started the main-floor renovations Maria began posting signs: *WE ARE OPEN. Please Excuse This Temporary Eyesore.*

Then: *Pardon the Mess; We're Getting a Makeover;.*

Followed by: *Don't Give Up On Us, the Wait Will Be Worth iI!*

Some of the customers became discouraged anyway, so when renovations moved up to the attic, Peter hung a banner stating

> ROME WASN'T BUILT IN A DAY
> *Maybe we shouldn't have used the same contractor!*

That brought them back laughing.

When the books were transferred upstairs, Bennett was in her element. She divided the books into categories, alphabetized them, and labeled all the shelves accordingly. She suggested having rolling stools in the aisles for better browsing. And she again began discovering books she wanted for herself, or for the children or Joe or Meyer or Juanita or Maria and now, Peter. The list of people she cared about had grown quite long.

Thanks to hard work on everyone's part, both floors of the shop and the basement were finished by early November. With the shop brightened and reorganized, Bennett felt the same sense of promise she'd felt when she first entered her light-filled house on Spring Street. There should be a law prohibiting dark houses and dreary workplaces. The world would be a much happier, more hopeful place.

As Thanksgiving grew near, Maria and Peter decided that a Grand Reopening would be just the thing to bring in holiday shoppers. They placed signs around the area, sent announcements to their old customers, put an ad in the local paper, and invited just about everyone they knew—including the young Sicilian couple from the restaurant.

Bennett called Meyer, hoping he could come, but the nurse said he was still under the weather but not to worry. It was just best not to be in a crowd.

The Grand Reopening brought a slew of first-time customers who came to browse and have a glass of wine, glad to have discovered a new place. Old customers came to reminisce, hoping to meet old friends, and found that much of what had brought them in all those years had not changed. They promised to return.

As the last of the customers left, Maria threw her arms around Bennett, and then even more enthusiastically around Peter, where they lingered quite a while longer.

"How can I ever thank you?" she said.

"How about a party?" Peter suggested. "Don't you think she deserves one, Benniehall?"

"Absolutely. We could combine it with Thanksgiving and do it at my house. Maybe Meyer could come then."

"We can't," Maria interjected, "Joe is planning a big feast at his house because it's Grace's first Thanksgiving and he wants it to be really special." Then she grinned at Peter. "You'll have to come dressed as a pilgrim. Or a turkey—what do you think, Bennett?"

46

Bennett had called Meyer Gold several times, only to be told every time that Meyer was fine, only a little tired and not up for visitors. She'd waited for Meyer to make the next move, but it never came so she still hadn't had the chance to thank him for encouraging her to go to Uganda. And now she had let far too much time pass. Why hadn't he called? If she didn't get to talk to him this time, she would go over to the apartment, invited or not. She was reaching for the phone to tell Maria she'd be late when it rang.

"Bennett? I hope I am not disturbing you."

"Meyer? I'm so happy to hear your voice, but where are you calling from? I didn't recognize the number."

Meyer hesitated. "I ... I borrowed the nurse's ..." His words were broken off by a deep and chesty cough. When he tried to speak his breath sounded labored, and he barely managed to say that he'd have to call back.

When twenty minutes had passed and he hadn't called, Bennett pulled up the number from the caller ID and called back.

The phone rang three times before a voice answered.

"Riverside Hospice, may I help you?"

"Oh, I'm sorry I must have the wrong ... no, wait. Do you have a patient named Meyer Gold?"

"Yes, we do. Would you like me to direct your call to his room?"

"Yes ... but wait, could you tell me first how long he has been there?"

There was the sound of fluttering paper.

"It will be five weeks tomorrow, ma'am."

"Five weeks? Why did no one ... ? I mean, what is wrong with him?"

People weren't in hospice unless they were dying.

"You are welcome to visit him, but I'm afraid I cannot discuss his condition with you unless you are an approved family member."

"He has no family. I am a friend. A good friend."

"I'm sorry. Perhaps if you talk to his doctor. He will be doing rounds later this morning."

"I'll be there."

Bennett pulled her Uganda folder off the shelf. She would show Meyer a few of the brochures; tell him about crossing the equator—that was silly, he'd probably crossed the equator a dozen times. The guidebook? No, she'd given that to Grace.

Bennett's hands were shaking. She had to pull herself together. What good would she be to Meyer like this?

The doll, of course, the doll for Elsie. She couldn't forget that. It would make him happy to know that Bennett had thought of it.

Bennett wrapped the doll in a sheet of tissue paper and placed it in a plain shoe box. She glanced at the clock on the wall. It was still early. That would give her time to sit with Meyer until the doctor made his rounds. She'd ask the doctor for permission to bring Meyer to Joe's for Thanksgiving. That would do him good, wouldn't it?

∼

Meyer's room was big and sunny, much grander than his little walk-up apartment. His bed was next to floor-to-ceiling windows that overlooked the hospice garden and the meadow beyond it. The back of his bed was elevated to let him look out, and to prevent fluid from filling his lungs. Two IV bags dripped saline solution and antibiotics into a picc line attached to the vein on the inside of his elbow. An oxygen tank stood at the ready on the side of his bed.

"I have pneumonia," Meyer said. "Nothing to worry about. They're giving me megadoses of antibiotics. I should be up and about in no time."

"Why didn't you let me know, Meyer? I would have come much sooner. The receptionist told me you've been here for five weeks. I thought you were home. I feel terrible."

"Doctors are too cautious. I was thinking of suing them for over-attentiveness and then taking the money and running off to the Caribbean. What do you think?"

"I'm serious, Meyer. You should have let me or Maria know."

"You have enough to think about. I'm fine. They're taking good care of me. So let's not talk about that. I want to hear about Uganda. You don't mind if I close my eyes. It's how I listen best."

When Bennett finished, Meyer opened his eyes and aid, "You have done a wonderful thing, my dear. You have given the child a future, a future filled with possibilities. Did you bring me a picture? I would like to see her."

"I did, and I intend for you to meet her, but first I want to give you this —it's something for your collection. For Elsie's collection."

Meyer's hands trembled as he opened the box and saw the doll. His eyes welled up and he had to swallow hard before he could speak.

"Thank you, my dear friend. It's exactly what she would have chosen."

Bennett spent the next three days at Meyer's bedside, arriving early and leaving late. The doctor said he didn't have long. It wasn't only pneumonia. Meyer's heart was failing. That was the reason for the fluid in his lungs. It was too late for surgery. He wasn't strong enough.

Sometimes Bennett and Meyer talked. Sometimes she read to him. Sometimes they just sat in comfortable and comforting silence.

"Were you always a reader, Meyer?"

Meyer nodded, pointing to a half-dozen books on his night table. "And you?"

"After my parents died, I read to fill the emptiness. But I read mostly reference books. They were safe, practical choices that introduced me to knowledge I might not have had—as they were meant to—but sadly they did not inspire me to dream or to act. There was a time, where there was this boy...but that is long ago. It's because of Mr. Schimmerling that I rediscovered fiction, and learned to think of books as friends."

"Do you have regrets, Bennett?"

"Yes. Too many. The greatest is that I've wasted so much time, so I will not waste anymore by regretting."

"You are a wise woman."

"How about you, Meyer? Do you have regrets?"

"Only one, but it's a big one." Meyer took Bennett's hand and pulled her closer. "When my sister died I lost the person I loved most in the world, so I thought I could show how much I loved her by following her list to the letter. But I was wrong. I didn't understand that she had made that list out of love for me, as a way to give me the world —so that I would go out and live in it, not so that I would check off places as if they were items on a grocery list. I loved my sister but I didn't understand that love needs to be practiced and nourished—on people and by people. Use it or lose it. Isn't that what they say now? Well, I didn't use it. I wasted it on a list. Until you gave me New Orleans. That's when I understood."

"And you gave me Uganda."

"No, it wasn't me and it wasn't the list. It was your love for Joe that gave you Uganda, that led you to find Grace and complete a family. You've made me feel a part of that and for that I truly thank you."

Meyer closed his eyes. It was late and Bennett thought he'd fallen asleep this time, but when she rose to leave, Meyer put out his hand to stop her.

"Don't assume Joe knows how you feel. You have to tell him."

"I don't think ..."

"Don't think. Speak. He needs to hear the words. Remember—practice and nourish."

On the fourth day, Bennett returned with a small parade behind him: Joe and the children, Maria, Juanita, and Isabella. The children unfolded a long banner they'd decorated with drawings of birds and flowers, and the words *We Love Meyer*, and hung it over his window. He asked the children what they most enjoyed doing and listened to each of their answers with great interest.

When Bennett returned the next day, Meyer told her that he'd asked them to disconnect the picc line so that Bennett could take him into the garden. He wanted to see the last of the chrysanthemums while they were still in bloom.

"Would you wait for me in the hall, Bennett, while the nurse helps me dress? Then we can go."

Bennett walked quietly up and down the hall, careful not to disturb the other patients. Many of them were alone and sleeping, attached to machines that kept them nourished and comfortable. Some had their families with them and she could hear soft conversations and even laughter.

When she returned to Meyer's room, Meyer was sitting in a wheel chair, wearing the suit Bennett had first seen him in. He was so frail now that it was a size too big, but he had lost none of his dignity.

"I think I should bring a blanket, Meyer. It's sunny but the breeze is rather chilly."

"Of course, Bennett. I wouldn't want you to catch cold," Meyer said, his eyes twinkling.

When they reached outside Bennett wrapped the blanket around Meyer's lap and legs and pushed the wheel chair into the garden. The gardeners had already started cutting back the chrysanthemums that had faded.

"Let's go a little further, Bennett. Down the street a bit. There's a school down there. Maybe the children are at recess. It's such a nice day and it would be fun to watch them for a bit. Maybe we could even go for a cup of coffee afterwards. It's been a long time since I've had an espresso."

The sun moved under a cloud as they walked, and she saw Meyer shiver.

"I'm feeling a little cold," Bennett said. "Do you mind if we go back?"

"Not at all, Bennett. I think I might take a nap, and I'm sure you have much to do. I've monopolized a lot of your time, and Maria must miss you at the shop."

He reached up and took Bennett's hand. His grip was still strong.

"Don't forget to talk to Joe."

Bennett stopped by a florist on the way to the hospice the next morning. When she reached Meyer's room she found it empty and the bed stripped but not yet remade.

As she stood in the doorway looking lost, a young nurse came up to her.

"May I help you?"

"I'm looking for Mr. Gold."

"Are you Miss Hall?"

"Yes." Her stomach cramped into a knot.

"I'm sorry, Miss Hall, but Mr. Gold passed away early this morning. We were about to call you."

Bennett stared into the room.

"Was he alone?" she asked after a moment.

"He looked very peaceful when I arrived," the nurse replied. "He was holding a doll in his hand. It was really sweet." When Bennett didn't respond, she added, "It was a cloth doll with a long skirt."

"Yes, I know it."

"It was handmade and must have held a special meaning for him."

"It was his sister's."

Bennett felt her knees grow weak as she said it. She reached out to hold on to the door but it gave way and she began to sway. The nurse took her by the elbow to support her and led her to the waiting room.

"Miss Hall, you are looking a bit pale. It's the shock. Come sit down. A glass of juice will make you feel better."

She returned with the juice and sat with her for a minute.

"When you are ready, Miss Hall, I believe there is a box Mr. Gold wanted you to have."

"How do you know?"

She hesitated and then, putting her hand gently on Bennett's shoulder, she said that Riverside was a place where patients arranged such things.

She brought her a cardboard box and said that she could take it home if she preferred to open it in private.

Bennett thanked her and, not knowing what else to do, went out to the parking lot and, with the box in her hands, sat in her car for twenty minutes before she turned on the engine and drove home.

47

Bennett glanced up at Joe's window. No one was home, of course. It was almost eleven and she should be at work as well. This was a busy time at the shop and she should be there, not sitting in her car in front of her house but she couldn't face having to tell Maria about Meyer. She needed time to absorb it herself.

She walked up her steps and unlocked the door. Lost in thought, she stood for a moment in the vestibule until a gust of wind propelled her to the kitchen, making the door slam shut behind her.

When her father died, she was so young, her mother thought it best not to have her attend the funeral so she'd be spared the tears and condolences. It was as if her father had merely moved into a part of the apartment Bennett couldn't reach. Months, perhaps even years, passed before Bennett fully grasped the permanence of his death. By then it was too late to cry. It was even worse when her mother died. Aunt Mary would break down at the mention of her name. So it became one of the many things they didn't talk about.

Even poor Mrs. McElroy's death had been so darkened by guilt that it had crowded out any sense of loss Bennet might have—should have—felt.

Bennett placed Meyer's box on the kitchen table, gently stroking the lid as if to console it. When at last she opened it, she found, perched on top of the cloth doll, Meyer's worn leather wallet, a watch, and an envelope neatly marked *For Bennett*.

My dear friend,

Please forgive me for choosing to burden you with my last wishes, but I know that I can trust you to do your best to grant them and to understand the reason for them.

Inside my wallet is the key to my apartment. The rent has been paid for another two months. That should give you enough time to do what needs to be done without having to rush.

The gifts that I have collected over these many years were meant for a child, and so I would like them to go to children. Elsie would find a certain harmony to the Ugandan doll being given to Grace. She, Medi, Hope, and Isabella should choose whatever trinkets delight them. The rest please give to children at a homeless shelter and tell them to dream big dreams, as Elsie did, no matter their obstacles.

Among my books are some that you grown-ups might enjoy, and I'd like to think that a part of me would then be with each of you. The rest you may sell at the shop, for many came from there. Perhaps they will bring a little extra money to help Maria continue with her renovations.

You will also find, in the closet, that I kept travel journals. They were, I suppose, my way of sharing thoughts and observations with Elsie, which is why I couldn't bear to throw them out. You are welcome to read them and join me in my travels. But if you are not interested, please feel free to dispose of them for they have no monetary let alone literary value.

There are also some bureaucratic details to take care of, such as closing my bank account and letting Social Security know they need not concern themselves with me any longer. I wish I could spare you these annoyances, and apologize that I did not ask your permission in advance. It especially pains me that the few dollars in the bank will be little compensation for these unpleasant chores.

I have saved the worst for last. What to do with my body. It goes against Jewish tradition, but I have no family that will object, no family grave to spend eternity in, so I have arranged to be cremated and have asked for you to receive my ashes. You will not be pleased by this, and I sincerely apologize, but it is only temporary. I would like, if and when you can do it, for my ashes to be scattered in the ocean where I spent so many years.

Having burdened you so heavily, I hope I can now lift the burden a little at least by telling you how greatly you've enriched my last days and thoughts with your friendship. I leave this world a happy man.

Meyer

Bennett her head in her hands. Her shoulders shaking, she felt the full weight of all the grief she had ever felt but never expressed.

48

Thanksgiving dinner wasn't to be served until late afternoon, so while Joe was finishing his rounds at the hospital, and the others were cooking and baking and preparing the table, Peter found himself left with the manly chore of chopping wood for the fireplace, but since the day turned out to be unseasonably warm he asked Bennett to help him wash everyone's cars instead.

"Maria's daughter is a nice child, don't you think?" Peter said, not looking up as he dipped a sponge into a bucket of soapy water and then energetically scrubbed the wheels of Maria's car.

"Yes, she's a sweetheart," Bennett replied, wondering what Peter was getting at.

"Is her father in the picture?" Peter asked, moving on to the doors. "No one ever talks about him."

"No, he never was. He died some time ago."

This time Peter did look up. "Oh, good."

"And why is that?" Bennett asked, suppressing a grin.

"Just curious." He dipped his sponge into the bucket again, and then added. "And I was thinking I should get a Delaware driver's license. What do you think?"

"Yes, I see the connection," Bennett said, starting to laugh. "And exactly how long are you thinking of staying? And have you told Maria?"

"Of course! I just wanted to see how you felt about it."

"What about your other plans? Have you given up on them?"

"Yeah, well. Winter's coming. Not the right time to work in a national park ... besides, Maria and I have this great idea of turning the storage room into a café. I'm going to put in French doors and fix up the area behind the building so we can have an outdoor patio in the summer—you know, with umbrellas and potted plants, maybe even a wall with a trellis."

"A touch of Provence in Wilmington?"

"Exactly. Good idea for a name, Benniehall, but why do you look so serious?" Peter said.

"I just want to make sure you have good intentions…"

"Toward Maria? Yes, I do, and she feels the same way. But before we take any real steps we want Isabella to be sure about me. In the meantime, I'm going to look for a little place of my own."

Bennett put her hand on Peter's shoulder.

"You don't have to do that. You can stay with me as long as you like—as long as you make your bed, or at least close the door."

Peter laughed.

"Yeah, sorry about that. And I promise to keep forks with forks and spoons with spoons."

This time it was Bennett who laughed.

"Maria likes things in order, too, you know. She'll appreciate my training you."

"It's three o'clock!" Medi shouted from the window. "Mama says you have to finish the cars and come in. And Grace says you can't look at the table until we're ready to eat. She and Hope decorated it special."

Joe returned from his rounds at three, and by 3:30 they were all gathered in the living room, with the children on the floor, sitting with their arms around their knees, listening attentively as Joe told the story of the first Thanksgiving.

"See, Bennie," whispered Grace, "you do have stories just like the Buganda have."

Maria and Peter sat on the sofa holding hands. Juanita leaned against the kitchen doorway to listen, while Bennett stood by the fireplace and watched it all. Her life would be complete if Joe and the children were truly hers. Meyer was right. She couldn't let this escape her. She had to tell Joe how she felt—but not today, not when everything was perfect and there was a chance of spoiling it. She would tell him when she was sure the time was right.

"Bennie," Joe said, shaking her out of her thoughts, "You are a better historian than I am. Grace wants to know more about the Pilgrims and why they came here and what happened to them after their first Thanksgiving, so I'm giving the floor to you."

Someday when they were alone and he called her Bennie again. That's when she would tell him.

49

One Saturday evening in December, when Peter was out with Maria, Joe at a school function with the children, and no one was at the shop, Bennett decided to sort through the dusty, long-neglected closet in the boiler room.

The latch on the door had rusted and Bennett had to pry it open. Except for a worn-out corn broom, all she found were four dusty cartons marked *VECCHIETTI*. Why had he put them there, she wondered, as she dusted them off and pulled them into the office.

A sudden wind rattled the basement window, blowing it open. The window latch was bent and Bennett had to jiggle it to make it close. Another thing that had to be fixed. She'd better make a note of it for Peter.

She shivered and put her jacket back on. It was colder than usual in the basement, despite the insulation and fresh drywall Peter had put up. Sooner or later they'd have to put proper heat down there, but for the time being Mr. Vecchietti's old kerosene heater would do. Bennett dragged it out of the boiler room and over to the long table along the wall, and lit it. Then she pulled the cartons closer to the table, and lined them up next to her chair.

The first was full of musty-smelling but clean magazines: *LIFE* from the 30's, 40's and 50's, an assortment of 1920's *National Geographics*, several issues of the Italian *Oggi* and *L'Espresso,* and a few copies of *Vogue* with covers by Erté. She separated them into four stacks on the table and made a note to order plastic covers for them. A magazine section in the attic book shop could be of interest to many of their customers, especially if they kept the prices reasonable.

A page fluttered and Bennett felt a chill as the small basement window above the table swung open and banged against the wall. The latch on that window would have to be fixed too. No point having new insulation if the windows didn't stay shut. She pushed the window closed, turned the kerosene heater up some more and hoped the latch would hold.

The second carton contained hundreds of yellowed articles clipped from newspapers and magazines, recipes written on scraps of paper, and who knew what else. She thought they might have been Mrs. Vecchietti's. She would take them home and go through them thoroughly when she had time.

Decades worth of Playbills, opera and concert programs filled the third carton. Clearly all performances that Mr. and Mrs. Vecchietti had attended, for Mrs. Vecchietti —from the feminine look of the handwriting—had marked each program with the date they'd attended, sometimes adding a few words of commentary or description: *Delightful and funny, great cast but mediocre story, good sets, enchanting, moving, devastating, a waste of time.*

Bennett pulled up a chair and sorted the programs into piles on the table. She enjoyed looking through them, and wondered why she had gone to so few plays and concerts herself. She'd barely even gone to the movies, settling for them on TV. How foolish to have missed so much for no reason but inertia.

The Playbills might be of interest to theatre memorabilia collectors. A few of them had autographs, which were of special interest to fans and might command higher prices.

At the bottom of the carton, under an oversized movie souvenir book, she found a small stack of programs tied together with a ribbon. On the top was a glossy placard of the type posted in concert halls, with a black-and-white photograph of a fine-featured, dark-haired young man in a tuxedo, seated, one hand in his pocket, his face in semi-profile—and the words:

WILLIAM HALL
pianist
Carnegie Chamber Music Hall
Monday Evening, March 23, at 8:30 o'clock

It took Bennett a moment to grasp that she was looking at her father. As she turned the placard over she saw that her father had written *To Amalia and Lorenzo, my friends and most loyal fans, with gratitude and affection, Will.*

Bennett passed her fingers gently over the image of her father's face. Poor Father. Poor Will. He had so much talent. Why had he given up?

Bennett had never heard him called Will, had never even seen a photograph of him. The memory of his face had faded so long ago that she could not have described it. But Mr Vecchietti must have remembered, and seen the young pianist's image reflected in Bennett's face the day Maria brought her into the shop. How strange to suddenly realize she looked like her father.

There were several programs of her father's other concerts and recitals—in New York, Philadelphia, Baltimore and, of course, Wilmington. How amazing that Mr. Vecchietti had been to all of them, and had known her father well enough to call him Will.

Bennett spent two more hours leafing through theatre programs of Broadway productions, regional plays and even high school performances, and reading the newspaper reviews that the Vecchiettis had slipped between the program pages.

When she finished, she tied the ribbon around her father's concert programs again and held them tightly to her chest. She was not going to be like her father. She would fight for Joe. For Joe and the children. For life.

She put the bundle to one side as her cell phone rang. As if he knew what she was thinking, it was Joe.

"Are you at the shop?" he asked. "How about going out for dinner? The kids are having a pajama party at Maria's. "

"I'd love to. Could you meet me here? I'd like to show you some things I found. I'll be in the basement, but I'll be glad to get out of here."

Bennett put her phone back in her pocket and stood up. Her head felt heavy, as if her neck could not hold it up. The mustiness of all the old papers was making her queasy. Overcome by a sudden wave of nausea, she clutched at the back of the chair, stumbled and fell.

50

*J*oe left the house, turning the corner of Spring Street, and found the street blocked by a fallen tree and a municipal public works truck. He couldn't back up because of the line of cars behind him. When it was clear the truck wasn't moving, he turned the car sharply to the left, drove up on the sidewalk and back to where he'd started. The streets on the longer route were empty but he hit one red light after the other.

"Bennett, I'm so sorry it took me so long," he called out, when he finally reached the shop.

No answer.

He ran down the steps to the basement and called out again.

No answer.

At the far end of the basement room, in front of the table on which Bennett had spread the contents of the cartons, she lay motionless on the floor next to an overturned chair.

"Oh my God, Bennie, are you all right?"

Joe felt his own breath becoming more labored. Looking around, he spotted the old kerosene heater. Realizing what had happened, he turned the heater off and opened the window.

"I'm calling an ambulance. We have to get you out of here," he said.

He gently checked Bennett's arms and legs. Nothing broken. Fighting his own increasing nausea, he raised Bennett into a standing position, put his left arm around her waist, and flung her right arm around his neck.

"Hold on, Bennie, hold on. I'm taking you upstairs. One step at a time. We can make it."

One ... two ... three ... four ...... eleven ... twelve ..... fifteen ... sixteen.

His body aching, Joe managed to reach the top, and staggered to the front door. With one hand, he opened it and took a deep breath of the cold air just as the ambulance arrived.

The medics lifted Bennett onto a stretcher and into the ambulance, and connected her to oxygen and a heart monitor.

"Are you all right, doc?" the younger medic asked, recognizing him.

"I will be. I just need to sit down and catch my breath. You can leave. I'll follow."

"Are you sure you can drive?"

"Yes, yes! I can, in a minute. Please, hurry."

"We'll take good care of her, doc, don't worry."

"I'll be right behind you," Joe said, getting up.

With the windows open, he raced to keep up with them, ignoring the screeching brakes of an oncoming car as he sped through a red light. Finally at the hospital, he squeezed his car into a narrow space near the emergency room entrance.

The revolving doors moved at a glacial pace.

"Faster, for God's sake," he muttered as he pushed at the glass door. It stopped revolving in protest. He put his hands to his side, and the door began to move again.

"What bay is she in? The woman they brought in? Her names's Hall, Bennett Hall.""Eight, Dr. Muir. Down the hall to the left, and then through the double doors on your right. You can't miss it."

"I know."

Joe opened the curtain to bay 8 and saw a doctor and nurse at Bennett's side. An oxygen mask covered her mouth, a blood pressure cuff squeezed her arm, making the numbers on the monitor rise and fall until they settled on 130/78. A little high.

"Is she conscious?"

"Not yet," the doctor answered in a normal voice. "But her vitals are stable and her breathing has improved. Do you know how long she inhaled the carbon monoxide?"

"I'm not sure. Less than thirty minutes, I would think."

If only he hadn't been delayed.

"Where was she when you found her?" the doctor asked.

"On the floor next to an overturned chair."

"So she might have hit her head. I do feel a small contusion on the right side." He turned to the nurse. "Put in an order for a CT scan in case she's suffered a concussion. We should have the results of his blood tests in an hour."

"Wakeup, Bennie. We need you, the children and I."

Joe sat for more than an hour, stroking her hand, and talking.

When they came to take Bennett to radiology, he called Maria.

Shortly after midnight, Joe saw Bennett's eyelids flutter then open.

"What are you doing here, Joe?"

"Keeping you company. You had an accident, but you'll be fine."

"Was it the stove?"

"Yup. We're getting rid of it, don't worry."

"Can I go home now?"

"Tomorrow."

"Good," she said and smiled, her eyes drooping again. "I think I'll sleep a little more."

Joe, pulled up her blanket and kissed her cheek.

"I'll be back in the morning."

51

"How are you feeling?' Joe asked, when he arrived the next day.

"Much better. Just a little headache."

"Good, but you might have had a minor concussion, so you have to tell me if you have any problems with vision or memory; if you notice any personality changes, or sensitivity to light or noise; or have problems concentrating or lose your sense of taste or smell. And you can't drive or drink alcohol. And don't make any important decisions."

"I feel fine, really."

"In any case, you're staying with us for a while. Can't have you falling down the stairs or passing out. The kids insist."

"I guess I have no choice then," Bennett said, with a grin.

When Bennett and Joe arrived home, Maria, Peter, Juanita and the children were already there, waiting. The living room was festooned with multicolored balloons and crêpe-paper ribbons. An eight-foot long banner painted in fluorescent colors and covered with misshapen paper hearts hung from the ceiling. WELCOME HOME, BENNIE! it said, in fat letters of varied heights.

Hope threw her arms around Bennett's waist.

"Do you like it? Medi and I did it all by ourselves except that Grace told us how to spell welcome 'cause it's a long word."

"I love it. I'm going to keep it forever," Bennett said.

"We fixed up Medi's room for you," Grace said, "and Juanita and I are making dinner."

"I can't put you out like that, Medi."

"Papa said you could get dizzy and fall down the stairs," Medi interjected.

Bennett laughed and looked at Joe. "Did he now?"

"Cross my heart," Medi said, looking very serious.

"I just meant that you shouldn't be alone," Joe said.

"See?" Grace whispered to Medi. "I told you he likes her."

"And I already brought all the paperwork from the shop so you can work here," Maria said, winking at her.

The next few days flew by. Although Bennett was supposed to be recuperating, she found herself thrown into the midst of all their everyday activities. She realized how little she knew about the minutia of normal family life: morning cereal spilled and quickly cleaned up; scrambling to find missing socks before the school bus arrived (when had Joe stopped driving them?); more laundry than she'd ever thought possible, to be divided into light and dark piles before it was washed, and neatly sorted and folded by wearer after; arguments about who left the water running in the bathroom, or whose turn it was to choose a television program or take out the trash.

When the children asked her help with homework, her attentiveness was soon as prized as it was taken for granted. In the quiet hours she and Joe were alone, they talked or worked side by side—she on the shop's paperwork, he on an article he was writing about pediatric oncology developments.

Joe discovered that Bennett hummed and curled her hair around her finger when she concentrated.

Bennett noticed that Joe stole glances at her and smiled when he thought she wasn't looking. Maybe what she feared was impossible was possible after all? If only she could be sure.

A few days later, as the children were doing their homework at the kitchen table, Bennett went to the front door to check for the mail and heard Grace whispering.

"It's just like we're a real family now. Do you remember the story I told you? How Kintu proved his love for Nambi by being brave and clever and overcoming every hurdle?"

"Yes, we remember," Hope said.

"Don't you think Papa is Bennie's Kintu?"

Bennett didn't move.

"You have to ask Papa that," Medi answered.

Sensible boy, Bennett thought as she opened the door and reached into the mailbox. And if Grace asked, what would Joe say? Could he say anything without knowing how Bennett felt?

Sunset had turned the sky red and gold and there wasn't a wisp of a cloud to be seen. Red sky at night, sailor's delight, Meyer would have said. A sign of promise and hope. Tomorrow, when they were alone, she would tell Joe how she felt. It was time. The right time.

But as darkness fell and Joe said he had work to do, her niggling doubts began their march—one by one, like an army of ants. She and Joe were friends. Good friends. Why not leave it at that? The children liked spending time with her, turned to her when they had questions or needed help. Wouldn't she be risking that? How would they feel if Joe rejected her? Wouldn't they side with him, their father? What if he kept them from her? What if she made Joe so uncomfortable with her unwanted show of affection that he decided to move somewhere else? Leave the house. Leave the country. She could lose everything. Everything that mattered to her.

That night, as she stood in the bathroom brushing her teeth, she wondered when her hair had gone so gray? She wasn't young anymore. What if it was too late?

52

Bennett woke earlier than usual the next morning, dressed quietly, and went outside to wait for the newspaper. The air was brisk, the early morning sky red again. Sailors take warning, *But that doesn't mean run and hide,* Meyer would have said. No goal was ever achieved without risk. Think of Uganda. Talk to Joe. It was time.

Encouraged at having overcome her doubts, she went back inside, and set the table for breakfast. She was soon joined by Joe and the children. After they'd all eaten and Joe had left for work, Bennett walked the children to the corner and waited with them until the school bus came.

Peter was waiting on her front stoop when she returned.

"I'm on my way to the shop," Peter said, handing her a piece of paper, "would you mind looking at this invoice? I think we were charged for materials we didn't order."

"Sure. How's the café construction coming along?"

"Good. French doors are in. Back patio flagstones have been laid, and I've started building the pergola. Since Juanita hasn't had to come here, she's been helping us."

"Good way to get to know your future mother-in-law, Peter."

Peter grinned. "Just what I thought. How are you feeling?"

"Much better. It's time I moved back home."

"Then you have work to do before you leave."

"At the shop?"

"No. I mean with Joe. Grace firmly believes Joe is your destiny, you know, so you might as well make it happen," Peter said, giving her a friendly shove. "Go for it, Benniehall!"

Bennett blushed.

"Go to work, Peter."

"You have no choice, no point chickening out," Peter said, laughing as he bounded down the steps.

Peter had a way of making anything seem possible—but dreams were fragile, and could shatter on a word or a glance. So Bennett knew she had to find just the right moment to tell Joe that she loved him and needed him and never wanted to live another day without him.

No, no, no. That was much too much! Joe would feel ambushed if she blurted out her feelings like that, completely out of the blue.

On the other hand... he might be happy to have her feelings out in the open so he could ask her to marry him then and there.

No, hold on. A proposal was serious business, not just an invitation for a stroll in the park. Grace might believe this was their destiny, but they were adults who knew the difference between myths and real life.

Maybe she was rushing this. Shouldn't he be courting her first? Isn't that how it was in books? She'd know more if she'd read more novels instead of dictionaries. Joe was a down-to-earth sort of person. He might think her declarations of love were silly or worse. She would be devastated if he thought her ridiculous.

On the other hand, even practical people liked to feel special. She'd read once that charm was the ability to make the other person feel they were the most fascinating person in the room. So that's what she needed to do. Charm him.

Of course, she had no clue how to do that. It's not as if she'd spent her life practicing. If only she could ask Meyer.

She'd have to sleep on it.

When she awoke the next morning, Joe was in the kitchen and the table was already set for breakfast.

"I would have done that, Joe."

"I know, but I've taken advantage of you long enough," he said.

"Oh. Guess I'd better move my things back home then," she said, trying to smile.

"No rush, and we'll still have dinner together, won't we? Can I drive you to work? Maria said you were going back today."

"No, that's all right. It's time I got on with things on my own again."

After he left, Bennett wondered why she'd said that, as if she was eager to be on her own. She made Medi's and Hope's beds—Grace always made hers herself—threw a load of laundry into the washing machine, tidied up the kitchen, then packed up her belongings and took them home.

She decided to walk to work. It always helped her think.

She knew what she wanted now. If only she knew how to achieve it.

By noon, she was back at work.

"Come look at what we've done in the basement," Maria said. "We can't have anything happening to you again. The new heater is in and Peter fixed the window latch so it's nice and warm—and clean, thanks to Mama. And I left you a bunch of mail. I hope you don't mind going through it."

"Not at all, especially now that it's so nice down here."

Bennett saw that Juanita had boxed up all the papers she'd left lying on the table that awful night. When she had a minute she'd sort through them again and show Joe the photos of her father. But shouldn't she do something that had meaning for him instead? A special evening somewhere, just the two of them?

A trip would be even better. To... Naples! Joe had often said he wanted to see where his mother was born and his parents met. They could all go for Christmas.

Perfect.

Impossible. Ridiculous.

Christmas was only a couple of weeks away and Joe couldn't take leave again so soon. Besides, he might already have plans.

Of course he'd have made plans. It would be Grace's first Christmas with him, and the first with Medi and Hope since their parents died.

"Bennett? What are you up to? You look so serious."

She hadn't heard Maria coming down.

"Just thinking."

She could see Maria was waiting for her to tell her about what, but then she'd give her advice and this was something Bennett had to figure out for herself.

"Was there a reason you ordered this rose catalogue?" she asked. "It was in with the invoices."

"Oh, yeah. I meant to tell you. Peter and I were thinking of ordering some of the fragrant ones for our garden café. We thought that would create a European cottage atmosphere, but we can't decide which ones. There are so many. You did such a nice job with your garden, I thought maybe you could take a look."

"I'd be glad to."

Maria was right. There were hundreds—tea roses, shrubs, heirlooms, little ones, big ones; roses named after famous people, roses with romantic names, and some with names that made no sense to her at all, like Oregon Trail.

One called Mme Legras de St. Germain caught her eye. Very fragrant, easy to grow and almost thornless, which was a good idea for a space where people would be moving around. Perfect. She ordered four.

Maybe she should order a few for their garden, too. Their garden. Hers and Joe's. She was starting to think like Grace.

She liked the really fragrant ones too and looked for roses whose names sounded like they'd been expressly chosen. She turned the page and saw a yellow rose with double blooms called Happy Child. She would order that one for Hope. For Medi she found one called Safari. After turning several more pages she came upon a rose called Amazing Grace—highly fragrant, with up to eighty pink and cream petals. Grace would love it.

And Joe? Were there any named for men? An Albert Schweitzer rose was unlikely. Romantic names like Perpetual Love, Falling in Love, Over the Moon all sounded like cheap perfume. With only a few pages left she was afraid she'd have to settle for one called Love which was striking with it scales and white petals ... but then there it was, on the second to last page. A perfect, fragrant, miniature pink rose called Jo.

Destiny, Grace would say. Or at least, close enough.

Bennett picked up the phone and dialed the grower's 800 number and placed the order.

It wasn't a trip, but it was something. Maybe Joe would find it charming.

∼

At 5:30 Bennett called it a day. The evening skies had grown heavy and the first drops of rain were already falling. She should have brought her car. She didn't relish walking home in a downpour so when she turned the corner and saw a cab letting someone off she ran toward it.

"123 Spring Street," she said, as she got in.

"Caught me just in time, lady. It's going to pour," the cabbie said. "I was in the Army, stationed in Germany, and it looked like this all the time. Hardly ever saw the sun …" He was a talker. "Are you a traveler? I knew a guy once who kept a list of places in the world he'd seen. Sometimes, when business was slow, I'd hang around the lobby of the hotel he worked at and he'd describe all the places he'd been. Always made me feel like I'd been there myself. All I ever saw …"

Meyer! Bennett knew just what to do now. They'd brought New Orleans to Meyer because he couldn't go himself. Now Bennett could do the same for Joe.

She leaned forward and said, "Thank you for reminding me. Now I need a CD of Neapolitan songs. Do you know where I might find one?"

"On the internet. My grandkids download things all the time, though it's a mystery to me how they do it. Or you could order one from Amazon."

"I would like to get one today."

The cabbie drummed his fingers on the steering wheel.

"Concord Pike! There's an Italian market there. They've got all kinds of things. Even movies. They're open late."

On the way, Bennett called Juanita.

By the time they reached the market it was pouring.

"I can wait for you, if you want," the cabbie said.

"It might take me a while."

"That's OK. I won't charge ya."

"Don't want me to try Uber and deprive you of a fare?"

"That's right," the cabbie said, laughing. "Gotta adjust to the times."

When they finally reached home, Bennett shook the cabbie's hand, gave him a generous tip, and stepped out into the rain.

Hours later it occurred to her that she should have asked the cabbie's phone number. It would have been nice to be able to call someone who'd known Meyer.

53

*B*ennett ran up Joe's steps, knocked on his door, and waited less than a second before knocking again. Her heart was pounding so hard she barely noticed the water dripping from her hair into her eyes and seeping into her jacket. What if he wasn't answering because he'd had enough of her and wanted a break? Maybe he didn't want to see her at all. Ever.

The door opened and Joe pulled her in. "My God, Bennie, you're drenched. Where have you been?"

"I had ... I mean ..."

"Come in and warm up. You can explain later. Let me get you a towel."

She stood helplessly as a puddle formed around her feet.

"I have to talk to you, Joe—"

"Sure," he said, "but first let me have your jacket."

He hung the dripping jacket on the doorknob and put a towel around her shoulders, and another over her head. Gently, he dried her hair.

"What is it you want to talk about?" Joe asked.

"Oh no, not now ... I meant tomorrow. I have it all planned."

"All right." Joe looked puzzled.

"No, you don't understand. I talked to Juanita. She said she'd watch the kids. Then we can talk at my house. Just you and me ... I mean if you're free. Maybe this is too last minute?"

This had gone so much more smoothly in her head.

"I'm free," Joe said, "but if it's important we can talk tonight."

"No, it's not ... I mean, yes, it is, but tomorrow ... not like this. I'm not ready."

Joe looked worried. He probably thought she had something terrible to tell him, like she was dying of cancer. This was not how it was supposed to go.

After an awkward silence, Joe said, "Okay, but come in and have something to eat."

Bennett shook her head and handed him the towel from her shoulders. "I have to go but I'll see you tomorrow. Seven o'clock?"

"Can I get you some hot soup, at least, just to warm you up?"

"I can't stay," she said. "I have things to do."

She took her jacket off the doorknob, flung it over her shoulders, and ran down his steps and up hers. Why did they have that stupid railing between them anyway?

The house was dark. Peter probably wouldn't be back until late. He spent most of his time with Maria now.

Bennett carried her bag upstairs and put away the few belongings she'd kept at Joe's, then went into her office to print out the menu from the website of the caterer that Vinny, a man at the market, had recommended. The caterer was his cousin and had been a top chef in

Naples, supposedly. With Vinny's help Bennett had ordered two vegetable antipasti, two pastas, a meat dish and a fish dish. He'd also added spinach, because it was Joe's favorite vegetable. And for dessert she'd ordered a chocolate and almond torta Caprese. She hoped it was all as good as it sounded.

Joe said he'd come. That was the important thing.

Downstairs, Bennett set the dining table with the English china Maria had given her. It would have been nice to have two candlesticks, except that she didn't have any. Maybe she should put the menorah in the middle. No. If they sat opposite each other, their view would be blocked and they'd be shifting their heads from left to right in an attempt to see each other. She'd leave the menorah where she always kept it now, on her Sorrentine desk under the Ugandan painting.

She dusted off the stereo and put on the CD of Neapolitan songs she'd bought. Vinny at the market had told him that Roberto Murolo's melancholy voice was more authentic than Pavarotti's. Bennett wondered if Joe's mother had ever played those songs for Joe, or sung them even.

Dinner was scheduled to arrive at seven-fifteen. Should she push it up to seven? Or push it back to eight in case Joe wanted to get the children settled first? The caterer was bringing an espresso machine and cups since all Bennett had was her Mr. Coffee. If Joe really liked it maybe she'd get him a machine for his birthday. That would be a good gift.

Preparing and reviewing the details of her plan was good medicine for she slept well that night and woke refreshed the next morning.

Maria called at nine.

"I take it you're not coming in this morning, though you forgot to tell me. What are you up to, Bennett?" she teased. "Not that I really have to ask. Mama told me she is babysitting, and Peter stopped at the house and told me you were singing in the shower. He also said you'd set the table."

"I don't know what you're talking about."

Maria laughed. "Good luck, Bennett, though I don't think you'll need it. We're all rooting for you. Wear a nice dress. And make sure you tell me all the details tomorrow."

She was glad Maria couldn't see her blushing.

How much did Joe know about Naples? Bennett's knowledge of the city was limited to pasta, *O Sole Mio*, and the fact that the city had once been Greek. Soon she was lost in a google search. Naples, she learned, was one of the oldest continuously inhabited cities in the world, and had been ruled, after the Greeks, by a string of other invaders until Italy was unified in 1871. She pitied the poor Italian children who had to learn all that history in detail.

It was one o'clock when she first noticed that the sky had turned the bright, backlit gray that portended snow; and two o'clock when the first flakes floated to the ground. Increasingly heavy and wet, they soon covered the streets, turning them as bright as the sky.

It was almost four when she heard the children laughing as they ran up their steps.

Bennett opened her door. The children waved and asked if she was coming over while Juanita removed their boots and admonished them not to tramp through the house in their wet clothes.

"I can't now," she said.

"We were lucky to make it back," Juanita said. "The streets are a mess—and it isn't even night yet. Do you have everything you need?"

"Just about."

At 6:10, the caterer called. *Mi dispiace tanto*, he was terribly sorry but the snow was so heavy someone skidded into his car and all the food is *rovinato*, but not to worry, he would give Bennett a full refund unless she wanted to reschedule. Bennett didn't. It was now or never—though she didn't say that to the unfortunate chef.

Bennett hung up and called Joe's number.

Grace answered.

"Has Joe returned from work yet? I'm afraid everything's changed. I had such a nice evening planned but now the caterer can't come—"

"You can't cancel!" Grace said. "I will make you something, something special, I promise. And I'll do it all myself. I've been learning. Don't worry."

"All right then." Bennett was touched that Grace sounded so happy. It was just food, after all.

"I'll bring it over by eight," Grace added before hanging up.

Eight might be late. She'd have to have something to serve before then. She rummaged through the kitchen for something interesting but all she could find was tuna fish in a can, which seemed inappropriate, so she put out some crackers and an inadequate piece of cheese. At least she had wine. Why hadn't she thought of buying an aperitif?

At seven, she heard the feeble groaning of a car engine. Afraid it was Joe's, she looked out and saw a car struggling to pull out of the snow. She put on her coat and boots and took a shovel out of the coat closet, but by the time she made her way down to the street the car had managed to start and was gone, leaving only tire tracks behind.

Bennett turned and cleared the path back to the house, as well as the steps to both their front doors, hoping they wouldn't be completely covered again before Joe got back.

At ten after eight, Grace brought over a covered casserole dish.

"Put it in the oven on low, but don't look," she said. "It's a surprise."

She gave Bennett a kiss and told her she looked nice before rushing out.

"Be careful on the stairs," Bennett called after her, but she'd already climbed over the railing separating her house from Joe's.

"I am so sorry to be so late!" Joe said, when he finally arrived shortly after nine o'clock. "You can't imagine all the disruption and delays the snow caused at the hospital and on the road. I wouldn't have gotten home at all if one of the nurses hadn't had a four-wheel drive ... You had something special planned, didn't you? I stopped home to change but Grace wouldn't let me in and insisted I come over immediately. She was quite mysterious about it."

Bennett helped him off with his coat and boots. He closed his eyes and shook his head as the last of the snowflakes on his hair melted and trickled down his cheek, and she thought how handsome he looked, even in the teddy-bear scrubs he wore for his youngest patients.

"This isn't exactly how I planned things, Joe, but we do have dinner thanks to Grace."

"Mm, it smells good. She takes cooking very seriously, you know. I think she might become a chef."

She led him into the dining room and turned on the stereo.

"Everything looks so nice," Joe said.

Bennett noticed that he wasn't wearing his wedding band.

"*Vicino a Mare*," Joe said, recognizing the melody coming from the stereo. "My mother used to sing that when she thought no one was listening. It was a happy memory for her. How lovely of you to remind me of that."

"There's a church in Naples," Bennett said, "that has Roman ruins under it and Greek ruins under that."

Joe nodded. "San Lorenzo Maggiore, I read about it. Someday we'll have to go."

He said we.

"Peter's a really good carpenter, isn't he?" Bennett said.

"Is he building a church?" Joe asked, his eyes laughing.

There was no going back now.

"I mean ... if we had him take down our connecting wall, we'd have a really big living room. We could even get a piano for Medi—"

"And we wouldn't need two kitchens," Joe said, moving his chair closer so that his leg was touching hers.

"And with six bedrooms we could use one as a library—"

"Which would be perfect," he said, his smile washing over her.

"He'd probably be done by the time we got back from Naples..."

EPILOGUE

The U.S. Antique Dealers Association Newsletter

An unusual double wedding took place on Saturday morning at the newly renovated Vecchietti-Schimmerling Antiques, Books, and Café (known locally as The ABC).

Miss Bennett Hall, business manager of The ABC was married to Dr. Giordano Muir, head of Memorial Hospital's new pediatric oncology wing. Dr. Muir's daughter Grace Muir was maid of honor. Peter Carrington was best man. Their vows were immediately followed by those of Maria Morales, owner of The ABC and Mr. Carrington, founder and CEO of The Grace Foundation, an NGO which provides training in construction skills to at-risk youth, who then use their skills to provide home improvements to those in need. Mrs. Bennett Hall-Muir was matron of honor, Dr. Muir was best man. Hope Muir and Isabella Morales served as flower girls and Medi Muir as ring bearer for both couples. All the members of both wedding parties left for a honeymoon in Naples, Italy immediately following the ceremony. The ABC will reopen upon their return.

NOTES ABOUT THE AUTHOR

Irene Wittig has found inspiration in the many aspects of her life.

Her immigrant experiences and memories of her Viennese family inspired the historical novel *ALL THAT LINGERS,* which is available in all formats including audiobook.

Her husband's anti-corruption work in Uganda, and her own experiences volunteering at an orphanage during a visit there, inspired the Uganda portion of *THE BEST THING ABOUT BENNETT.*

Thoughts and memories inspired the short stories in *SHORT TALES AND RUMINATIONS.*

Her art and art history education, and her many years as a ceramic painter led to publication of the *CLAY CANVAS,* and the later updated and revised and lavishly illustrated *CREATIVE PAINTING ON EVERYDAY CERAMICS (paperback)* and THE CLAY CANVAS, REVISED EDITION *(ebook).*

Her love of language and design led to the whimsically illustrated and alliterative picture book for preschoolers: *AN AMUSING ALPHABET.*

Further information on these books can be found on her website https://all-that-lingers.com, where readers can also explore the historic, cultural and gastronomic Vienna of her novel.

Ms. Wittig enjoys hearing from her readers and is always greatly appreciative of reviews.

www.ingramcontent.com/pod-product-compliance
Lightning Source LLC
LaVergne TN
LVHW011943060526
838201LV00061B/4190